HARD TARGET

A TOM ROLLINS THRILLER

PAUL HEATLEY

INKUBATOR
BOOKS

Published by Inkubator Books
www.inkubatorbooks.com

Copyright © 2022 by Paul Heatley

Paul Heatley has asserted his right to be identified as the
author of this work.

ISBN (eBook): 978-1-83756-071-4
ISBN (Paperback): 978-1-83756-072-1

For Aidan

PROLOGUE

Cindy Vaughan is out getting food when she finds out she can't ever go back to her apartment.

It's late evening, late summer, and the day has been hot. The sidewalks of Lubbock, Texas, are still radiating heat, despite the darkening sky. Cindy has sheltered in her apartment all day, thick curtains drawn, the AC on, and the fan on her desk whirring non-stop. It remained hot, though. It always does, with a monitor and a couple of laptops perpetually running. Still, it was preferable to being outside, and risking a sunburn. Cindy, despite living all of her life in Texas, and suffering through its stifling summers, has never coped well with heat.

It started getting dark, and Cindy was hungry. She was in the mood for Chinese, and her favorite place, just a couple of blocks away, didn't deliver. Outside seemed as cool as it was going to get, so she risked it. She'd supposed the exercise and fresh air wouldn't kill her.

If she'd stayed inside – if she'd decided it was just easier to order a pizza, or something from any of the other myriad restaurants that *did* deliver – *that* could have killed her.

She's sitting on a bench and eating noodles from a carton when an alert sounds on her phone. The phone is on silent, but it buzzes aggressively against her thigh. She pulls it out and checks it, and feels her stomach drop. Her appetite is gone. Someone has broken into her apartment.

She unlocks her phone and accesses the security cameras in her apartment. She has one in every room, and another in the hall just outside her door, concealed behind one of the lamp fittings on the wall.

There are two men inside her home. They're both big, and they're broad, though one of them is clearly bigger than the other. They're dressed all in black, and they're wearing balaclavas. She feels bile rising up in her throat as one of them roughly searches through her living area, checking her laptops and then her furniture. The other, the bigger of the two, is in her bedroom. He sifts through her drawers and her wardrobe. He even looks under the bed. He tears her clothes out and rummages through them, though she doesn't know what he might be looking for. She doesn't keep anything important in her apartment. If they're thieves, all of her money is stored online, save for an emergency stash of cash that she carries on her at all times. She feels it now, hot and crumpled in her back pocket. The most the two men can hope to take are her electronics, but she has fail-safes built into them, so they'll never be able to unlock them. They're unusable to anyone but her.

It doesn't look like they're interested in taking anything, though. They're searching. Searching for what? For her? For signs of where she may be right now?

The thought makes her blood run cold. Sends electric chills down the back of her neck. While they continue their fruitless search, she accesses the camera in the hall. She rewinds it to their first appearance. It doesn't take long. Sees them coming down the hallway, to her door. They're already wearing the masks. Cindy curses under her breath. She has another camera, elsewhere in the building. It's in the lobby. Hidden behind another lamp fixture, and pointing straight at the entrance. She goes to this one, and rewinds it again. Again, they enter the building in their masks. There's no one around to see them. They probably waited outside before they entered, watching the building. Making sure no one was coming in or out, or loitering. Cindy checks the time. She's only been out the building a half-hour. They could have arrived just after she'd left, the two of them passing like ships in the night.

Cindy's knee bounces. She checks back in her apartment. The two men have come together in the living room. Their heads move, like they're talking. Cindy raises her head and looks around, makes sure no one is near, then rewinds the footage and turns up the volume.

"She's not here."

"I can see that. Any sign where she's gone?"

"Not that I can see. What do we do now?"

The bigger man goes to one of her windows, looks down to the streets below. "All of her stuff is still here. Her computers, her clothes. She hasn't left. She's just gone out. Store, or something. She's coming back. She's coming back soon, I'd bet. We close that door and we wait for her."

Cindy feels like she could be sick. She gets to her feet and she starts walking, her carton of noodles left behind on the bench, forgotten. She walks to the bus station. It takes her an hour and forty-five minutes. She's conscious all the way that she is being hunted. She glances back over her shoulder, telling herself it's silly, that she knows where the men are. When she checks her phone and the cameras in her apartment, they're still there. Still waiting for her, but they're growing impatient. They're pacing the floors, and checking the windows.

Next to the emergency cash in the back pocket of her black jeans, there is a key. A locker key. In her front pocket there is a phone. A burner phone, with only one number on it. She never leaves home without any of these objects. All these years, feeling foolish about carrying them with her – and now it's paying off. Everything she has worried about has caught up with her, although she doesn't know exactly what. Not yet.

She has a locker in the bus station. Inside, there's an emergency pack. It has a change of clothes, a jacket, and a laptop. The laptop hasn't been switched on in a while. She finds a quiet corner of the station, takes a seat, and charges it up. She keeps her face turned down, away from the security cameras inside the building. She pulls out a baseball cap from the pack, pulls it on over her short, bleached-blonde hair, the peak low and covering her features. The laptop finally comes to life. She logs in. On her phone, she checks her apartment. The men have given up. They've left.

Outside her apartment, watching the street, there is a CCTV camera. Cindy hacks into it, checks its footage. She rewinds it. Sees the two masked men leave her building only ten minutes before. They get into a car. It's a nice car. A new car. A sleek black BMW. It speeds away when the men get inside. Neither of them gets behind the wheel. The car moves too fast for her to see who is driving. She rewinds. Goes all the way back to when it first arrived at her building. Her stomach does a flip when she sees herself walking away, and then the car arrives less than two minutes later. It sits outside for ten minutes, then the two men go inside, already masked. Only the driver remains.

Cindy pauses the footage, and puts her face close to the screen. It's blurred. She downloads the image onto her laptop and tries her best to clear it up. It takes a while. The image remains pixelated, but she gets it clear enough that she knows who the driver is. She knows him without fully being able to see his face.

She could never forget one of the men who killed her sister.

Suddenly, the frame of the bigger man that was in her apartment is familiar to her. The sound of his voice. She knows who *he* is, too.

After all these years, they've tracked her down.

Cindy closes her laptop. She grits her teeth and stares at the hard ground in front of her, her hands either side of the laptop, squeezing it.

They've found her. They broke through her defenses, and they tracked her to her *home*. She doesn't know how, and right now that doesn't matter.

She inhales deeply through her nose. She needs to think. This is no time to panic. They're coming for her. They're powerful, and they're coming. Nothing can stop them now.

Cindy needs help.

She shifts her weight and reaches into her front pocket. The burner phone. She calls the one number saved in it.

Tom Rollins.

1

Tom keeps an eye on a couple of guys in the corner of the bar. There's another guy comes here regularly, a wannabe writer, and he always drags his girlfriend along. She looks bored, but he insists on coming to 'soak up the atmosphere'. He tells this to anyone who'll listen, same way he'll tell them he's a writer. Just waiting on his big break.

His bored girlfriend, though, she's attractive. She looks out of the writer's league, yet she's with him every time he comes. There must be something there that Tom doesn't see. Perhaps, when he's not being a pretentious asshole in here, he might be a really nice guy.

The writer isn't paying any attention to the two guys in the corner of the bar. He's too busy scribbling away in his notebook. He used to ask Tom a lot of questions, shortly after Tom first arrived and took the job of doorman. He got real excited after the first time he'd seen Tom bust a couple of heads. "You must've had training, right? Or do you just study martial arts, is that it? Maybe karate, or boxing?"

Tom knew what he was doing. Sizing him up, working out

if he was interesting enough to turn into a character. Tom has no interest in being a character. He was polite – he's always polite – but he didn't give him anything to work with. The writer eventually gave up trying.

The two guys in the corner are paying a lot of attention to the writer's girlfriend. She's aware of their eyes. She keeps her back to them and looks uncomfortable. She's wearing jeans and an army jacket, and Tom notices how she keeps tucking the bottom of the jacket under herself, to hide her hips and her backside from their eyes. She tries not to look back at them over her shoulder. Her writer boyfriend remains oblivious.

Tom isn't working alone tonight. Billy is tending bar. "I think it might be time to cut those two off," Tom says to him.

Billy is playing on his phone. He's a young guy, early twenties, and has a perpetually bored expression on his face, but he's always respectful to Tom. He's seen Tom work. "What's that?"

"We keep giving them drinks, they're gonna be trouble."

Billy looks over. The two men have their heads lowered. They look in their forties. One of them has a shaved head. The other has some scars in his eyebrows and a crooked nose, showing he's no stranger to a brawl. "They're not regulars," Billy says, as if he's seeing them for the first time. "Not that I've seen, anyway. You know them?"

Tom shakes his head. "No more drinks," he says. "They wanna make a problem of that, I'll talk to them."

Tom was hoping for a quiet night. He's expecting someone. It's been a couple of years since they last saw each other in person. It's been a couple of weeks since they spoke on the phone, though they've kept in touch via messages since. She checks in daily. She never tells him where she is, but she lets him know she's all right. She's taking her time coming to him. She hasn't told Tom the full story yet, but it's clear she's paranoid. Worried about something. Thinks she's being followed. She chose to lay low for a while, before she came to LA.

While not watching the two men, he watches the door, awaiting her arrival. She didn't give a time. Just said it would be tonight.

"I'm gonna step outside," Tom says. "Get some air. Keep an eye on things in here. Anything happens, give me a shout."

Billy nods. Tom rounds the bar and crosses the room to the door. There's a few other people in tonight, but they're having quiet drinks and minding their own business. They're regulars, and they recognize Tom and nod at him as he passes. He returns their nods. He steps outside. The night air is cool. The road in front of the bar is quiet. He checks the time. It's almost ten. Somewhere, far off in the distance, he can hear a coyote howl.

He folds his arms and leans against the wall by the door. He watches the darkness. There's no sign of her. The bar is out the way. She'd need wheels to get here. Either she's got a vehicle of her own, or she'll take a taxi, or an Uber. No buses stop out this way.

Tom takes a couple of deep, clean breaths. He steps closer to the road again, looking up and down. Sees no one. No vehicles. Not even a distant headlight. He goes back inside the bar. Nothing much has changed. Everything is as he left it. The two in the corner keep their heads close, stealing glances at the writer's girlfriend. She still looks uncomfortable. Tom goes to her.

"You all right?" he says.

She looks up with a start. She didn't realize he was approaching. "I'm, yeah, I'm fine. Thanks." She doesn't look fine.

The boyfriend looks up from his notebook, oblivious. "What? Oh, hey, Tom."

Tom ignores him. Keeps his eyes on the girlfriend. "I can ask them to leave, if you want."

She shakes her head. "It's fine," she says. "I'm just... I'll just ignore them. They're not causing any trouble."

Tom feels like trouble could just be a matter of time.

He goes back behind the bar. The two men saw him talking to the object of their looks. One of them, the one with the scars, glares at him. Tom stares back. The scarred man looks away first.

"How's it been?"

"Nothing changed," Billy says. "Sold a couple of drinks to a couple of regulars."

"No more for them," Tom says, tilting his head toward the two men.

"I know, I know," Billy says. "I didn't forget. They've just been nursing the ones they've got."

Tom nods.

The front door opens.

It's Cindy.

Tom feels himself smile. She's looking around the room, searching for him. A few heads turn her way. The regulars aren't used to seeing a woman like Cindy in here, with her short, bleached hair, her ripped black jeans, and a Godflesh T-shirt. She's wearing a thick jacket, and has a rucksack on her back looped over both arms. She spots Tom behind the bar, and she smiles, too. She looks relieved, Tom thinks. He sees her shoulders slump a little, as if a weight has been lifted off them.

He goes to her and they embrace. "Been a while," Tom says.

"Wouldn't kill you to keep in touch," Cindy says.

"You have my number."

"And I called it," Cindy says. "I just wish it had been under better circumstances."

"Mm," Tom says, letting go of her and taking a step back. "You wanna tell me about it?"

Cindy looks around. "Maybe not in here."

"Sure," Tom says. "We can go to my apartment when I finish. We close in a couple of hours. You all right to wait? I can make you something to eat if you're hungry."

"Y'know, I'm *really* fucking hungry. I'll take you up on that." She looks around again. "Although, I gotta ask, is the kitchen cleaner than the rest of this place?"

"It's the cleanest area we've got," Tom says, winking. He motions to a booth in the corner. "Second only to this sitting area."

Cindy smirks. "Don't I feel like a queen." She takes the bag off her back and slides into the booth. "And what a *view*," she says, widening her eyes, her words dripping with sarcasm. "I can see why you like it."

"You grow accustomed to its charms."

Cindy grins. She tilts her head, looking at his left arm. She can see some of the Santa Muerte tattoo on his left shoulder poking out the bottom of his sleeve. "That's new," she says. She reaches out, pulls up his sleeve. "Let me get a proper look."

Tom twists so she can see it better. Cindy whistles low. "I like it," she says. "Never would have pegged you as a tattoo guy." She smiles, but then she frowns, letting his sleeve fall back down and looking beyond him. Something catches her attention.

He's heard it, too. The rising commotion, behind him at the bar. The voices getting louder, and more aggressive. He turns. One of the men is trying to get drinks. Billy has told him no. Tom turns back to Cindy. "I'll go deal with this," he says. "And when I come back, I'll have a grilled cheese for you."

"Deal with it quick," Cindy says, "or else you're gonna hear my stomach growling all the way over there."

Tom makes his way back across the bar. It's the one with the scarred eyebrows kicking up a fuss. He's cursing Billy out. "Damn it, get me and my buddy a couple of fucking beers, before I drag your sorry ass over this counter!"

Billy isn't a fighter. The way this bar had been before Tom started working here, Billy would never have dreamed of working here. He wouldn't have made it through his first shift. He takes a step further back from the counter so the man can't grab him and make good on his promise.

"You're not gonna do anything," Tom says. He keeps a safe distance back, and keeps the other guy in view to his right.

Scarface turns to Tom, sneering. "You wanna make this your problem, buddy?"

Tom stares at him.

The guy to Tom's right, still at the table, begins to stand.

"Stay sitting," Tom says, "or you're gonna get hurt, too."

The guy at the table hesitates.

"Ignore this asshole," Scarface says.

The guy at the table straightens.

"The two of you aren't regulars here," Tom says, planting his feet. "So I'm going to give you a chance. Pay your tab, apologize to the lady here for how uncomfortable you've made her feel all night" – he motions to the writer's girlfriend – "and then get out. Nice and easy. There doesn't need to be any trouble. No one needs to get hurt."

Scarface smirks. He looks at the writer's girlfriend, runs the tip of his tongue over his lips and winks at her. She shudders. The writer looks confused as to why his girlfriend is being brought into things. She drags him up to his feet and gets him out the way.

"I'll see you real soon, baby," Scarface says to her back. "I've just gotta deal with this asshole first."

"That's enough," Tom says. "Get out, now, or I throw you out."

Scarface reaches into his pocket. Grinning, he pulls out a switchblade. He pops it.

"That looks like it'll hurt," Tom says, "when I take it off you and stick it through your hand. You'll never be able to pop that thing again."

"I'm gonna shove it up your ass," Scarface says.

"You're gonna *try*."

Scarface makes the first move. Tom expects him to. He slashes through the air to back him up. He's keeping Tom distracted, so the guy on the right can make his move. The guy on the right is half-drunk, though, and he's untrained. His lunge is clumsy. Tom strikes at him with an elbow. The point of it connects with the bridge of his nose. It breaks. He goes down, clutching at his face.

Scarface is moving in, jabbing with the switchblade now. Tom blocks him with his left forearm, then takes control of his wrist. He twists, and strikes Scarface with a chop across both eyebrows. The skin there is thin with scar tissue, and it bleeds easily. The blood gets into his eyes. Tom jabs him in the ribs to keep him docile, then takes control of his arm, holding it against his own ribs. He takes the switchblade from his weakened grip, then judo throws him onto the ground. Scarface lands with a thud. Tom drives the switchblade down through his palm. Scarface screams.

"You were warned," Tom says.

The other guy is up now, holding his broken nose, but the fight has gone out of him. With his other hand he's begging off.

"Pay your tab," Tom says, "then pick up your trash." He indicates Scarface. "Then get the fuck out and don't come back."

Broken-nose guy goes to the bar, pulling notes from his

pocket. He drops them on the counter, more than they owe, then hurries back to Scarface, helping him up off the ground. The knife is still in his hand. If they have any sense, they'll leave it in until they get him to a hospital. Tom doesn't care whether they have enough sense or not.

Cindy appears nearby. She looks at the drops of blood on the ground. "So how *have* you been these last couple of years?" she says. "Keeping your head down? Staying out of trouble? Living the quiet life?"

"Take a seat," Tom says. "I'll bring you that grilled cheese."

2

Cindy yawns as she enters Tom's apartment.

"You tired?" he says, setting her bag down in the corner of the room. He's carried it from the bar. It's not a long walk.

"I haven't slept much lately," Cindy says, taking a seat on the edge of the bed. She looks around. It's not a big apartment. It's all crammed into one small room, save for the bathroom, which is through a door off the kitchen area. "So, what?" she says. "Between the bar and this place, you've developed a real taste for shit-hole dives?"

Tom laughs. "I didn't plan on staying here long."

"Uh-huh. How long have you been here now?"

"Few months." He shrugs. "It's cheap. I've stayed in worse places."

"I don't doubt it. When you said you were already in LA, I thought you might've been in a nicer part of it."

"What's ever given you the impression I like to take myself to the *nicer* parts of town?"

"True," Cindy says. "You don't find as much trouble there."

Tom considers this. He supposes it's true. He came here because he thought it would be easier to find work. The kind of work that comes with no questions asked. He doesn't *think* he goes looking for trouble. At least, he didn't. Lately, he hasn't been so sure.

"How about the last couple of years?" Cindy says. "You managed to keep your head down?"

Tom grunts. "For the most part."

"I'll take that as a no."

"Well, there was this long period of time in Alaska where it was *real* quiet."

"Oh yeah? *Then* what happened?"

"Stuff got blown up."

Cindy laughs. She pushes herself up the bed and rests her back against the headboard. She yawns. Stretches her arms out. "Jesus," she says, blinking. "I *must* be tired, because even *this* mattress is feeling comfortable to me right now."

There aren't any other chairs in the apartment. Tom gets on the bed next to her. He looks at her. She's struggling to keep her eyes open.

"You wanna talk tonight?" he says. "Or do you wanna wait until the morning? Get some rest first?"

Cindy opens her eyes. She pushes herself up. "I wanna talk *now*," she says. She looks at him, suddenly alert, remembering why she has come here.

"So what's happened?" Tom says.

Cindy takes a deep breath. "Couple of weeks ago, I went out for some food. While I'm out, I get an alert on my phone which basically tells me someone's breaking into my apartment. Couple of guys in masks. I've got cameras in the place, so I just sit there and watch them ransacking it, wondering what it is they're looking for. Except they're not taking anything. They're looking for clues, and then when they don't find any of them, they're waiting. Waiting for me. It's me they're searching for."

Tom's eyes narrow. "Did you see their faces?"

"Never took the masks off, from the moment they got to the building to the moment they left."

"They must've known enough about you to suspect you'd have security footage," Tom says. "Any idea who they could've been? Why they might've wanted you? Someone you might've pissed off, perhaps?"

"I didn't see them, but I know who they were," Cindy says. "Or, at least, I know who sent them, and I've got a pretty good idea who one of those masked guys was."

"Okay," Tom says, waiting for her explanation.

"I got a look at the driver waiting outside for them. *Him* I knew, for sure. I'll never forget that son of a bitch."

"Who was he?"

"He's called Hugh. And I think one of the masked guys, the bigger of the two, was his buddy, Lenny. His bodyguard."

"Who are they to you? You upset them?"

Cindy grits her teeth. "Yeah, I upset them. And they upset me." Her voice wavers a little, sounds like it might break. She blinks hard.

Tom waits while she takes a deep breath. She's composing herself. She's going to tell him who they are. He doesn't need to rush her.

She closes her eyes. She's steeling herself for what she says next. She's trying hard not to cry. Tom has never seen her like this before. She opens her eyes and she looks at him. Her face is firm now. Her eyes are clear. "They killed my sister," she says.

Tom didn't know Cindy had a sister, but they've never talked much about her personal life. In the past, when Tom has needed her help, she's given it and kept her personal life exactly that – personal. It's been a couple of years since he saw her last. He's been meaning to reach out, to get back in touch. It's a shame that they're meeting again under these kinds of circumstances. "I'm sorry," he says. "When did that happen? Was it recent?"

Cindy shakes her head. "It was a long time ago now. But they're looking for me. They've tracked me down."

"And you need help."

She nods. "I want justice."

"You want vengeance."

"Justice *is* vengeance," she says.

Tom nods. He stands. "You sleep. We'll talk more in the morning. We'll make plans. Decide what we're gonna do next."

"We can do that now," Cindy says. "I've come all this way—"

"No," Tom says. "You've come all this way and now you're tired. You need to sleep."

Cindy starts to protest, but she knows he's right. She *is* tired. "All right," she says. She deflates a little, everything catching up to her. "Fine. But what are you gonna do? This is your bed. I don't mind sharing. I trust you not to try anything untoward." She gives him a tired grin.

"I need to keep watch," Tom says. "If they've found you once, they might still be following."

Cindy looks perturbed at the thought they may have tracked her all the way to LA.

Tom reaches over the bed, places a hand on her shoulder. He squeezes comfortingly. "Even if they come, they won't get you. I won't let them. Go to sleep, Cindy. You're safe here."

She's not used to having to ask for help. She's used to doing everything herself. Tom can see it in the way she struggles to relax. In the way she struggles to accept his help, despite coming all this way.

"All right," she says, finally, hesitantly. She starts to lie down. "All right."

3

Cameron Brewer lives in the Hollywood Hills. It's a beautiful home, but he doesn't spend as much time here as people would expect. Usually, he's in Balboa East, where his facilities and factories are located. However, now it's close to midnight. He got home less than half an hour ago.

It's a sprawling mansion, Spanish-villa style. Its exterior is white, with orange tile roof. The premises are walled off, an eight-foot-tall barrier ensuring privacy. Outside the walls, where the ground slopes down the hill, there is a smattering of eucalyptus trees. Beyond that, down in the valley, is the shining city of Los Angeles. Its many lights twinkle in the dark, a sea of illuminations that looks deep enough to swim in.

Out the back of the house is a pool. Olympic-sized. Cameron is no Olympic athlete, but he keeps himself in shape. He usually takes a swim first thing in the morning, before he sets off for the office. His girlfriend, Amy Pernier, is swimming in it now. It's well-lit. She does slow, leisurely laps. Breast stroke. When she's not swimming, she's usually either going to nightclubs or throwing parties here at the house. Amy is a socialite. Her father is an industrialist up in Montreal. Amy has never had a real job. She's paid to attend parties. To open nightclubs. Cameron doesn't hold it against her. She's beautiful enough to make a living from something so ludicrous. If he was in her position, he'd do the same. These days, now that she's with him, she doesn't have to concern herself with making money at all. He makes more than enough for the both of them. All she has to concern herself with, as far as he cares, is keeping her body tight. Is keeping him happy. She's doing well enough on both counts.

Cameron sits on a lounger near to the pool, watching Amy swim. Stephen Hawke, his head of security, perches himself on the edge of the lounger next to him.

"Is Hugh home yet?" Cameron says, looking down to the pool house. It's in darkness, but that doesn't mean he's not back. He could be asleep.

"He got back a few hours ago," Stephen says, rubbing his chin. "He went straight back out, though. Probably to Titty City."

Cameron rolls his eyes. "I wanted to talk to him. I expect him back to work tomorrow – did you tell him that?"

"We didn't really speak."

"Then I assume you don't know if he dealt with his business."

"No." Stephen shakes his head. "I don't even know what his 'business' was."

Cameron grunts.

"Kept it close to his chest, didn't he?" Stephen says. "That's not like Hugh. Wouldn't even tell me where he was going." He grins.

"I know where he went," Cameron says, waving a hand. "Don't concern yourself with it."

Stephen falls silent for a moment. His grin slips. He clears his throat, says, "I'm surprised you gave him a full two weeks off."

Cameron shrugs. "It was important. And besides, it gave me two weeks with him out my hair. But now that two weeks are over, and if he wants to continue to get paid, then he needs to get his ass back to work."

He watches Amy doing her laps. On her way by, she sees him watching and winks. Cameron smiles.

"I don't feel comfortable not knowing what he was doing," Stephen says. "We know what he's like. He can be careless. He could have done something while he's been off that might come back on the company, on *you*."

Cameron sighs. Stephen is good at his job – he has to be, or else Cameron would get rid of him. One thing about him, though, is that he's a little too moral for Cameron's liking. A little too much of a straight arrow. He doesn't have the stomach for a lot of things that are expected of him. Cameron doesn't believe morals get anyone very far. He *knows* they don't. He didn't get as far as he has by worrying about little things like right and wrong. "Don't worry about it," he says. "If he did anything I'm unhappy about, *I'll* deal with it. Understand? He knows better than to do anything that would upset me."

Stephen looks away, toward the lights of Los Angeles. Cameron notices how he makes sure he doesn't look in Amy's direction. Doesn't want it to seem like he might be checking her out.

"Speaking of things that might upset me," Cameron says, staring at Stephen until he looks back at him, "where is Kylie?"

Stephen grits his teeth, and already Cameron can tell it's not good news. Stephen is hesitant, but there's only so long he can hesitate before he has to answer. He shakes his head. "We haven't been able to find her. Not yet."

"Not *yet*?" Cameron says. "Been a while now, hasn't it, Stephen?"

Stephen doesn't answer.

"How long's it been, Stephen?" Cameron stares at him.

Stephen takes a deep breath. "About three months."

"Three months *exactly*," Cameron says. "To the *day*. We know she hasn't left LA, Stephen. I've greased enough palms and programmed enough software to be sure of that." Facial recognition software. They haven't had a hit yet. Cameron had expected to find her within a few days of her disappearance. She's proven smarter than he anticipated. She's somehow managed to avoid all cameras. No one can do that unless they're doing it on purpose.

Stephen says exactly this. "She'll know that, though. She knows what you can do, what you're capable of, the technology you have at your disposal. She could've found a way to sneak out."

"I'm aware of that, Stephen. And if that *has* somehow happened, I expect you to be the one that finds that out and tells me about it."

Stephen looks suitably chastised.

"Three months, Stephen," Cameron repeats. "I pay you and your men a lot of money. I expect results. And I expect them a lot sooner than *three months*."

"I'm sorry, Mr Brewer," Stephen says, not meeting his eye.

"Three months is three months *too long*. I want her found – I *need* her found – before *she* finds someone that *will* listen to what she has to say."

"We don't need to worry about that," Stephen says. "As soon as she raises her head above the parapet, shows her hand, you can just pay off the people she's trying to talk to again. They could even direct us to her, and I could talk to her – I could get her to sign an NDA and—"

"I don't *want* to have to pay off every Tom, Dick and

Harry, Stephen!" Cameron glares. "Do you think I got this rich by giving away money at every fucking available opportunity?"

"No, Mr Brewer. That was presumptuous of me."

"I want her found, Stephen. I want her found by the end of this fucking week." He's leaning over in the lounger, leaning closer to Stephen, sneering and jabbing the tip of a finger into his thigh. "And if you can't do it, if you're not up to the task, then, damn it, I'll hire someone who *is*. This is no fucking time for your namby-pamby bleeding-heart *bullshit*. If you let me down again, I'll throw you out on the fucking *street*. Is that clear? I'll *ruin* you, Stephen. You'll have nothing left – you'll *be* nothing – by the time I get through."

Stephen is trembling. His jaw is clenched. He's taken aback. He's not used to seeing Cameron this way.

"*Do* you understand?" Cameron says.

"I, uh, yes – *yes*, I understand, Mr Brewer. I'm...I'm sorry it's taken me this long."

Cameron hears gentle splashing at the pool as Amy pulls herself out. He turns to her, watches as she walks, dripping, to a nearby lounger, where she has draped her towel. The water runs down her tanned body in rivulets. Cameron smiles. He feels a stirring. His annoyance at Stephen is promptly forgotten. He glances back at him over his shoulder. "Get on with it, then," he says.

Stephen nods, then gets to his feet and hurries away toward the house.

Amy towels herself off, watching him go with a bored expression. Cameron calls to her, tells her to come to him. She does so, drying her hair. "I need a shower," she says, her French accent a soft purr. "I smell of chlorine."

"I don't mind," Cameron says, reaching and taking her by the wrists, pulling her into his lap. He starts kissing her chest and shoulders.

She places her hands upon his chest. "Shall we go inside?"

"No," Cameron says, tugging her bikini bottoms down.

"*Here?*" she says, laughing.

Cameron nods, pulling aside a bikini cup and sucking on her nipple.

She gasps in his ear. "Security might see us," she says, running her hands back through his hair. "Or your brother."

Cameron doesn't care. He unzips his trousers, takes her hand and places it there. "Let them watch," he says.

4

In the early morning, Tom and Cindy go to a diner for breakfast. It's not close. Tom has to drive them there.

"Did you sleep at all last night?" Cindy says on the way.

"I took some cat naps, here and there," Tom says. He feels fine. He slept in yesterday, in preparation for the late shift at the bar. He doesn't feel like he needs to catch up on his sleep just yet. "How'd you find the bed? You sleep all right?"

"Save for a few bad dreams, I slept like a baby," Cindy says, grinning.

They reach the diner and go inside. They sit by the window in the far corner where Tom can see the rest of the room and the parking lot. They both order eggs. Cindy asks for some orange juice, too.

"So," Tom says, taking a sip from his iced water. "Give me some background."

"How much?" Cindy says.

"Tell me what you think I need to know. Everything relevant."

Cindy takes a deep breath. She looks out the window. "I suppose I'd better start at the beginning."

"It's usually best."

"My sister's name was Erica," Cindy says. She sighs. It's clear to Tom that she doesn't talk about her sister often. Clear that – no matter how much time has passed, this remains a fresh wound. "She was five years older than me. When I was thirteen, and she was eighteen, our parents died. They were in a car crash. Erica stepped up. She became my guardian. She raised me. It was hard, though. We weren't able to stay in the home we grew up in. The landlord kicked us out. We had to move into this tiny apartment. It wasn't much bigger than the one you've been staying in. It was all we could afford. All *she* could afford. Erica had to sacrifice a lot to take care of me. She found a part-time job, working in a convenience store on weekends. She was tired all the time. I could see it.

"Part-time wasn't enough to pay the rent and bills, though. Erica dropped out of school and went full-time. Did all the hours she could. I barely saw her, but I knew why she was doing it. She'd given up everything, because all of a sudden she had to be a single mother to me."

The waitress brings their eggs. They start eating.

"I got my first computer when I was thirteen, right before our parents died," Cindy says, in between chewing. "When Erica and I had to leave our childhood home, she told me to only pack the essentials. I made sure to bring the laptop with me. By the time I was fourteen, I'd learned how to write code, program, and hack."

"And how did you learn that?" Tom says.

"Like I said, Erica wasn't around much. She had no idea who I was friends with, who I was hanging around with. At first, I was spending time with some older guys who were really into computers. When I say older, I only mean a couple of years.

They were just some nerdy guys who had a computer club that met up on lunch breaks and sometimes for a couple of hours after the school day was over. I learnt some basic ins and outs with them, and through them I met a couple of other guys, older still, finished school, who were into more heavy stuff. Like, hardcore hacking. Dark web kind of stuff. Everything else, I learned from them. I'm not gonna lie, it wasn't all legal. Kids would pay us to get into the school systems and change their grades – basic stuff like that, right? At first, anyway. We made some fake IDs. Erased some security footage, or, y'know, saved some. The guys I was learning from, they said I was a natural. Said I could teach them more than they could teach me.

"Anyway, once I started doing that kind of work, more and more of it would come my way. I was doing it on my own pretty soon, no backup, just me, making some extra money. Just to help Erica out, y'know? I'd slip some notes into her purse, or put them in the cookie jar on top of the fridge. I didn't want her to know what I was doing. Part of me had a feeling she wouldn't like it. She'd try and get me to stop. I mean, like I said, it wasn't exactly legal. She'd probably worry about me getting into trouble."

Cindy sighs. She looks out the window while she chews. Tom watches the side of her face. She was twenty-seven when they first met. She's twenty-nine now. She usually looks younger, but today she looks older. Her features are pinched. Strained from two weeks on the road, on the run. She brushes a short strand of bleached hair back out of her eyes. Near her scalp, her darker roots are showing.

She turns back to her plate. "When I turned eighteen, I got a place of my own. I told Erica I'd found a job working with computers. It wasn't a total lie. Besides, once I was out, it meant she could finally live a life of her own, right? She was twenty-three then. Still young. She didn't have to worry about me any more. Didn't have to spend all her time trying to take care of me or provide for me.

"Before I knew it, a couple of years had gone by. Me and Erica, we stayed close. We kept in touch often enough. She'd come visit, or I'd go to see her. She'd tell me about her latest relationship, and how and why it fell apart. I'd tell her the same." She grins and shrugs a shoulder. There isn't much left on her plate. She pushes the remaining scraps of egg around with her fork. "It was around that time that Hugh found me. I always remember, because it was a couple of weeks before I turned twenty-one."

"What's Hugh's story?" Tom says. "Was he a hacker, too?"

"He thought he was," Cindy says. "He was no good at it."

"Did you know him already?"

Cindy shakes her head. "I'd never seen him before in my life. But he wasn't from Texas. He was from around here – California."

"What was he doing down in Texas?"

"He'd been living there a little while. He wouldn't tell me that much about his history, but from what I've been able to figure out over time, seems like he's the black sheep of his family. I think he'd done something back at home and his parents got so upset they sent him away. Maybe even told him to lay low for a while, so he went south."

"You haven't been able to find the details?"

"They've been scrubbed. Completely. All trace is gone."

"So he's from a powerful family?"

"Yes, but that's not the half of it. We'll get to his family." Cindy's face darkens.

"How old is he?"

"Couple of years older than you," she says. "Mid-thirties. Anyway, how he found me in the first place, I'm not sure. All he'd say was that he'd been told good things. He gave me a couple of jobs to do, and he paid well, and I didn't think anything of it. To cut a long story short, those jobs were tests. He wanted an idea of what I was capable of. Once he knew what I could do, he moved himself into my place and introduced me to Lenny."

"I assume that was without an invite."

"You assume correctly."

"Who's Lenny?"

"His bodyguard. Never goes anywhere without him. And one of the guys that tore up my apartment. Lenny's job, once we'd been introduced, was to make sure I did exactly as Hugh said. These jobs, he wasn't paying. There was a gun to my head. And I mean that literally."

"Jesus. What were they getting you to do?"

"Well, Hugh had acquainted himself with certain criminal elements and not just in the local area. Throughout Texas and across almost all the states. He didn't know them all personally. Some he'd just heard of, or about. What he'd get me to do was rip them off. Electronically. He'd get me to raid their hidden online and offshore bank accounts, transfer all the money to a hidden account of his own. Scrub all trace, so it could never be followed back to him."

"How much are we talking?"

"Hundreds of thousands. Once it was in that account he got me to set up for him, he could access it freely, do what he wanted with it. And he *did* do what he wanted – he was frittering it away. I had no idea what he was spending it on. Still don't. I wasn't thinking about it too much, though. I was busy thinking about how I was gonna get myself out of that situation. There was a gun to my head daily, and I knew that meant once they were done with me, they were *done*. They weren't going to leave a witness. I was gonna end up in a ditch somewhere."

"So what'd you do?" Tom finished eating. He rests his elbows on the table, his hands clasped next to his mouth.

"I ratted them out," Cindy says. "I sent messages to some of the guys they'd had me rip off and told them exactly who had stolen from them, and where to find them. Then I went into Hugh's secret account and I drained it for what little was left – fifty thousand. I know that sounds like a decent number, but I know what had been taken. There could have been a hell of a lot more in it than that."

"How'd you manage to get away?"

"Lenny was in my apartment at all times, but Hugh wasn't. He was out living it up with his stolen money. I got used to Lenny. He didn't say much, but he didn't need to. I was watching him. I was listening. I got used to his routine. Every night, he'd handcuff me to my bed when it was time for me to sleep. Always by the left wrist." Cindy holds out her arm to indicate. "Then he'd go into the next room and watch television. A couple of hours later, he'd fall asleep in the chair in front of the TV. He was a *deep* sleeper. He snored, too. But I knew he was a deep sleeper because one night I needed to piss and no matter how loud I screamed for him, he didn't hear."

"That's not a great characteristic for a bodyguard."

Cindy grunts. "Maybe not, but it sure helped me out. So anyway, when the time came and I was getting myself ready to get free of the two of them, I taught myself how to pick locks. I practiced on the cuffs every night until I was able to pop it right off. All it took was a hair pin. For another two weeks, I practiced every night to make sure I could get it open with ease. When I was ready to run, I was gonna run *fast*. I didn't want anything to hold me up."

"And I know that you got free," Tom says.

Cindy takes a deep breath. She nods. "I got free. I ran. Left everything behind and went into hiding. I knew I had enough money to start over. I'm still living on some of it now, topped up with freelance work." She takes another deep breath, and this time it shudders, like she might be about to cry. She grinds her jaw. She tries to be strong, but her eyes are glassy. "I forgot one thing, though," she says, her voice distorted by repressed tears. "I forgot...I didn't think... I didn't think they'd find out about Erica. I didn't think they knew about her. I didn't...I didn't *think*. I should have taken her with me. I thought I was keeping her safe, keeping her out of it."

Tom reaches across the table. He covers her hand with his own. She looks down at where he holds her, comforts her. Tears fall from her eyes.

"You don't have to say any more," Tom says.

Cindy nods, but she continues. "They killed her. They beat her to death." She slips her hand out from under Tom's, but she doesn't take it away. She locks her fingers into his and squeezes. With her other hand, she covers her eyes. "They killed her, and it was all my fault. I was too busy thinking about myself, and all Erica ever did was think about *me*."

Tom gives her a moment. It doesn't take Cindy long. She wipes at her eyes and drains off the last of her orange juice.

"They went into hiding after that," she says. "I think they fled to Europe for a few months."

"Did you talk to the police?"

Cindy shakes her head.

"How come? You said you wanted justice. You might have got in some trouble too, for what you'd been doing, but what they'd done was much worse."

"I wasn't thinking about justice then," Cindy says, shaking her head. "I was very much thinking about vengeance at that time. *Bloody* vengeance. I was determined to hunt them down, both of them, and make them pay. But..." She looks at Tom. "Do you know who Cameron Brewer is?"

Tom blinks. "No," he says. "Should I?"

"I suppose you wouldn't. He's a tech bro billionaire. He's also Hugh's older brother. The golden boy of the family. The one Hugh was always trying to match up to. *That's* where Hugh and Lenny eventually ran to, and hid out."

"Does he know what they did?"

She takes a deep breath. "A lot of time has passed between then and now, and I've spent a lot of that time looking into what they did to Erica. I would go over the same things, over and over, obsessively, like maybe I would spot something that could help me, right? I never knew what kind of code I was looking to crack. But then one day I *did* find something. All that money I'd stolen for Hugh – he hadn't completely wasted all of it. A lot of it he was sending back to his brother." She purses her lips, remembering. "I was able to get into phone records and emails from back then. There was a lot of correspondence between the two of them." She trails off, looking out the window.

"What did you find?" Tom says.

She turns back. "Cameron sent them to me," she says. "Cameron wanted Hugh to get me to steal all that money. Cameron was the one who had tracked me down in the first place. He needed money for a new start-up. He'd been kicked out of college and needed the cash to get a project off the ground." Tom can see how the sinews pulse in her cheeks as she grinds her teeth. "After I'd disappeared, Hugh reached out to his brother, told him what had happened. It was Cameron who reminded him I had a sister. He wanted Hugh and Lenny to go talk to her, to use her to find out where I was. Maybe hold her hostage so I would give myself up. I don't know what happened. I don't know why they ended up killing her.

"All this time, I've been a problem for Cameron, just as much as for Hugh and Lenny. And this is how they found me. Hugh couldn't have done it on his own. He's needed Cameron's resources, his workers, *his* hackers. How could I get my vengeance when I was up against Cameron and all of his money? I knew they would still be looking for me. I was no hunter – I was the prey. I needed to put up guards against them. It's because of Cameron's team that they would've found me. That's how they broke through. And I know they'll still be looking now. Hugh and Lenny and Cameron are always going to look for me, just like I'll never forget about them and what they did. They know *that*, too. There hasn't been a day gone by that I don't think about them. And when you think about someone you hate that much, you start to think that maybe vengeance isn't enough. Not for any of them. Erica deserves *justice* – against the men that killed her, and anyone that helped them to cover it up."

"And do you have a plan to get that justice?"

"I have a plan," Cindy says, leaning her arms on the table and leaning forward. "I don't know how long it's going to take. You don't have to help me with all of it."

"I'm already in," Tom says.

"The bar will miss you."

"I'm sure it will. What's the plan?"

"We find Hugh," Cindy says. "And we find Lenny. And we get a confession. Hugh is weak. He'll break at the sight of you, I know he will. But through them, we get Cameron, too. And if they try to take me down with them, then so be it. I'm done with hiding."

5

Hugh was out late, but he wakes up early. Before his alarm goes off. It's not even five a.m. yet, which is Cameron's preferred time to set off for the factory. Hugh's not trying to impress his brother: it's his first morning back at work, and he knows Cameron expects he's going to have to wake him up, so this is to throw it back in his face.

He stayed out late last night. Took Lenny and went to his favourite strip club – Titty City. His trip down south didn't go quite how he'd wanted it to. He didn't find Cindy Vaughan. Found her apartment, sure, but that was the easy part. She got away. Disappeared. It was like she knew he was coming, somehow. Of course, bitch like that, she probably has all kinds of security protocols in place. In her line of work, chances are she's probably pissed off a lot of people over the years.

But none of them, he's certain, are as mad at her as he is. Or his brother.

The last thing they'd wanted nearly ten years ago was to have to smooth everything over with the dangerous men Cindy ratted him out to. Cameron had to send him and

Lenny to Europe, told them to keep their heads down while things blew over. In the meantime, Cameron built his empire, those men he'd stolen from, having no idea *he* was the one who'd really ripped them off.

Still, Cindy can run, but she can't run forever. There are men that work for Cameron that are very good at what they do, and what they do is the same as Cindy. Some of them are probably better at it, he'd wager. They managed to break through her walls once. He's sure they'll do it again. They *will* do it again. That's what his brother pays them for.

Titty City had been a welcome distraction after the failure of the preceding weeks. He'd needed to see some naked women covered in baby oil writhing around on stage, swinging from a pole. Now, though, at four-thirty, he's regretting staying out so late. Just a little. It hurts, though, getting up this early. No matter how much his brother forces him to, he just can't get accustomed to it.

He stands in the kitchen of the pool house he calls home and makes himself a coffee. Outside, the sun is slowly rising. He looks up to the main house. He can see a couple of lights on. One of them is sure to be Cameron. He's probably meditating or some shit. Getting himself mentally ready for the day. Hugh doesn't know. He doesn't care. He's not into that kind of bullshit.

What he *is* interested in, however, is Cameron's latest piece of ass. They've been together a couple of years now. Amy Pernier. Amy Pernier, with her sweet little body and her sexy French accent. Hugh would very much like to know what she's doing right now. Still sleeping, most likely. She doesn't have to be up at this ungodly hour, so why would she?

Hugh sighs, downs his bitter coffee, and goes to take a shower. By the time five a.m. comes, and Cameron is on his way to the pool house to rouse him, Hugh is already waiting for him by the door. Dressed and ready to go.

"Tah-dah," he says, as his older brother approaches.

Cameron looks neither surprised nor impressed. He looks at Hugh the same way he always does. There's a hint of distaste in his glance. He runs his tongue around the inside of his mouth. "Let's go," he says, moving away from the pool house, barely breaking stride.

Lenny is following close behind Cameron. He slows, waiting for Hugh. Hugh steps out of the pool house, shaking his head and holding out his hands. "Can't win with this fucking guy," he says, exasperated.

Lenny grunts.

Lenny isn't a morning person, either. He doesn't grumble about it so vocally, though, or make his displeasure so apparent. He gets up, gets dressed, and gets on with the day.

Back when they first moved in with Cameron, shortly after their return from Europe, Lenny had lived in the pool house with Hugh. He'd slept in the spare room. Hugh likes to keep him close. The pool house was a little *too* close, though. Lenny's snoring would reverberate through the thin wall between them. Felt like it was shaking the whole building. Hugh had to send him up to the main house. Cameron put him in a room in the far wing, where his snoring can't disturb anyone, save for the other security guards still awake and doing their rounds.

They follow Cameron down the side of the house, walking under the shadow of the wall. The pathway on either side of them is bordered with white pebbles and shrubbery. They reach the garage. Lenny steps forward.

"Which vehicle today, Mr Brewer?" he says.

Cameron doesn't answer right away. He ponders this for a moment, his hands in his pockets. Lenny presses the remote control that opens the garage door. There are half a dozen cars inside. Half of them are sleek, gleaming, expensive sports cars. A red Lamborghini Veneno. A black Bugatti Chiron Pur

Sport. A silver Ferrari 812. These vehicles are for pleasure. The other half are just as gleaming, but they're bigger. They're for business. One of them is the black BMW Hugh and Lenny and a guy they'd hired online had driven down to Texas. Another of the vehicles is the Hercules SUV.

When Cameron was a child, he'd gone through a phase of obsession with Greek mythology. At least, Hugh had thought it was a phase. Their parents, naturally, indulged him. They bought him all the books, comic books, and movies they could find about the myths. Anything for their golden boy, who, even then, as a pre-teen, was higher on their pedestal than Hugh could ever hope to be.

When Hugh heard Cameron had named his business enterprises Zeus Conglomerates, he realized the obsession had never really faded. When he found out Cameron had moved into renewable energies, he had to admit he was a little surprised. He'd never imagined his brother as any kind of conservationist. The name Zeus made sense after that. The God of Lightning. But not just that. The God of *Gods*. That about summed Cameron up perfectly – his idea of himself, at least.

The electric car company he started a few years ago he named Zeus Motors. They produce the Hercules SUV. They produce the Olympus, too, and the Athena, the latter of which is aimed more at the female market. At the minute, the car manufacturing is proving to be the bane of Cameron's existence.

"We'll take the Hercules," Cameron says. Hugh knows why. He wants to prove a point. Wants people to see it on the road. Wants them to believe that there's nothing wrong at the factory. That production hasn't ceased. That they haven't run into a colossal brick wall due to supply chain issues.

Lenny steps into the garage and takes the key for the Hercules from a hook on the wall. As he pulls it out, Hugh can't help but needle his brother while they wait. "Putting a brave face on it, right?"

Cameron barely glances at him. "What?"

"Drive the Hercules around town. Don't let anyone know the factory's in trouble." Hugh is grinning.

"The factory isn't in trouble," Cameron says, bluntly.

"You know that story doesn't run in the media."

"I don't give a shit what the media has to say about anything." Cameron turns to his brother now. "The factory isn't in any trouble, Hugh, because we're not going to have to worry about those supply chain issues for much longer, are we?"

Hugh rolls his eyes. "Are you even gonna ask me how it went?"

"You took two weeks, and you couldn't find her. That tells me all I need to know."

"It wasn't for lack of trying. Damn it, you think I'm happy about it? We got a hit, and I dropped everything and went after her. I ran everything by you first. You're awful pissy considering I made sure you signed off on everything first. What – should I have just up and gone, never told you?"

Cameron glares at him. "I gave you three *days*. You *took* the additional eleven, and you didn't check in with me about *that*."

Hugh wants to chuckle about this, but he refrains. "Sorry," he says. "It was pressing. Hey, if we *had* got her, you'd be pretty happy right now –"

"But you *didn't*." Cameron shakes his head. "But it's done. We can't get that wasted time back. And now that you're back from your little sojourn into the south, you can get back to fucking work, and get me what I need. Isn't that right?"

Hugh smirks, unfazed. "Sure," he says. "You know I will. You can always count on me."

Cameron snorts and looks away. "If that were true, you

wouldn't be working for me, or living in my pool house. If that were true" – he looks at Hugh again, as Lenny pulls the jet-black Hercules to a stop alongside them – "I'd have those minerals by now. That land would be mine." He gets into the back of the SUV and closes the door after himself.

Hugh doesn't get straight in after him. This last barb has stung him a little. Cameron forgets, sometimes, that he didn't accomplish all of this by himself. He buys into his own hype a little too much. Believes that he's a self-made man. If it wasn't for Hugh, and Lenny, he wouldn't have *any* of this. The reason Cameron gave Hugh a job, and a place to live, is because he *owes* Hugh, big time.

Hugh takes a deep breath, calms himself. He knows the truth. That's what matters, and when the time comes, if necessary, he'll remind Cameron of these details.

Usually, Hugh rides in the back with his brother. It's clear that today Cameron does not want him near. Instead, Hugh sits up front with Lenny. He glances back. Cameron is looking out the window, his chin resting on his fist. Hugh turns back around. Lenny opens the main gate and pulls out onto the road. It's quiet. No one else is around. No one in their right mind would see any need to be up this early.

Hugh makes himself comfortable. He looks up at the house as they pass by. The lights he saw on earlier are off now. Amy is in there. Still sleeping. Nice and peaceful. Hugh pictures her. Her bow lips puckered, like she's waiting for a kiss. Later, she'll probably go for a swim. There isn't a day goes by she doesn't go in the pool. Hugh sees her, sometimes. When he's home. He watches her through the window. Sometimes she catches him, but she never does anything. Or if she complains to Cameron, he never does anything. Hugh doesn't care. He watches her glistening, lithe body doing laps, imagines having her in his bed. Many long nights he's comforted himself with the fantasy of her coming to the pool house to see him.

No one talks on the way to the factory. Hugh doesn't mind. He thinks of Amy in the pool. Thinks how he'd rather spend the day sitting around in a lounger, watching her swim.

6

Cindy finds directions online to Balboa East, the district where they'll find Cameron Brewer's facilities. His office building, and his labs, and his car factory. It's early. Cindy has read interviews online with Cameron, and he's bragged about how he wakes up at four every morning, and gets to his facility, ready to start, at six a.m. Bragged, too, about how he sometimes works sixteen-hour days, six to seven days a week. Tom and Cindy figured they'd best get there early if they hope to see him arrive.

Yesterday, after Tom called the bar and told them he wouldn't be coming back, he and Cindy made their way across LA to get close to Hugh and Lenny. Yesterday was all preparation. They booked into a hotel near to the Hollywood Hills, where Cameron's home is. Cindy paid for the hotel. They set the room up as their base of operations. They paid a visit to a local electrical store, where Cindy picked up some surveillance cameras and other bits and pieces she thought they might need. There's a camera in the hotel room, keeping an eye on the place while they're not there. They can't be too careful. Hugh managed to track her down once. If he manages to do it while they're here, closer to him, they want to know about it and be prepared for what would come next.

The rest of the day, they rested. Tom cleaned his Beretta. Sharpened his KA-BAR. Cindy did research, looking into Cameron Brewer and his business.

"Are there other businesses out there?" Tom says. He's driving.

"A couple," Cindy says. "But none of them are as big as his." They grabbed some breakfast from a drive-through on their way over. It sits in a bag at Cindy's feet. Tom stopped off at a convenience store, too. He bought a glass jar of jam, but outside he promptly emptied the jar and rinsed it out in a public restroom. Cindy regarded him as he put the empty jar in the bag with their breakfast, snacks, and drinks for the day.

"What's with the jar?" she asked.

"You'll find out," Tom said. He didn't want to tell her then. He wasn't sure how she'd react.

"And what did you say the name of his company was?" Tom says.

"Zeus Conglomerates."

"That's an interesting name. What's he deal in, other than cars?"

"Renewable energies."

"Really? That surprises me. I guess the name makes sense."

"He's probably got some kind of angle," Cindy says. "People like him always do. They follow money, not morals."

Tom grins. "I don't doubt it."

The road to Balboa East is lined with other business districts. Factories, mostly. Early on, they passed a couple of outlet stores. Now, it's all manufacturing. These places are mostly quiet. It's getting close to six in the morning. It's too early for these businesses. Tom and Cindy are one of the only vehicles on the road.

It becomes clear when they've reached the area where Cameron's facilities are. Tom doesn't need Cindy to tell him they've arrived. Balboa East is the biggest of the districts they've passed through. There's more open space, too – land that has been filled with solar panels and wind turbines that are likely powering the immediate buildings and factories.

"I'm gonna drive through," Tom says. "Keep an eye out for anywhere we can park. We'll turn around and come back."

Cindy has her laptop open. "That's an interesting design," she says, looking up and squinting. They pass by the main building. It's squat and square, but seems to be made up mostly of windows. The sun is getting higher, and it catches the light and throws it back. When the sun will be at its highest, the reflection will likely be blinding. "You think it causes many accidents on this road?"

"I wouldn't be surprised," Tom says, driving on. This building is on their left. The car park to the side of it is quiet for now. There are plenty of spaces. Only a few of them are occupied. Security, more than likely. A delivery van is parked outside of the premises, at the side of the road. The driver is carrying a package toward the entrance. A security guard is holding the door open for him.

Further down, on the right side of the road, is Zeus Motors. Its design is a lot less avant-garde. It looks like any other car manufacturing plant Tom has ever seen. A corrugated metal warehouse. The name is on top of it, with a lightning bolt either side.

Tom leaves Cameron's buildings behind and continues on down the road a way. The Zeus facilities are at the end of Balboa East. Beyond is miles of dried-out scrubland. Tom turns around. They go back the way they came. They see the delivery driver turn his truck around and drive off. Tom pulls their car to a stop at the side of the road outside the main building, a little further down from where the delivery driver stopped. They have a good view of both the building and the factory, now to their right and left respectively, and they're in an inconspicuous space next to the chain-link fence that surrounds the parking lot.

"So what do we watch for?" Cindy says, though she's not watching, she's busy typing on her laptop, her fingers moving fast across the keys.

"For Hugh and Lenny," Tom says. Cindy has shown him a picture of them both. A recent picture, taken onstage at an event where Cameron was unveiling his latest electric car design, the Olympus. Hugh and Lenny were both stood to one side, watching as Cameron made his presentation. Lenny's face was a blank. A professional doing his job. Hugh looked bored. "We get an idea of their routines. If they leave and they go somewhere, we follow."

Cindy nods, still typing. She's frowning.

"What are you doing?" Tom says.

"I'm trying to access their security," she says. "To get into their cameras. If I can get into them, we can see inside. Watch them that way."

"You don't look like you're having much success."

"I'm not. This is some heavy security." She looks at him. "I'll break it, though." She winks. "I always do."

"You might break it faster when you've eaten," Tom says, reaching for the bag and pulling out food. He hands her a sandwich. "Keep your strength up."

They're still eating when they see Cameron arrive. They don't know it's him at first, though judging from the time, they have an idea that it is. "The fuck is that thing?" Tom says, eyeing the vehicle coming down the road and signalling into the entrance.

It's an SUV, but it's bulky, and looks almost like an armoured vehicle. It's black in color, and has tinted windows and strange angles on its wings. It isn't exactly streamlined.

Cindy snorts. "That's the Hercules SUV," she says. "It's Zeus Motors' premier sports utility vehicle." She's grinning.

"It's one of the ugliest vehicles I've ever seen," Tom says. "And I've been to war. It looks like being blown up would improve it."

Cindy laughs. "It's one of their bestsellers."

"Can't account for taste."

The SUV goes to the front of the building, then stops. Two men get out – one from the back, one from the front.

"That's Cameron," Cindy says, her face dark, pointing at the man who gets out the back. Then she sits up, her eyes wide.

She doesn't need to say anything. Tom has seen who the front passenger is. It's Hugh. He hears how Cindy's breath comes in short gasps. Tom reaches over, places a hand on her shoulder to comfort her. She takes the hand from her shoulder and slips her fingers through. She holds tight. "I didn't—" She tries to speak, but sounds like she's battling hiccups. She takes a deep breath, so she can talk. "I didn't realize how much it would affect me," she says. "Actually seeing him."

Tom watches. Cameron goes into the building, leaving Hugh behind. Hugh follows at a leisurely pace. He doesn't go inside, though. He waits by the door, looking back to the SUV, like he's waiting for the driver. The SUV pulls away, goes around to the parking lot. It parks close to the building. The driver gets out. Cindy's grip on Tom's hand manages to get tighter. It's Lenny.

She's breathing harder, now. She sounds like she might cry. She moves the laptop from her legs and puts it on the dashboard. She turns into Tom, wraps her arms around him. She's trembling. Close to tears.

Tom holds her, but he keeps an eye on the building. Lenny catches up to Hugh. They go inside together. "They're gone," he says. Her reaction to Hugh and Lenny was stronger than it was to Cameron. Tom knows why. Cameron is the figure behind the scenes, pulling strings, barking orders. Hugh and Lenny were the ones who got their hands dirty. They were the ones who killed her sister.

Cindy holds him a moment longer. "I'm sorry," she says, speaking into the side of his neck.

"It's all right," Tom says. "Take your time. I'm here for you."

7

The parking lot has gradually filled as the hours have gone by. Most of the workers for the main building turned up at eight a.m. The parking lot is full now. Overflowing, in fact. Some vehicles have parked along the road in front of where Tom and Cindy are seated.

It's getting hot in the car. September is still feeling like the height of summer. Tom turns to look at the car factory. The staff there arrived later, which surprised him. He thought they would've got here sooner than the office and lab workers. Instead, it was closer to nine. He hasn't heard or seen much activity since then. Now, he sees workers hanging around outside. They wear overalls, but most of them have dropped them and tied them around their waists. They're standing around, or leaning against the side of the building. One of them is sitting cross-legged on the ground. Tom counts seven of them, but beyond that, inside the building, he can see more workers. They're standing around in there, too. Talking to each other. They're not working. None of them are working. They all look bored.

Tom checks the time. It's only just after ten-thirty. Too

early for a lunch break. He winds his window down a little. He can't hear the sounds of any machinery. Nothing coming from inside the building.

"They're not doing anything in the factory," he says.

Cindy glances up from her computer, looks over. "Doesn't look like it," she says. "Hmm. I'll take a look into that later. See if I can find a reason why. For now, I wanna keep on at their security systems."

She returns to her laptop, and Tom turns back to the main building. There isn't much activity there. It seems like once people go inside, they stay there. He hasn't seen any sign of Cameron, Hugh, or Lenny since they arrived. He wonders what they're doing in there. Wonders if it's all people sitting at desks, in cubicles, at computers, doing research, making phone calls. Or if it's more practical – maybe they're in labs, wearing white coats. Perhaps they're putting together solar panels. It could be a combination of all three. The building is certainly big enough, and that's not to mention the other smaller buildings dotted around nearby. If Cindy is able to crack the security and get a view inside, he'll be interested to see.

It's hard to stare at it too long. The way it reflects the light hurts his eyes. It's probably done on purpose. To maintain a level of privacy. To stop rival companies from seeing in, poaching ideas.

"You know how we found Cameron's home address easy enough?" Cindy says suddenly, not looking up from her screen.

"Yeah," Tom says, sipping from a bottle of water. The water has already warmed.

"I've been trying to find an address for Hugh," she says. "And for Lenny, too. Been trying since yesterday." She shakes her head. "Can't find anything."

"They're not public figures like Cameron is," Tom suggests.

"Yeah, but I've searched the census, and there's nothing there, either."

"Could they have scrubbed that information from online?"

"I don't think it's that," she says. "I wonder if they're living with Cameron."

"They *did* arrive here with him. Lenny was driving."

Cindy nods. "And from what I've seen online, his house would be big enough. *More* than."

Tom nods. His eyes never leave the front of the building, watching the entrance. Occasionally he glances back over at the car manufacturing plant. Some of the workers there are still standing outside, but most of the ones he saw earlier have gone back inside. He can see them milling around, looking bored. The ones still outside have their faces turned to the sun, catching its rays.

"You said Cameron had already made some money when he sent Hugh and Lenny to you," he says, turning back to the main building.

Cindy nods. She looks up from the laptop now, blinking and rubbing at her eyes. She laces her fingers and pops her knuckles. Takes a rest from the computer screen. "Uh-huh." She raises her eyebrows. She doesn't sound impressed. "You wanna hear how?"

"Something tells me I probably don't, but I suppose I'd better," Tom says. "Important to get all the details."

Cindy nods. "Typical rich asshole story, though with maybe a little more assholery."

"All right, then."

"I'm sure it won't come as a surprise to hear they already come from money?"

"Not really."

"Yeah. Not like billionaire money, nothing like what Cameron has now. But they were definitely a *lot* more comfortable than most. Their grandfather was a landowner, he got rich selling a lot of it off, and after he died, all that money and remaining land went to his son, Cameron and Hugh's father. So Cameron had a pretty good start to begin with. And like I've said before, he was the favorite son. Hugh was the younger problem child. Cameron was the shining star who could do no wrong.

"When he went to college, that's when he first got noticed by everyone else. He got into MIT. The thing with Cameron is, so far as I can tell, he *is* smart. He's more than capable. He's also just a spoiled little rich boy, and he had his choice of colleges and universities. But, a couple of years into MIT, he got into some trouble. Big trouble. It actually got him kicked out of the school. But like I said, it's also where he got noticed, so when they kicked him out it didn't mean a damn thing."

"What did he do?"

"He developed an app. It was called Rate It. It's an innocuous name – it doesn't sound like it's anything bad. It just sounds like somewhere you go to review stuff. And that's what it was, effectively. Except it was exclusively for college boys, and what they were doing was rating their one night stands, their fuck buddies, sometimes even their girlfriends. It was gross."

Tom grunts agreement.

"Anyway, the school found out about it and the kicked him out. Didn't matter by then, because there was already interest in the app. A company bought it for hundreds or thousands of dollars. They reframed it as a hook-up site and opened it up to women, too. The members get to rate each other based on their sexual prowess – or, y'know, just what they were like on the date. If they were a gentleman, if they paid, if they told boring stories or only talked about themselves, whatever. The idea is that the users get more dates and hook-ups based on their reviews. It's still going today, apparently.

"So, this company buys his app for thousands of dollars. He's got his own money now, but it's still not enough. He starts investing it. Like I said, he's not a stupid guy. He knows how to play systems. He knows how to get the best return on his stocks, how to grow his money. So he does that, through cryptocurrency, through index funds, through land. But it didn't work fast enough for him. That's where Hugh, and Lenny, and *me* come into his story. So all that money Hugh was getting me to steal, and then sending on to his brother, he invested *that* into electronics, and he branched out from there. Into renewable energies, starting with solar panels and turbines, and eventually into vehicles. Do you see what I mean? There's always an angle. He goes where the money is. And that's what's led him to all of this." She gestures at the main building and the car manufacturing plant.

Tom nods. Cindy pulls her laptop back onto her legs. She sighs, then cracks her knuckles again. "You familiar with Rate It, Tom?"

He laughs.

The hours pass by. Cindy begins to shift in her seat, and Tom knows what this means. "How you getting on?" he says.

"Trouble is," Cindy says, "there's a hell of a lot of them in there, and there's only one of me out here." She shifts again. "You know, the problem with this all-day stakeout thing, and especially when we don't know when exactly they're gonna leave, is that I'm really starting to need to piss. You don't need to piss?"

"I've got a strong bladder," Tom says. "It's from doing this so many times. Too many times." Tom reaches into the bag that's carrying their supplies. He pulls out the empty glass jar, holds it up to her.

Cindy's eyes narrow. "What's this?"

"Your toilet," Tom says.

She looks at him.

"I've been told it's difficult for women to piss into a bottle, the way I'm going to when I need to. I've been told a jar is better."

Cindy stares at him for a while, like she's trying to work out if he's joking or not, then finally takes the jar from him. "I suppose this is very considerate," she says, starting to climb through the middle of the front seats into the back. "And yet somehow I still find myself annoyed at you. No peeking."

"Wouldn't dream of it."

"And maybe put the radio on or something. I'm pee-shy. I'm gonna really struggle if I think you're sat up there listening and judging me."

"What would I be judging?" Tom says, laughing, but he turns the radio on as she requests.

The day rolls on. People come and go, but none of them are Cameron or Hugh. They haven't left the building since they first arrived. Cindy naps for a couple of hours. She hasn't been able to break through the security yet. She said she'd sleep on it. Come back with a fresh perspective. Tom thinks the heat's probably tired her out. He lets her nap.

When it gets to five, Tom expects a mass exodus from the building. Workers leaving for the day, heading home. It doesn't happen.

It's a different story at the car plant, though. The workers are all fleeing at five minutes to the hour. The shutters are put down and the doors are locked. It's empty.

"You think Cameron expects everyone in the main building to leave the same time he does?" Tom says.

Cindy is awake now. She rests her head on her arm,

staring at the building. "Maybe even later. Wouldn't surprise me. Although he did get here before everyone else."

Gradually, people do begin to leave. Not a mass exodus like at the plant. Judging from the vehicles, a lot of people remain inside.

"This is gonna be one of his long days, like he bragged about, isn't it?" Cindy says. "We're gonna be here all night. Until it's dark. Until the moon's shining."

"We knew this was a possibility when we started. You can always stay at the hotel, if you want. I don't mind coming here alone."

Cindy shakes her head, straightens up in her seat. "No," she says. "I'm here. This is *my* fight. Where you go, I'm going too. I've waited a long time for this. A few hours of discomfort here and there isn't gonna stop me now."

As Cindy finishes, someone leaves the building. Tom recognizes him instantly. Cindy stiffens, and he knows she does too. It's Lenny. There's no sign of the other two. Not yet. Lenny goes down the side of the building. Gets the Hercules SUV. He pulls it around the front. Cameron and Hugh come into view, stepping outside. They stand apart from each other. They don't appear to be talking. Tom wonders about their relationship. If they're close, or if Hugh's reputation as the problem child has meant it's strained. That Hugh is an albatross around his older brother's neck. Lenny stops the SUV in front of them. They get in. Same as this morning – Cameron in the back, Hugh in the front.

Tom waits until they've pulled away from the building. Gives them some distance. He starts the car and follows.

"Finally," Cindy says, but her face is set. She's not crying this time. She's determined.

8

They follow the Hercules SUV into the Hollywood Hills. They keep a distance. Do nothing to arouse suspicion. When they reach the street where Cameron's house is, they stay down the road and watch as the gate at the house rolls open for the SUV to pull inside. It closes after them.

"They've all gone in," Cindy says. "That pays into our theory that Hugh is living there."

Tom nods. "We'll give it some time to be sure."

Cindy reaches into the backseat, and grabs one of the small security cameras they bought at the electrical store yesterday. Tom takes it from her, but he doesn't get out of the car yet. It's too soon. Cameron and the others have only just gotten back.

"You remember how I told you to use it?" Cindy says.

Tom nods, but he already has experience with planting cameras like this. They watch the gate. It remains closed.

"They're not coming back out," Cindy says.

Tom nods. "We wait for dark," he says. "Then I'll go plant the camera."

The house is big. All the houses on this road, this whole area, are. They're spaced out. No one has an immediate neighbor. It looks like the kind of place where, if a resident sees someone they don't like the look of, or the look of their vehicle, they'll call the cops to come check things out. And it's the kind of affluent area that the police will come rushing to. Tom remains aware of this. He wants to hang around until it's dark, but he doesn't want to stay too long. The last thing they need is for cops to roll up on them, lights flashing, drawing attention.

Cindy pulls out her laptop. She turns it on, then starts typing.

"What are you doing?" Tom says.

"Seeing what kind of security he has in his house," she says. She types and clicks. She turns the laptop toward him. "You see this?"

Tom looks. He can see a radar signal emitting, scanning the area. He sees the vague outline of Cameron's house, and the radar picking up on something from within it. A few somethings. He's not sure what they're scanning for, so he doesn't know what the items the radar is highlighting are. "I see it," he says.

"This scanner is picking up on nearby security features. I've got it pointed at Cameron's house." She turns the laptop back to herself. "He takes his security very seriously. He's got pressure sensors. He's got internal cameras. Chances are, the place is probably crawling with security, too, but I can't pick up on them through this."

"You gonna try to get into the cameras?"

"I'm gonna try, but this is his home – I reckon it's gonna be as difficult as at his business. But, like that, this is a start. Gives me an idea what I'm working with, and going up against."

As it gets darker, the house lights up. It's like a beacon.

Hugh and Lenny still haven't left. The gate remains closed. Tom is certain now that Hugh and Lenny aren't going to leave.

"I'll be right back," Tom says. He makes sure the internal light is switched off before he opens the door, then he gets out of the car and walks down the opposite side of the street. He has both hands in his pockets, the camera in his left. There are trees to his side. He walks under them, under their shadows, away from the lights of the house.

He steps back deeper into the darkness when he's directly opposite. Looks to the house. The lights are security lights. A lot of the windows aren't lit up. They're in darkness. Tom spots security cameras near the lights. It looks like they're all over the outside of the house. From what Cindy has told him, they're all over the inside of it, too.

Tom looks down the road. Headlights approach. He steps back further. The headlights come to a stop in front of the house, at the gate. The gate stays closed. The car is a taxi. A woman gets out. She's wearing a green sparkling dress. It twinkles when she moves, striding away from the taxi. She's on her cell phone. The gate opens up for her. Then promptly closes when she's inside. The taxi rolls on.

Tom plants the camera. He hides it in the crook of a tree's branches, aims it toward the gate. He steps away, then pulls out his phone. Calls Cindy. "How's that?"

"Little to the left," she says. The camera is switched on, and she watches its feed through her laptop. "Like, an inch."

Tom does so.

"Right there," Cindy says. "Perfect."

Tom takes one last look back up at the house, then returns to the car. Cindy is still typing. "You good?" he says. "You get through? We shouldn't hang around here too much longer."

Cindy closes her laptop. "Let's go," she says. "I'm not

gonna break through tonight. Let's get back to the hotel. I wanna shower, and to lie down and stretch out. I'm not built for this the way you are."

9

The early start has caught up to Hugh. He took a nap while he was at work, in his office, but it wasn't enough.

Hugh's job is easy, though, so it's not like it tires him out. Truth be told, the hardest part of his job is just turning up. He doesn't have to do anything else. He gets an office, and a secretary, but it's a made-up position. Hugh can't even remember what it is – 'Head of Urban Clean-Up Department', or something like that. Cameron came up with it. Hugh thinks it gets him some kind of tax breaks. Hugh's real job is clearing out Los Tierras Bajas – though he supposes that might be where the 'Urban Clean-Up' part makes sense. They don't do that during work hours, though. They do that at night, after dark.

The rest of the time, Hugh sits with his feet up on the desk and streams shows on his tablet. Lenny sits in the corner of the office, either reading a magazine or streaming something on his own phone, his headphones in. What they really do is spend their days waiting for Cameron to finish.

"You don't really need me here," Hugh has said to him, in

the past. "You've given me a job, like Dad asked, and that's all he needs to know, right? I don't actually have to be in the office. We just need to say I am. It's not like he's gonna call around and check."

Cameron had looked at him. "If I'm paying you – if you're taking money from me – you're gonna be in that office. I don't care if you sit in there and twiddle your thumbs all day long. That's where I want you. That's where I *know* you are. You turn up."

Hugh is woken from his after-work nap by noise outside the pool house. There's splashing in the pool. There's whooping and calling. Laughter. He can hear people running around. Realizes, too, he can faintly hear music. The kind of stuff that would be played in a nightclub.

Hugh rolls onto his back, pulls the pillow over his face. "Lenny," he calls through it, though it must be muffled, as there's no answer. He pulls the pillow from his face. "*Lenny Campbell!* You there?"

Hugh hears footsteps approach his room. Lenny opens the door, peers in. Hugh switches on the bedside lamp. "The fuck is going on out there?" he says, though he already knows the answer. He's been woken from his nap, and he's grouchy, and he wants to complain about it.

"Miss Pernier is having one of her parties," Lenny says. "She got back about an hour ago. I saw her return. She was on her phone, and I don't think she put it down until everyone started to arrive about fifteen minutes ago. I assume she was inviting her usual crowd of hangers-on."

Hugh snorts. Exactly as he expected. "Is Cameron out there with them?"

"I haven't seen him," Lenny says. "That doesn't mean he's not, or that he won't join them soon."

Hugh grunts. "What's the time?"

"Just after ten."

"When did I say we'd head out?"

"Eleven. To get there at midnight."

"What time did we get there last time?"

"It was midnight then, too."

"Then let's set off at half-past," Hugh says. "Get an earlier start tonight. Slightly. We've missed the last two weeks, after all. I'm sure they miss us."

"All right," Lenny says. "I'll go let everyone else know." Lenny leaves the room. Leaves the pool house.

Hugh lies back on the bed, but then pushes himself up and goes to the window. He peers out. There are a lot of bodies out there, in the water, and around it. It's dark, but it's still warm, and nearly everyone is in a swimsuit. A couple of people are naked, male and female. Hugh grimaces at the flopping dicks, but he eyes up the women.

Through the dancing and cavorting throng, he searches out Amy. Spots her finally, in the pool, at the edge, talking to someone sitting at the side with their feet dangling in the water. Her hair is wet and slicked back, tucked behind her ears. He can see her shoulders, and the straps of her bikini. Disappointingly, she is not one of the nudists.

Hugh realizes the person she's talking to, sitting on the edge of the pool, is his brother. Hugh shakes his head. Cameron is a machine. No doubt he'll stay up all tonight, indulging Amy and her gathering, and he'll still be up before dawn tomorrow and hassling Hugh, dragging him out of bed and to Balboa East, just to sit in his office all day.

Hugh takes a little longer to stare at Amy. To admire her. She pushes away from the edge of the pool, away from Cameron, and she starts swimming with one of her girl-friends. Cameron watches them go. He's in swimming shorts, and an open shirt, but he doesn't go any further into the water.

After eyeing up a few more toned, tanned nudes, Hugh

leaves the window and gets dressed for the night. For his *real* job. He pulls on dark clothes, then makes himself a coffee and waits for Lenny to return. He's not waiting long.

He knocks first, then steps inside. "Everyone knows. They're just getting ready. They'll be good to go soon."

"Let's set off," Hugh says. "They can catch us up."

Lenny nods, and they leave the pool house. The revellers at Amy's impromptu gathering don't pay the two black-clad men any attention. Cameron sees, though, with his feet still dangling in the water. Hugh nods at him. Cameron knows where they're going. What they're doing. It's for him. This is where Hugh earns his keep, as if he didn't already help bankroll everything Cameron has. Hugh volunteered for this job. He could tell Cameron was surprised, maybe even a little impressed, but it didn't take long for him to return to his usual level of disappointment in his little brother.

Cameron does not return his nod. Instead, he turns back to the pool. To the party. To these people that surround him, who aren't his friends. Not really. They're not Amy's friends, either. They're here because they're like vultures drawn to money, and power. They go where that is. They see an opportunity to be around wealth, and take advantage of what it's offering, and they seize it greedily. Hugh isn't impressed by them. He sees through them, even if his brother blinds himself to what they're doing. Hugh knows an argument could be made that he's doing the same thing. It's not the same. He's earned his place here, whether Cameron likes to acknowledge that or not. And he's family. He's blood. Cameron is his brother. No one else here can say that.

Hugh looks around as he and Lenny leave. He sees the naked flesh he spied from his window up close, indulging in their bacchanalian displays. He spots Amy. She's getting out of the pool. She's standing there, dripping wet, talking to someone. Hugh doesn't care who. He stares at her. At the contours of her body. At the way the water runs down her. He licks his lips without thinking. His breath quickens.

Then she's gone from view. Hugh and Lenny are leaving the grounds. They go to a car parked around the corner. A nondescript Volkswagen – not a Zeus vehicle, and not a flashy sport car. Lenny gets into the driver's seat, and Hugh sits up front. "You think they'll still be there when we get back?"

"I don't know," Lenny says. "Maybe. It certainly looked like they were all settling in for the night."

Hugh nods. "Yeah," he says. He grins. "They did." He chuckles. If he's lucky, one of the drunk and drugged-up girls might accept his invite back to the pool house. Maybe even a couple of them. They could have a wonderful night together.

They wouldn't be Amy, though, but that doesn't matter. He'll make do.

Hugh folds his arms and settles down in the chair, and thinks about what could be. It'll make the night go faster.

10

Cindy is sitting at the vanity table on her laptop. She's sitting by the window. They're up on the fifth floor. She's typing. Tom isn't sure what she's doing. He lies on the bed, his back against the headboard. The television is on. Tom isn't focusing on it. It's background noise. Cindy requested it.

She sits up suddenly. "Tom," she says. "Tom. *Tom!*"

"I'm right here," he says.

She looks up, as if startled by how close he is, like she's forgotten he's in the room with her. She sits cross-legged on the chair, her jeans off, wearing an oversized Swans T-shirt. She drops her legs and starts grabbing for her jeans, where she's dumped them in a heap on the floor. "They're on the move," she says, glancing at the computer screen.

Tom swings his legs over the side of the bed, into his boots. He starts tying his laces. "Who? All of them?"

"Hugh and Lenny," she says, pulling up her zip while watching the screen. "They're on foot." She frowns. "Shit, *shit* – they're moving out of view – oh, wait." She leans in closer. "They're getting in a car. It's parked outside."

She pulls out her cell phone, starts punching in details. "A VW. I've got their license plate." She slams her laptop shut and heads for the door. Tom grabs the car keys and follows.

"You get an idea of what they were doing?" he says.

"I dunno, I dunno," Cindy says, frantic, rushing down the stairs. "*Shit*," she says. "They were all in black. I just – if we get on the move, I can track them with surveillance cameras across the city. I can hack in, and we can follow them that way. But we're gonna need to catch up with them! How far out are we from Cameron's?"

"Twenty minutes," Tom says, keeping up with her. "Wherever they're going, we can catch up."

"Right, right," Cindy says, nodding, trying to persuade herself. "It's not like they're gonna go far. Not at this time of night. Right?"

They reach the bottom of the building, pass through the lobby of the hotel. It's quiet. The only person present is a young guy on the desk. He's on his computer. He glances up as they hurry through, watching them go.

They get outside, to the car. "Head to the house," Cindy says, opening her laptop up before she's strapped herself in. "We can head down the road they took. Unless I pick up on them and there's a faster way."

Tom starts driving. He heads up into the Hills. Returning to Cameron's house. Cindy is typing, searching for them. They're almost at the house when she says, "Got them!" She's almost laughing with relief. "Okay, okay – I think there's a faster way to catch up. Take a right here."

Tom follows her directions. They drive for a while, toward the outskirts of LA, but not quite as far.

"I don't—" Cindy says. She's still typing, but she sounds confused. "Something's happened. I've lost them. It's like...it's like they've driven into a black spot. They've completely disappeared."

"Then we head to where you last saw them," Tom says.

"I'm trying to check around this black spot," she says. "See if I can see them coming out the other side."

"Anything?"

"Not yet. Maybe not at all. I think they might've stopped inside it."

They get closer to the black spot. The area is looking rundown. Where they're going seems to be in a canyon. "Maybe head up there," Cindy says, pointing. "There's an overlook. If they *are* in the canyon, we'll have a better view of them from up there."

Tom does. The road is lined with trees. Tom peers down, looking through the trees, though they're still ascending and not too high yet. He makes out the roofs of some houses. There's an estate. "Where is this?" he says. He can see a few streetlights, but not as many as he would expect for an estate that looks so large through the trees.

"It's called Los Tierras Bajas," Cindy says, looking at her screen. "It means 'The Lowlands'. It's a low-income estate."

Tom turns off the headlights. He motions to the glow of Cindy's laptop. "Dim that light," he says. "If anyone's down there, we don't want them to see us."

Cindy nods and closes the lid. She puts it down by her feet.

The ascent evens out a little. They're at the peak, before the descent down the other side begins. Tom lets the car roll to a stop, getting it close to the trees. They're thick here, and they can't see through them as much as they'd like. They get out the car and step through. The edge is not far from the treeline. Cindy reaches out for Tom, grabs hold of his arm. He steadies her, holding her by the elbow. They stand close to the thickest tree near them and look down.

Cindy frowns, then points. "That's them. That's their VW."

Tom had already spotted it, along with the other vehicles parked next to it. There's five of them in total. They all have their headlights on. They're parked next to each other, across the road, like they're blocking the way in and out of Los Tierras Bajas.

Tom looks over the houses. A lot of them are in darkness. Like they've been abandoned. There are boards over windows. Some doors are hanging off their hinges. Walls have spray-painted graffiti on them. There is trash in the street. Most of the gardens are wild.

Not all of them, though. Some are still well-cared for. These are the ones with the lights still on. Signs that people still live inside. Tom sees that some panes of their windows are smashed, too. Their doors are damaged. One sits with a sunken car on its driveway, its tires all flat.

"What's going on here?" Cindy says. She must be seeing the same things Tom is.

The men who have arrived, who have parked their cars across the road, are out of their vehicles. They're all dressed in dark clothes. Hugh and Lenny are standing in the middle of the road. The men come and join them. Ten extra men – twelve in total, with Hugh and Lenny. Hugh turns and speaks to them.

At the houses, Tom can see curtains twitch. Can see the homeowners peering out.

Hugh turns to the houses. He shouts. At this distance, Tom can't make out what he's saying as he calls to the people inside their homes.

"I can't hear a word," Cindy says, leaning a little closer, like that might help. Tom tightens his grip on her arm, not wanting her to fall.

Someone steps out of one of the houses. An older Black man with a bald head and a white beard. He's cautious. His empty hands are raised. He approaches Hugh, taking his time. Lenny steps closer to Hugh. Right by his shoulder. The older man reaches Hugh. He's talking, keeping his arms raised all the while.

"I wish I could hear what they're saying," Cindy says.

Tom does, too. They're too far for him to read either of their lips. He sees Hugh start laughing about something, though. He turns to his gathered men. Repeats something. Starts laughing again. The men join in, whether they think what he's said is funny or not. Hugh is clearly their boss.

Hugh turns back to the old man. He says something, then he hits him. The old man keeps his hands up. He stumbles back a step, but he doesn't go down. Lenny steps in and hits the man from the other side. He knocks him down. Hugh turns back to the others. He waves an arm in the air. The other men move in. They move on the houses that have lights on, or look like they have people inside. They start busting down doors and charging inside. Windows are smashed. No doubt the insides of the houses are being trashed.

The old man is left fallen in the middle of the road. He looks unconscious.

"Where are the cops?" Cindy says, looking to the distance.

There are no signs. No approaching blue and red lights. If anyone in the houses has called the police, they're not in any kind of rush to get here.

"Could it have something to do with the black spot?" Tom says. "Could it be killing their phone signal?"

"Maybe," Cindy says. "I'd have to check. But I think that black spot only extends to any cameras in the area. They still have power. We can see the lights on. Presumably their landlines are still intact." She reaches into her pocket, checks her cell phone. "I've got signal. You?"

Tom checks. He nods.

The attack goes on for another ten minutes. Hugh stands to one side with Lenny, watching the other men go in and out of the houses, smashing things up, destroying property. No one tries to stand up to them. The only man who came out was the old Black man, who is only now just pushing himself up from the ground, still dazed. Everyone else stays inside their homes. If they're attacked in there, as the old man was, Tom can't know.

Hugh's men leave the homes. They smash some more windows on their way out. A television is thrown through one, rolling across the lawn. They return to their cars. Hugh and Lenny are already inside theirs. The vehicles come to life, their lights on. They turn around and leave.

The old man has made it to his lawn. Finally, someone comes out to help him. An older Black lady. His wife, presumably. She takes him by the arm, steadies him. They head back inside the house. They close the door behind them, except it doesn't close all the way. It's been damaged. It hangs loose.

Tom and Cindy look at each other. They're both frowning, both thinking the same unvoiced question. *What just happened?*

11

Tom starts early. He takes the car and returns to Los Tierras Bajas as the sun begins to rise. Cindy stays behind, at the hotel. She's online, looking into why last night happened. Checking if there's any news about it online – if it's happened before, or if complaints have been raised.

Last night, when they got back to the hotel, they were both in agreement that it looked like those men paid regular trips to the estate. The existing damage was likely their handiwork. On the camera they planted outside Cameron's house, they watched as Hugh and Lenny returned home, parking the VW on the road outside. The other men didn't go to the house. It was late, and they probably returned to their own homes.

Tom parks at the entrance to the estate. He looks around. The television that was thrown through the window is no longer there. There's a white woman, middle-aged, on the lawn, clearing up the bits of broken glass. The inside of the broken window has been covered with a sheet of cardboard. She turns, a handful of glass in her left palm. She sees Tom.

She frowns, glances left to right, then she goes inside her house. The door closes. Tom thinks he hears it lock.

On the other side of the street, he sees people peering out. When they see him looking back at them, they pull away. Hide themselves. He can hear a couple of keys scraping in nearby locks. The people here are wary of him. They don't trust him. From what he saw last night, he doesn't blame them. To the residents, he probably looks like one of the heavies. He wonders if they ever make daytime visits, or if their raids are strictly nocturnal.

Tom goes to the house where the old man who was hit lives. The door has been propped into place in its jamb, but it's clearly still broken. The wood around the hinges is splintered. He rings the doorbell. Waits. He isn't sure anyone is going to answer.

He rings the doorbell again. He can hear it sound inside. Then he hears movement. Someone is approaching, cautiously. The door begins to move. It's inched aside. Opens only a little. It's the man who was hit. Tom sees how the skin around his left eye is swollen and darkened. It shines.

The man frowns, staring out at Tom. "Help you?" he says.

"Hello, sir," Tom says. "I saw what happened last night."

The man's frown deepens.

"I was passing by, up on the ridge there." Tom nods back toward where last night he and Cindy stood.

Before Tom can continue, the old man cuts him off. "No one goes up there," he says. "Nothing up there, not any more."

"I got lost," Tom says.

The old man peers past Tom, looking to the road. "Who are you, man?" he says. "What do you want?"

Tom runs his tongue around the inside of his mouth. "I'm someone who saw what happened," he says. "And I might be able to help. But first, I need to know *why* it happened."

The old man laughs, but there's no humor in it. "You might be able to help?" He shakes his head. "Ain't no one can help us. No one *wants* to. No one cares."

"Have you called the cops?"

The old man laughs again. "I know better than most around here that cops don't do shit. Some of my neighbors don't know that. They make the call – you think anything happens? They don't turn up. We ain't as important, and we ain't as rich, as the boys turning up here every night."

"John – who you talking to?"

The voice comes from inside the house. The old man's – John's – wife. John calls back over his shoulder. "Don't worry about it none, Maggie," he says. "They're just leaving." He turns back to Tom.

"All right," Tom says. He can take a hint. "You don't want to talk, I get that. You don't know who I am, so why should you trust me? But I've come across situations like this before, and I've helped people in these predicaments. They're always scared to talk. I get it. But one thing they always have in common is that I could've helped them a lot sooner if they just told me what the problem was."

John looks at him. He sucks his teeth. A tentative finger probes at his swollen eye. "Here's what I *will* tell you," he says. "Don't stick your nose in. Mind your business. Leave right now, before you get yourself into trouble. Hell, they already know you're here, believe that." He shakes his head and moves to put the door back into place. "Ain't nobody can help us," he says, and then the door is wedged back into the jamb.

Tom steps away. He thinks about ringing the doorbell again, but he doesn't. John doesn't want to talk. Hassling him isn't going to change that. Tom turns to leave. He notices twitching curtains at other houses. People have been watching.

A car approaches. Tom can hear its engine. It's coming

fast. He turns his head to watch. It gets close enough for him to see two men sitting in the front. It screeches to a halt. It's not far from where he stands on the sidewalk in front of John and Maggie's house.

The two men get out. He recognizes their type. Heavies. Pumped up from hours spent in the gym. They're both wearing jeans and tight-fitting T-shirts. One of them is bald-headed. The other has dark hair and a goatee. They're both eyeing Tom. They slam the doors of their vehicle, and they come closer.

12

Tom has been in this situation enough times. He knows how it's about to go. He stands his ground. They're thrown by this. They exchange brief glances. Clearly, they expect him to be intimidated. The bald one is a full foot taller than Tom. The other is around the same height as Tom.

The bald man talks. "You lost, buddy?" he says. "Car break down, something like that?"

Tom looks them both over. Looks through them, to their car. Makes sure there's no one else inside it, hiding in the back maybe. It looks empty. "No," Tom says. "No breakdown. The two of you having some kind of trouble?"

The guy with hair rolls his neck. Something pops. He shakes it loose.

The bald man is smiling. "Maybe you need some help finding your way out of this dump. That it?"

"I can find my way just fine," Tom says. "Why you so interested?"

"Just get outta here, buddy," the guy with hair says. "There's nothing for you here."

"Nothing but trouble," the bald guy says.

"I've seen my share of that," Tom says.

The guy with hair looks up to his partner. "He's pissing me off," he says. "He pissing you off?"

"Man, his *face* pisses me off," the bald guy says, grinning. "He's pissed me off since the first moment I laid eyes on him."

"Who do the two of you work for?" Tom says. He knows it's unlikely they'll answer. He just wants to get them off balance, mentally. And he doesn't want them to know that he knows about Hugh, or Cameron.

"Man, fuck you," the guy with hair says. "There's two of us. And you seen the size of him?" He tilts his head toward the bald guy. "Just get outta here before you get yourself hurt. And don't come back here."

Tom smirks. He looks the bald guy up and down. "He's a tall one," Tom says. "But I've had worse odds."

"I'm bored of this," the bald guy says, making his move.

Tom responds in kind. As the bald guy steps forward, reaching, Tom ducks through and kicks at the inside of his left knee. The bald guy's leg buckles and he goes down, his kneecap out of joint. Tom hears his screams, but he's not paying attention to them. He's moving on to the guy with hair.

The guy with hair isn't much of a fighter, though it's clear he thinks he is. He adopts a sloppy boxer's stance, bouncing on his heels. It's also clear, however, that Tom putting down his taller, balder friend has jarred his confidence. He wasn't expecting that. He starts jabbing at Tom, but Tom easily ducks and bats aside the shots. He catches the guy by his wrist, drags him closer while he twists, then flips him over his shoulder. The guy with hair lands hard on his back. Tom doesn't let go of his wrist. He drags him off the ground, up to a kneeling position, then brings up a knee of his own, burying it under his chin. The blow knocks him out.

Turning, Tom sees the bald guy is trying to get up. His knee is blown, but he's still trying. His right hand is on the ground. Tom stomps on his fingers, breaking them. The bald guy falls back, clutching the hand to his chest.

Tom looks around, wondering how these two knew he was here. Wondering if they were stationed nearby, and so able to get here so fast. He doubts anyone who lives here called them. There could be a camera hidden somewhere, like the one he and Cindy positioned outside Cameron's house. There could be a lot of cameras hidden around this estate.

The scuffle has been heard inside the houses. There are faces at windows, watching. Tom turns back. He sees John and his wife at their living room window. Tom turns away. He goes back to his car, leaving the two heavies in the middle of the road, the guy with hair out cold and the bald guy still writhing.

Tom turns the car around and heads back to the hotel, to Cindy. His trip to Los Tierras Bajas has answered no questions, only posed more. With luck, Cindy has had a more successful morning.

13

———

Hugh gets the morning off, after last night's excursion to Los Tierras Bajas. He told Cameron he'd come in after lunch. Hugh would rather have just taken the day off, but Cameron frowns on that kind of thing. It's amazing he gives his staff any kind of vacation time at all. He never takes days off himself, and he expects the same from everyone else. Hugh didn't see it, but he's heard about his brother firing an employee for requesting time off for a family emergency. Hugh doesn't doubt this happened. It sounds like the kind of thing Cameron would do. He's a bit more lenient with Hugh, on account of their shared blood. And, perhaps more so, because their father asked him to keep Hugh out of trouble.

The party was winding down when Hugh and Lenny got back last night. Only a few stragglers remained, and most of them were on the verge of passing out. There was no sign of Cameron or Amy. It looked like the people still at the house had already coupled up. No one left for Hugh. A shame, but he didn't let it get to him too much. He was tired, and passed out almost as soon as his head hit the pillow in the pool house.

He hasn't been awake for long. Usually, after he pays a visit to Los Tierras Bajas, he still goes in to work with Cameron in the morning. But after two weeks off, he had a feeling he'd need a little recovery time. They'll be going back tonight, though, and he'll soon get his stamina back up. He's just tired, is all. Going down to Texas took it out of him. The stress of not being able to find Cindy hasn't exactly helped, either. Not finding Cindy has obviously stressed Cameron, too. He's more tightly wound than usual, Hugh thinks.

He pushes Cindy from his mind now, as he gets dressed. Drinking coffee, he glances outside. There are still a few people present from last night, either passed out on the loungers or doing lazy laps in the pool.

Amy is among them. She's on a lounger, in a bikini, sunglasses obscuring her eyes. Hugh sucks in his bottom lip and chews on it while he thinks. Cameron isn't home. Hugh grins to himself. Coffee mug in hand, he heads outside.

Lenny is leaning against the wall next to the door outside the pool house. He's reading a magazine. He looks up as Hugh exits, surprised to see him. He starts to straighten. Hugh holds out a hand. "Easy there, big man," he says. "We're not setting off just yet."

Lenny remains by the pool house as Hugh goes to the lounger next to Amy, sits himself down beside her. "Good morning," he says, sipping coffee. "Surprised to see you up so early. You would've had a late one last night, I'm sure?"

Amy is facing away from him. She rolls her head his way, though her shades are dark and it's hard to tell whether her eyes are even open. "What?" she says. She sounds unimpressed. She sounds like conversing with anyone at this time of the morning is the last thing on her mind.

Hugh takes another drink, and with his face obscured

by the mug his eyes roam over her body. Her tanned body glistens with beads of sweat. Her legs are long. He finds himself studying them all the way down to the tips of her toes.

"Enjoying the view?" Amy says.

Hugh realizes he wasn't being as subtle as he thought. The coffee mug is empty now. He puts it to one side, then shrugs and smiles at Amy, seeing his shameless reflection in her shades. "Hungover?" he says. "I could get you a coffee, if you like."

"I'm fine," Amy says, rolling her face away from him and turning it to the sky.

"Or some water, if you'd prefer."

"*I'm fine*," she repeats.

"Sure," Hugh says. She doesn't need to look back at him. Doesn't need to pay him any kind of attention. Hugh doesn't care. He's getting what he wants. He watches her small breasts gently rise and fall with her breath. He sees the sparse, downy hair between her cleavage, looking extra blonde against her bronzed flesh.

"It's always a shame when you talk in monosyllables," he says, deciding to push his luck.

She turns her face back to him, but only a little.

"You have such a beautiful accent."

She grunts.

Hugh laughs. "See? Even that sounds like music."

"What do you want, Hugh?" she says.

"Ah, now *that's* better! How many words was that – five? And that way you say my name – *Hew* – that's great, it really is." He's grinning.

She doesn't look impressed. "Why don't you fuck off, Hugh, before I tell your brother you've been bothering me again."

"Ah, I'm not bothering you, Amy. I'm just being friendly.

What, you don't want me to be friendly with you? I heard you Canadians are supposed to be a real friendly people."

She lowers her shades so he can see her eyes as she glares at him.

"The rudeness must be the French part of you, right? Sexy accent, terrible manners."

"Leave me alone, Hugh," Amy says, turning away from him again and covering her eyes.

Hugh stares at her. He doesn't leave, but she treats him like he has. She ignores him. Doesn't even turn her head again to check if he's gone. Hugh glances back over his shoulder. Lenny is still standing by the door of the pool house, leaning against the wall. He's not reading his magazine any more. His arms are folded. He's not watching Hugh and Amy, not staring, but he's watching over the area. Standing stoic. Doing his job.

Hugh leans closer to Amy. He clasps his hands. "Let me ask you something, Amy," he says.

She doesn't make any indication that she's heard him.

"Where are you gonna go when Cameron gets bored of you?" He stares at her. "Back to Montreal? Back to Daddy?" He waits a beat. "Of course, what's to say he'd even take you? You came to America for a reason, right? I reckon a pretty girl like you, who makes her living – her *real* living, so don't give me any of that bullshit about what you *think* you do for money – who makes her living from getting with powerful and wealthy men...well, that kind of girl's gotta have some daddy issues, right?"

She turns back to him finally. She's sneering.

"No, he's not gonna want you, either," Hugh says. "And listen to me, Amy, because no matter how much you might think you know my brother, he's still *my* brother. You're never gonna know him better than I do. He won't just get bored of you. He'll get *rid* of you. No one will ever see you in this town again, and do you think anyone's gonna fucking *care*, or *remember* you, when you're back up in Canada?" He laughs. "He's gonna drop you like a bad habit, and forget you just as fast. And when that happens, you're gonna come *begging* to get just a little of my attention."

He stands and walks away from her before she can respond. He's put her in her place, he's sure. He feels better for it. He goes to Lenny without looking back at the bitch. She's watching him go, he's sure. "Come on," he says to Lenny. "Let's go get lunch."

14

Tom gets back to the hotel. Cindy looks up as he enters the room. She's on her laptop by the window. "How'd it go?" she says. "Anyone talk to you?"

Tom tells her what happened. The old man that wouldn't say anything. The two heavies that turned up and tried to cause trouble. Tom mentions how he was careful not to give his name to anyone, and didn't let the two heavies know he knew who they worked for. He tells her about his belief that Los Tierras Bajas is under surveillance, as how else would they have known he was there?

Cindy nods. "It sounds like it. All the security cameras near the area are blacked out, but if they've planted their own cameras, that would explain why my software wasn't picking up on them. They could have the same firewalls as at the factory and in the house."

Tom takes a seat on the edge of the bed, close to her. "Do you think Cameron is behind this?"

"I don't think Hugh would go there unless his brother wanted him to. But I don't know. He and Lenny left from Cameron's house, when there was clearly a gathering of some kind going on – Cameron had to know they were leaving, and dressed all in black. That would've raised an eyebrow, surely. And those other men that were there with them, we don't know where they came from exactly, but I wouldn't be surprised if they're on Cameron's payroll."

Tom nods. He's been thinking the same thing. He tilts his chin toward her laptop. "Have you been able to find anything concrete?"

Cindy sighs, looking back at the screen. "No," she says. "Nothing on Los Tierras Bajas. I mean, I've found out a lot *about* the estate – when it was built, who the contractors were, stuff like that. Nothing that would actually tell us why Hugh, or Cameron, might be interested in it, or why they're hassling the people that live there."

"What about the residents themselves?" Tom says, a thought occurring to him. "Have you looked into them?"

"Are you wondering about potential past employees?" Cindy says, reading his mind. He nods. "I've tried that. None of them – no one that still lives there, at least – has ever worked for Cameron or any of his affiliated businesses. They're all manual laborers, blue-collar work. Not the kind of people Cameron would hire at all. Even the guys out building his cars all seem to have engineering degrees."

Tom exhales through his nose, still thinking.

"*But*," Cindy says, "I did find something interesting. It raises more questions than it answers, though. And it's only tangentially related to Los Tierras Bajas."

"What is it?"

"Not what," Cindy says. "*Who*. Kylie Hood."

Tom doesn't know the name. "Who's that?"

"She used to work for Cameron." Cindy starts typing, bringing up some information. "I started searching on the dark web, just to see if there was anything there that could help us out, as I wasn't getting any hits via conventional means. Here it is." She reads, reminding herself of the details. "So, Kylie used to work for Zeus Conglomerates as a researcher of rare earth minerals. I don't know what her job entailed exactly, as there aren't all that many rare earth minerals to be found on American soil."

"They could ship them to her," Tom says. "If she's a researcher. Cameron has the money for it."

"True. But the words that come up in conjunction with Kylie Hood most often *aren't* 'rare earth minerals' – they're *whistle blower*."

Tom cocks his head, intrigued.

"I can see you're curious," Cindy says, "but that's about as much as I can tell you. That's about as much as anyone knows. Whatever she was trying to tell people about, whatever secrets she was trying to spill, they've all been suppressed. There's gag orders left and right. Kylie herself has gone into hiding."

"Has she," Tom says, "or has she disappeared?"

Cindy raises her eyebrows. She knows what he's getting at. She's thought the same thing. "No one knows for sure. What they *do* know for sure is that no body has turned up."

Tom grunts. That's not always a good sign. He thinks of Hugh, and Lenny. They've definitely killed someone, and they're walking around as free men. They work for Cameron. Does he use Hugh and Lenny to take care of dirty jobs – to make problems disappear? They killed Erica years ago, and it sounds like they did it sloppy, but, again, they're still free. Now, they've had plenty of time to get better at it. To clean up their techniques.

"If she's still alive," Cindy says. "*If* she's still alive, then she's gotta be someone worth talking to."

"Maybe," Tom says, "but is it worth expending the energy on someone we don't know is still alive? Even if she is, we can't guarantee she could give us anything we could use."

"I think it's worth a shot," Cindy says. "I've been trying to find out where she could be, but I haven't had much luck so far."

"Do you know what she looks like?"

"Not yet. It's like every trace of her has been wiped from Zeus Conglomerates. If I was able to break into their security, I'd maybe be able to delve a little deeper, find some kind of record of her there, but I haven't gotten through yet."

"Do you think you *can* find her?"

"I always find who I'm looking for," she says, with a wink. "Look, I'm hesitant to spend more time on this than it might deserve, but this sounds like a decent lead. I'll give it the rest of the day, see if we can find her, or at least get a scent. If I can't, we move on, try to root out some other leads."

Tom nods. "Okay."

"I *will* find her, though," Cindy says, getting back to work, her fingers flying across the keys. "Same way I *will* break through the Zeus security system."

15

One of the benefits of Hugh starting later in the day, Cameron thinks, is that they don't have to ride in the same car together. Hugh went home – hours ago, now – with Lenny driving. Cameron *could* have made his brother stay later, to make up for his later start, but he knows Hugh would complain about staying out last night to visit Los Tierras Bajas and how that is work time. So Cameron lets him roll in late and leave at the same time as everyone else. Instead, Cameron is heading back with another driver. One of Stephen's men.

Cameron sits in the back of the Hercules SUV, staring out the window. His thoughts are racing. He has more important things to think and worry about than his brother, and yet lately Hugh is always at the front of his mind. He hasn't calmed over the years. If anything, he's gotten worse – wilder.

Cameron stayed late at the office, but it doesn't matter how late he stays, it doesn't fix his problems in the factory. Production has ground to a halt. It's been this way for over a month now. It's costing him hundreds of thousands of dollars every day. He could save money, a little bit, if he closed the factory and sent the workers home. He doesn't want to do that, though – not out of loyalty to his workers. Not because he wants to make sure they still get paid. He keeps it open, keeps them at work, as a show of strength. So the competition doesn't think there's a problem. He can't show weakness. If he shows weakness, others will move in. Other magnates, tycoons, businessmen. They'll smell the blood in the water. They'll try to take what is his, what he's built, away from him. He won't let that happen, even if that means he has to burn some money first. These problems are temporary. They're not forever. He just has to keep reminding himself of this.

Amy is sitting in the living room when he gets back. He's surprised to see her home. He expected her to be out, at a club, to return with her usual gaggle of hangers-on to throw yet another all-night party. Instead, she sits in the center of one of the sofas, one leg crossed over the other, her foot bouncing. The television is not on. She's not listening to music. She's wearing a pale blue dress, her legs bare. Her lips are pursed. She doesn't look happy.

Cameron steps into the room, an eyebrow raised. "You're home," he says.

She looks up at his approach. Her face does not change. "I want to talk to you," she says.

"Sure," Cameron says. He remains standing. He slips his hands into his pockets.

"Your brother is an asshole."

"I know that already."

"He was bothering me today," she says. "He was being creepy. By the pool."

"I've told you to ignore him."

"I've tried ignoring him. It's difficult to do when he's so obnoxious, and he won't go away."

Cameron blows air out his nose. He's not interested in

this. It's a waste of his time. Domestic issues don't concern him. They never have. "What do you expect me to do?"

"Why does he have to live here?" she says. "I don't understand. He's a grown man – he should have his own place. You pay him, don't you? But he stays here, in the pool house, staring out at me all the time, and at my friends. I don't like to think about what he is doing when he's watching us."

Cameron grimaces. "Don't be disgusting."

"You make that face, but do you think *I* like it? *He* is the one who is disgusting. You are not the one he's looking at, Cameron. They are not his eyes you feel all over your body."

"What do you want? You want him out?" Cameron shakes his head. "That's not going to happen. He's my brother. And I promised our father—"

"Your father," Amy repeats with disdain. "*You* are a grown man, Cameron! What should you care what your father says? He is not here. He is far away. Do *you* even know where he is?"

"Last time I heard from him, he was in New York."

"Exactly! He is not here! Why do you fear what he thinks? Why do you do as he says? You are your own man, Cameron."

Cameron clenches his jaw. "Hugh can't be trusted," he says. "Not out there. Not on his own. Hugh is a fuck-up. Hugh has brought nothing but shame and disappointment to our family name. He needs to be *here*, where *I* can watch *him*. Do you understand that?" He can feel his temper rising.

Amy shakes her head at him and sits back, her arms folded. "So you will leave him to do as he pleases? You will let him *ogle* me?"

Cameron rolls his eyes. "Jesus Christ, I'll go talk to him. Is that going to make you happy?"

She looks at him. "You used to care, Cameron. Lately, I feel like you do not. Ever since Hugh left for those two weeks, you have been changed. Angry. Impatient. You did not use to be like this. What has he done? What has upset you so?"

Cameron takes his hands out his pockets, throws up his arms. "I'll go talk to him now."

"He's not here," she says.

Cameron pauses. "What?"

"He's not home."

"Where is he? He left the office hours ago."

Amy shrugs. "I don't know. I don't ask him where he goes. I don't *care*. I prefer it when he is not here."

Cameron checks the time. It's too early for him to have gone to Los Tierras Bajas. Of course, there's nothing to say he's going at all. He could just be sending men. Hugh doesn't always need to be there; Cameron just prefers it when he *does* go. At least then it feels like he's earning a *little* of the money Cameron pays him.

Footsteps approach, distracting Cameron before his thoughts can go any further. He turns to the sound. It's Stephen Hawke. He looks harried. "Mr Brewer," he says, when he's close.

"What is it?" Cameron says. His nerves are already fraught, and from the look on Stephen's face this is not going to be good news.

"There's some footage I think you'll want to see," Stephen says.

"Footage? What kind of footage?"

"From Los Tierras Bajas."

Cameron feels his stomach sink. He thinks of Hugh, wondering what he could have done this time.

Stephen turns on his heel and Cameron follows. Behind, he hears Amy click her tongue, unimpressed. He ignores her. Something more pressing has taken the place of her petty complaints.

Stephen leads Cameron to the back of the house, to the

surveillance room. A wall of this room is monitors. Most of them show various rooms in the house, as well as the surrounding grounds. A couple of them are covering Los Tierras Bajas. A member of the security team is sitting in front of the monitors, watching over them. He doesn't glance back as Stephen and Cameron enter. Stephen goes to the wall opposite the monitors. To a desk with a couple of computers on it. There's some footage, already paused, on one of them. Stephen goes to this one. Cameron recognizes the area. He's never been out there himself, but he's seen plenty of maps and pictures of the place. Los Tierras Bajas.

"What's happened?" he says, as Stephen sits down and prepares to hit play. He stops, looks back at Cameron. "What has Hugh done?"

Stephen looks confused. "This isn't anything to do with Hugh," he says.

"Okay," Cameron says, surprised. He nods at the screen, encouraging Stephen to show him whatever it is he wants him to see.

Stephen hits play. Cameron watches as a man pulls up on the estate. Stephen starts fast-forwarding, telling Cameron how this man knocks on a door, talks to one of the occupants.

"He was spotted on the footage, so a couple of the guys who were nearby went over," Stephen says. "To see what was up, who he was. What he was doing there."

"And?"

Stephen doesn't answer. Instead, he stops fast-forwarding. Shows the two men confronting the stranger, and the stranger going through them like they were nothing.

"Jesus," Cameron says, although he's impressed by the man's efficiency.

"They said he hit like a freight train, and moved just as fast," Stephen says.

"Who is he?"

"We don't know."

"Do we know what he was doing in Los Tierras Bajas?"

"Just asking questions," Stephen says. "Apparently he saw some of Hugh's attack there last night."

"And, what? Curiosity got the best of him?" Cameron shakes his head. "I don't buy it."

"Neither did I. But we pressed the old man he was talking to, and he swore that's all he told him. Judging by the footage of how long they talked – and it wasn't very long – I believe him."

Cameron folds his arms and strokes his chin. He stares at the screen. Stephen has paused it on the stranger's face, just after beating down two of Stephen's men. "Find out who he is," he says. "If he's gonna be trouble, I wanna know about it. And I want it nipped in the bud. That clear?"

Stephen nods. "I'm on it."

16

Tom goes out for food. He comes back with Chinese. He hands Cindy a carton. She hasn't moved from her laptop all day. She tears into the carton and starts scooping out noodles with chopsticks. Sitting cross-legged, she turns to him. She waits until she's finished chewing before she speaks.

"So, I haven't found Kylie," she says. "And every record of her having worked for Cameron, save for her job description, seems to have been wiped."

Tom scoops out his own noodles. "I get the feeling you've found something, though."

She grins. "They missed one little thing, and I didn't even need to break into their system to get it. A press release, talking about the various teams working in Zeus Conglomerates. There's a picture of Kylie."

She turns the laptop so Tom can see. There are two women in the picture. The picture is close up, so it's hard to tell what's around them, what kind of room they're in. It looks like it might be a laboratory, judging from the counter to their side and the white lab coats they're wearing over their pantsuits. Cindy points to the one on the left.

"This is Kylie Hood," she says.

She's pretty. She has long dark hair, tied back. She wears glasses. She's smiling into the camera. It doesn't look genuine. It looks forced. There's no sign of how long ago the picture was taken, or how long she'd been working for Cameron at that point, but she already looks like she's not enjoying it.

"Who's the other woman?" Tom says.

"Well," Cindy says, "she's who I'm excited about. Her name's Catherine Massey. She used to work for Cameron, too, but as of a few months ago – around the same time Kylie disappeared – she doesn't any more. And they look pretty friendly in this picture, right?"

"It's a work picture," Tom says. "It's hard to gauge how friendly they might actually be."

"Maybe, but she's a lead, isn't she?"

"She's worth talking to," Tom says. "Do you know where she is?"

"I do." Cindy nods. She scoops more noodles into her mouth, then puts the carton to one side. "She's still in the city. Like, an hour away from where we are."

Tom checks the time. It's not too late. He finishes his noodles. "Then let's go," he says.

17

Hugh is barely watching the strippers dance.

It was his idea to come here, to Titty City. He's brought Lenny with him. He won't go anywhere without Lenny. He just wants to kill a couple of hours before they have to go to Los Tierras Bajas. Hugh is losing patience with the routine. He didn't think it would take this long. It's been about four months now. Only the stalwarts remain, but they're holding out, no matter what Hugh and his men do.

Hugh has had a couple of beers already. He's working his way through his third. "I dunno, Lenny," he says, leaning in close. "How much more can I do to get rid of these mother-fuckers? Short of burning the damn place down..."

Lenny isn't drinking. It's hard to tell if he's even looking at the women. He sits with his arms crossed, staring into the distance. *Stoic.* That's the best way to describe Lenny. He's stoic. Like a moving, breathing statue.

Hugh takes a long drink. "I can't do that, though," he says, bitterly. "Cameron says I can't damage the ground." He blows air. "I dunno, man. It used to be *fun*, y'know? I don't get the same feeling I used to when we went there."

A woman dances on the stage near to them. She wears nothing but thigh-highs and a thong that looks like it's been made from dental floss. Hugh watches her. She crouches down, her thighs spread, her hips rocking side to side, mesmerizing him. Her breasts look pumped full of silicone, almost misshapen. Hugh doesn't care. He stares between her legs. His throat is suddenly dry. He has to take another drink.

When it becomes clear neither Hugh nor Lenny (the latter of whom has barely batted an eye in her direction) are going to slip her any notes, she moves on. The next group whoops at her. They stuff crumpled dollar bills into her barely-there underwear. It spills out and gathers at her feet.

Hugh sighs. "Y'know what I think it is?"

Lenny grunts.

"That bitch down in Texas," Hugh says, leaning on the edge of the stage and staring off into nothing, much like Lenny. "We were supposed to go down there, deal with things, then come back conquering heroes. And instead she got away. How can I think about anything else when she's still out there? And worse than that, she probably knows it was us." He shakes his head bitterly. "We might never find her now. We got lucky that one time. I don't know if we're gonna get that lucky again."

"We'll find her," Lenny says.

Hugh pushes himself up, turns to Lenny. Lenny is looking back at him now.

"We will," Lenny says. "Look on the bright side – we found her once, we can find her again. And next time she won't get so lucky and give us the slip."

Hugh manages to smile. He nods. Lenny is right.

It's funny. Lenny is his employee. Hugh pays him to always be around. Pays him for his protection. But, in a way, they've been together so long now, Lenny has become his oldest friend. His best friend.

His only friend.

He's closer to Lenny than he is to his own brother. "You're right," Hugh says. "You're right. Enough of this maudlin shit." He drains his beer and indicates to a waitress that he wants another. "Gotta look on the bright side, like you say. Gotta think positive. We get Los Tierras Bajas dealt with, we're gonna have a lot of free time on our hands. We'll track her down. Run her to ground. We'll fucking *get* her."

Hugh keeps nodding at his own words, convincing himself. "Yeah, yeah, that's what we'll do. We ain't gonna give this bitch a chance to breathe. We get her before she can get us. Yeah. We were lucky to get away with what we did to her sister. We can't let her persuade anyone to dig up old graves. Some things even Cameron can't keep us safe from."

A waitress brings him another bottle. Hugh takes a drink, then settles back and looks around the room. He's ready to enjoy the view now. Ready to enjoy himself.

He makes eye contact with Dental Floss Thong and motions her over. She looks hesitant. Hugh pulls out some notes, wriggles his eyebrows. At the sight of the cash, she relents. She starts dancing in front of him. Hugh waves her closer, so he can speak to her. She crouches down, still dancing.

"I apologize for before," he says. "I had some things on my mind, but now you have *all* of my attention." He grins. "Why don't we go into the back room there, for a little privacy?"

The stripper eyes the money. She sees how much she could make. She winks at him. "Follow me," she says, stepping down off the stage.

Hugh turns to Lenny. "Stay close," he says.

Wordless, Lenny stands. He keeps pace with Hugh. Hugh notices how he doesn't so much as glance at the stripper's behind, despite how shapely it is, and the way she rolls it while she leads the way.

She turns back when she reaches the door, then spots Lenny. "What does he think he's doing?" she says.

"He's joining us," Hugh says. "He's my friend. You don't gotta worry about him – he's real quiet. You'll barely notice he's there."

The stripper raises an eyebrow, looking doubtful.

Hugh waves the money again. "I got enough here for two," he says. "I'll cover him. You just get in there and dance."

The stripper shrugs, then goes through the door into the back room. Hugh has been in here plenty of times before. He doesn't mind throwing Cameron's money around for a private dance. They're the best kind, in here, in privacy, away from prying eyes. Sometimes he slips them enough that they give him a hand job, or use their mouth. This girl is new. He's seen her before, but she first appeared a couple of months ago. Hugh hasn't seen her in private yet. All the other times, she's been busy with someone else, or wrapping herself around a pole as part of her stage show. The kind of performance she can't be dragged away from.

But now he has her alone. Just the two of them – plus Lenny, standing at the back, out of the way. Seeing, but not watching.

The room isn't huge. It's about 12 by 12 feet. It's big enough that sometimes parties are brought back here, and there'll be a few women dancing. The back wall is taken up almost entirely by a padded sofa with a high back and sides. It's purple in color. The lights are dimmed, but the walls are purple, too. In front of the sofa, there is a low glass table, for drugs and drinks. Hugh has neither. Sometimes the women dance on the table. This stripper does not. She guides Hugh to the sofa and pushes him back into it. She starts to move her body. She turns and bends a little, and rubs her ass on his legs.

Hugh watches, but she's already naked and it doesn't take

long for him to get bored. "Hey," he says. Her movements have stirred him. She looks back at him over her shoulder. "How much for some action?"

She doesn't stop dancing, but she moves away from him. "I don't do that," she says, turning back around, her hands behind her head, fluffing up her hair. Her hips move side to side. Her movements have slowed, though.

"I've heard that before," Hugh says. "Everyone's got a price."

The stripper shakes her head. "Not everyone," she says. "Now, are you gonna settle your ass down and watch this dance, or are we done here?" She's stopped moving. Her arms fall down by her sides.

Hugh looks up into her eyes. He smirks. "We can do this easy, or we can do it hard," he says. "I *got* the money. You can see that. All the whores in here, all you want is some money. Isn't that right? That's why you're here. Either you dance for it, or you do...other things."

"No," she says.

Hugh sucks his teeth. Sometimes they play a little hard to get, but he's not getting that impression here. It feels like something more. Something firmer. He doesn't like it. He narrows his eyes. Tilts his chin back toward Lenny. "You see my friend there?"

The stripper looks back. She's uncomfortable now. She folds her arms to cover herself, feeling exposed without any clothes on. The thigh highs and the floss thong leave nothing to the imagination.

Lenny doesn't move. He knows his cues, though. His arms are folded and he's looking back at the stripper now.

"He's bigger than anyone that works here, ain't he?" Hugh says. "Bigger than the bartender. Bigger than any of the door-men. And...they're out *there*, aren't they? And he – he's in *here*. With us. With you."

The stripper turns back. She swallows. "I'll scream," she says. Her voice is barely a whisper, her throat so dry.

"No, you won't," Hugh says, still smirking. "You won't do shit. Only thing you're gonna do is what I tell you to do. That clear? Cause if you don't... Well, let's not think about that, huh? Cause you don't wanna get yourself hurt."

She's trembling a little. She swallows again. Then she does something Hugh wasn't expecting.

She screams.

18

There are lights on at Catherine Massey's house when Tom and Cindy arrive, and there is activity at the front door. A man and two kids, heading out. The driveway's security light illuminates them as they get into their car. Catherine is standing in the doorway, watching them go. Tom recognizes her from the picture Cindy showed him. The kids and the man are waving at her from the car. She waves back. She's smiling. The car drives off.

Tom and Cindy have pulled to the side down the road, watching the goodbyes take place. It's a nice, suburban neighbourhood. The road and sidewalk are clean, and the windows of the houses are all intact. The lawns are well kept. The estate stands in stark contrast to Los Tierras Bajas.

"Records say she's married," Cindy says, "with two kids. That must be them."

They wait until Catherine has finished watching the car leave and gone back inside the house. Tom rolls down the road, parks in front of her home.

"Let me do the talking," Cindy says before they get out the car. "Sometimes you have this intense look on your face and that intimidates people. This is a nice, suburban house. She's not expecting a CIA interrogation."

Tom looks at her, an eyebrow raised. "I can be plenty friendly," he says. "And look at you – if this is as conservative an area as you're making it out to be, what's she gonna think when a cyberpunk turns up at her door in the late evening?"

Cindy shakes her head as she gets out the car, but she's laughing. "I've never claimed to be a punk, Tom. You need to brush up on your subcultures." She leads the way to the door and rings the bell. Tom stands to one side, lets her take the lead. "If it looks like we're not getting anywhere, feel free to step in and give her that stare you do," she says.

Before Tom can respond, Catherine has opened the door. She looks surprised to have visitors, especially so soon after she's just stepped back inside. She looks Cindy and Tom over. "Hello?" she says.

"Hello, Mrs Massey," Cindy says, smiling as wide as she's able. "We're real sorry to disturb you so late in the day, but we're looking for someone, and we were hoping you could help us track them down."

Catherine doesn't say anything. She eyes them both warily.

"We're looking for Kylie Hood," Cindy says.

Catherine stiffens at the name, but her face doesn't change. "I can't help you," she says. "I'm sorry, but I can't."

"Please, if you could give us any kind of information at all, it would be a big help."

"I don't know where she is." Catherine is already making to close the door.

"You seem awful eager to shut us out," Tom says, "if you genuinely don't know where she is."

She pauses, looking back at him. She looks at Cindy then, and says, "I'm sorry, who are you both?"

"We think that Kylie might be in trouble," Cindy says, "and we just want to help."

Catherine keeps one hand on the door, ready to slam it in their faces. She hasn't yet, though. That means she's at least curious about what they have to say. "My husband will be back soon."

Cindy holds out her hands. "We're not looking to cause any problems," she says. "We just want to find her, so we can talk to her. You used to work with her, right? The two of you were friends."

There's no evidence they were ever friends, Tom thinks. Cindy is taking a chance. But he can see, from Catherine's face, that she was right to do so. They *were* friends. Still are, perhaps. She's torn. Deliberating. She chews her bottom lip. She leans forward and looks up and down the road. "Is this some kind of trick?" she says, pulling herself back inside, straightening up. "You work for Cameron, don't you?"

"Do we look like we work for Cameron?" Cindy says.

Catherine looks at Cindy, particularly. Looks at her Swans T-shirt and her ripped jeans. "He might," she says, pointing at Tom. "I've seen Cameron's *security*." She snorts. "His *heavies*. You look like you'd fit right in." She turns back to Cindy. "Not you. He'd never hire anyone that looks like you do."

"I'm flattered," Cindy says. "Because I'd never want to work for anyone like him." She motions to Tom. "This is my friend. I can vouch for him. I can guarantee he'd never work for anyone like Cameron, either."

"Why do you want to find Kylie?" Catherine says. "Cameron's the only person who's been looking for her since she disappeared three months ago."

"*That's* why we want to find her," Cindy says. "To ask her why Cameron is looking for her. To ask her what it was she was trying to reveal. What he's had suppressed."

Catherine goes pale. She swallows. "I think you should leave," she says. "You're going to get yourselves into trouble."

"We're already in trouble," Cindy says. "We're looking for a way out of it. Kylie could be that way."

Catherine shakes her head. "Kylie doesn't have any way out—" She cuts herself short, realizing what she's said. An admission.

Cindy doesn't leap on it. She keeps her tone gentle. "Look, maybe we don't need to find Kylie at all. Maybe you could tell us what they suppressed—"

Catherine is already shaking her head. "I have a family," she says. "And I – I signed an NDA. I promised I wouldn't speak, and they promised...they promised they wouldn't bother me..."

"That's all right, that's okay," Cindy says. "Then maybe we could be Kylie's way out. She could help us, and we could help her. Please, Catherine. You're the only connection I've been able to find who might be able to put us in touch with her. If you don't know where she is, we might never be able to find her. If we don't find her, she might never be able to leave hiding."

Catherine is torn. She's deliberating. Thinking hard. She looks up and down the street again. She wants to help her friend, that's clear, but at the same time she doesn't want to put her in any danger. She doesn't want to put herself, or her family, in danger, either. She doesn't want to be seen talking to them. She's aware of the repercussions.

"Do you know where Kylie is?" Cindy says.

Catherine shakes her head. "No," she says. "But I know how to get in touch with her." She turns and disappears inside the house, but she doesn't close the door. Tom and Cindy look at each other, wondering if they should follow, or wait. They decide on the latter.

Catherine comes back a moment later. She has a small

piece of paper in her hand. She holds it out to Cindy. There's something written on it. A number. The ink is still fresh. Cindy takes it.

"It's a burner," Catherine says, still torn, her jaw working. She looks close to tears, not sure she's doing the right thing. "I swear to God," she says, "if you're lying to me—"

"We'll find her," Cindy says, pocketing the number. "And we'll help her. I promise."

Catherine seals her lips and nods. "All right," she says. "I hope you do. Now please, leave before my family gets back."

19

Cameron doesn't come into the strip club himself. He sends Stephen, and Stephen brings a couple of his men.

Hugh isn't surprised. Cameron wouldn't be seen dead in a place like this. He couldn't. Pictures would be taken. It would be front page news tomorrow morning. It's more hassle than it's worth.

Titty City is in disarray. The lights are all on. The patrons are gathered to one side, the opposite side of the room to where Hugh and Lenny stand. There are paramedics present, tending to the doormen. The ones who tried to break the door down after the dancer screamed. It didn't do them, or her, any good. Now they're nursing wounds. They're bloodied, and they have broken bones, courtesy of Lenny. The dancers are all wrapped in oversized jackets. The one with the floss thong is nowhere to be seen. Hugh smirks to himself.

Stephen is desperately trying to smooth things over with the club owner. He's throwing money at the situation –

Cameron's money. To buy their silence, and guarantees that no charges will be pressed.

The owner of the club, a short man with a mustache and a mullet, is gesturing toward Hugh. His face is close to Stephen's, and full of blood. He's angry. Hugh turns to Lenny. "Cameron's not gonna be happy about this," he says. "Sorry, buddy, but I'm gonna throw you under the bus here."

Lenny grunts. Likely he was expecting this.

Things begin to calm with the mulleted club owner. He takes the payoff Stephen is offering him. He doesn't look happy about it, but the money will help numb the sting. He turns away, goes off to check on his girls.

Stephen comes to Hugh and Lenny. He doesn't look happy, either. No one, save for Hugh, is looking very happy right now. "What happened?" Stephen says.

Hugh shrugs.

Stephen is unimpressed. He looks around the club. "Jesus Christ," he says, shaking his head. "Let's get out of here. We've managed to hold off the cops and the press, but we can't do that forever. Come on. Cameron is waiting in the parking lot."

Hugh sighs, bracing himself for the inevitability of Cameron's fury. Stephen leads the way out. Hugh and Lenny follow. Hugh looks back at Lenny. Lenny is looking straight ahead. Hugh clenches his jaw. The strippers are glaring at him as he walks by. Hugh ignores them. Their eyes mean nothing next to his brother's anger.

Outside, Stephen turns back to him. "Needless to say," he says, "you can't come back here."

"Sure," Hugh says. He can see which vehicle Cameron is in. It's the Hercules SUV. He knows Cameron is in it, in the back of it, because it has blacked-out windows. He's come down here, but he's still going to maintain his anonymity.

"I'm serious, Hugh," Stephen says, stopping and placing a hand on his chest. "That was part of the deal. That was what paid for their silence. You *cannot* come back here. Not ever. You do, the deal goes out the window."

Hugh speaks through clenched teeth, his jaw aching. "Fine," he says.

Stephen and his men get into a van, and they wait while Hugh and Lenny get into the Hercules. Hugh gets in the back. Lenny gets in the front, next to the driver. The driver looks uncomfortable. No doubt he's picking up on the furious vibes Cameron is putting out. Hugh certainly is. He almost chokes on them.

Cameron stares a hole through him as he settles. He tries to speak, but he's too angry to get any words out. His nostrils flare as he blows air. "What the *fuck* happened here?" he says, leaning in close, his eyes wide and unblinking. They look like they're about to pop out of his skull.

Hugh can't hold Cameron's gaze. It's too intense. The driver hasn't started the car yet. Stephen's van hasn't left, either. They're all waiting on Cameron's say-so.

"Look, Cameron—" Hugh begins.

"Look me in the eye when you're talking to me," Cameron says.

Reluctantly, Hugh does. It's difficult to maintain. "Lenny... Lenny just got a bit carried away. That's what happened here. The girl got him all worked up. You know how it is. They're all like, 'you can look but don't touch'. Well, Lenny wanted to touch. The girl wasn't having it. He got caught up in the moment."

"I've heard exactly how carried away he got," Cameron says. "A broken nose, a dislocated jaw, and a fractured cheekbone? A couple of cracked ribs? And they say she was *tiny*. He could've killed her. I'd say that's more than a *bit* carried away, wouldn't you?"

"I couldn't stop him, Cameron," Hugh says. "What do you expect me to do?"

Cameron seethes. "I've had to cover her medical bills," he says. "Not to mention her lost earnings, plus some extra on top, just to keep her fucking mouth shut."

"Well, keeping her mouth shut shouldn't be too much of a problem..."

Cameron's eyes blaze. "Do you think this is *funny*?"

"I get it, Cameron, I really do," Hugh says, hands raised, begging off. "But tell *him*."

Lenny sits in the front, and he stares straight ahead.

Cameron narrows his eyes at his brother, then he turns on Lenny and slaps him in the back of the head. Lenny barely moves. "Look at me," Cameron says.

Lenny turns. He looks back at Cameron. He has no problem with holding his eye. Cameron looks unnerved by it. Lenny's face is fixed, impassive. He's like stone.

"You wanna explain yourself?" Cameron says.

Lenny clears his throat. "It's like Hugh said." He sounds bored. "I got carried away. I apologise, Mr Brewer."

"You think an *apology* is enough? Jesus, Lenny, you almost killed that girl! And for what? Because she wouldn't suck your dick? You need to get it together." He jabs his finger into Lenny's impassive face. "I expect you to be a professional, damnit. This kind of behavior isn't acceptable." He shakes his head. He's already softening. He's not as hard on Lenny as he is on Hugh. This is what Hugh was banking on. "If you ever need a woman to – to – to do *whatever* it is you want, then you come and see me. I can just buy you one, for Christ's sake!"

Lenny nods once. "Yes, sir, Mr Brewer."

Cameron sighs and falls back into his seat. "Let's go home," he says to the driver.

They go back to the Hills in silence. Cameron stares out the window, his left fist balled and resting against his mouth. When they get back, he gets out of the car and storms inside without a word. The driver goes out after him. Hugh and

Lenny are left alone in the Hercules, parked in the garage. Stephen and his men park elsewhere.

"Sorry to do that, man," Hugh says.

Lenny doesn't turn.

"But you know what he's like," Hugh goes on. "If it was me – if he thought I was responsible for what happened to the girl – he would've kicked me out of the house. He would've kicked us *both* out. You know how he feels about me. You're on firmer ground, though. He likes you. He thinks you've got worth. And, y'know, he probably knows it wasn't really you. I reckon he knows it was me. I can't admit to it, though. If I admit to it, then he can do what he wants with us, and he doesn't have to worry about any repercussions from Dad."

Lenny doesn't respond. They sit in silence for a moment. Hugh fidgets with his hands.

"Listen, I'll make it up to you," he says. "You're gonna get a bonus this month. And I really appreciate you dealing with the bouncers how you did."

Lenny grunts. "He shouldn't have hit me," he says.

Hugh doesn't remember any of the doormen managing to land a shot on him. Then he remembers Cameron slapping him. "No, he shouldn't have."

"If it was anyone else, I would've broken their arm."

"I know you would, big guy. I know you would."

They sit in silence a moment longer. Lenny stares straight ahead, at the wall.

"Let's go inside now, shall we?" Hugh says.

Lenny doesn't respond. He gets out of the SUV and waits for Hugh to do the same. Hugh does. Out of the vehicle, he pats Lenny on the arm. "I appreciate you, big man. You know that."

Together, they return to the pool house.

20

Tom and Cindy don't go straight back to the hotel. They leave Catherine's home, leave her street, but they find somewhere to pull over under some low-hanging trees.

"It's getting late," Cindy says, staring at the number Catherine gave them. "Should I call now? Should we wait until morning?"

"There's no time like the present," Tom says. "The question is, how likely is she to answer a number she doesn't recognize?"

Cindy nods. "But if I send her a message, and that spooks her, she might just up and get rid of this number completely."

They both stare at the scrap of paper Catherine gave them. They read the numbers over and over.

Finally, Cindy takes a deep breath, and she pulls out her phone. "I'm gonna call."

"And if she doesn't answer?"

"I'll leave a voicemail. In fact, a voicemail might be the best way to go. Then she can hear my voice. You can't get tone through a text."

"Provided she listens to it," Tom says.

"Try not to be so negative, Tom."

"Not negative," he says. "Just considering every possibility."

Cindy stares at the number, then punches it into her cell. She braces herself before she hits dial. "We've got one shot at this," she says.

Tom nods.

Cindy dials the number. They both listen as it rings. It rings for a while. There's no answer. Neither of them is surprised. It goes to voicemail. Cindy swallows. She starts to speak.

"Kylie, my name is Cindy Vaughan. I got this number from Catherine Massey. I'm sat here with my friend, Tom Rollins. I don't expect you to trust us, but I hope you'll listen to this message and call us back. We want to help you. Nearly ten years ago, my sister was killed by Hugh Brewer and his bodyguard on the orders of his older brother, Cameron. I've been hiding from them ever since that day, so I know what you're going through right now. But recently, they tracked me down. They almost got me. I've come here to LA to stop them before they can hurt anyone else. I don't know what's happened between you and Cameron Brewer, but I'm not shocked you're hiding from him. Please, call me back. Let's meet up. Let's talk. Let's see if we can help each other out." She hesitates, and then she hangs up. She turns to Tom. "How did that sound?"

"As good as it could," Tom says.

Cindy nods, staring at her phone, willing it to ring. Even if Kylie has chosen to listen to the message, she won't be through with it yet. "How long do we wait?" Cindy says.

Tom starts the engine. "We don't," he says, pulling away from under the trees and heading back to the hotel. "We prepare our next course of action. If Kylie Hood is potentially a dead end, we need to treat her as such and leave her behind. Move on to something that could prove useful. If we *do* hear from her in the meantime, then good. But we need to keep our options open."

Cindy nods. She knows he's right. She keeps her cell phone in her lap, though, staring down at it.

When they pull into the hotel's parking lot, before Tom has killed the engine, the phone begins to ring. Cindy's eyes go wide. "It's her," she says. She answers, putting the phone on speaker so Tom can hear.

Kylie's voice comes through. It's harsh, and rough. Three months of being hounded, and hiding out, has sharpened her tone. "I won't talk on the phone," she says. "Tomorrow morning, ten a.m., you come where I tell you. I'll see you before you see me. I see anything I don't like, I'm out. That clear?"

"That's clear," Cindy says.

"I'll message you the location," Kylie says. She sounds like she's walking, fast. Like she keeps checking back over her shoulder. "Send me a picture of you both. One at a time. Full body, front and back."

"I will," Cindy says, and then Kylie has hung up.

Cindy looks at Tom. "Okay," she says, sounding suddenly as breathless as Kylie did. "She'll see us."

"I heard," Tom says.

Cindy stares at the phone, waiting for the location to come through. "Let's get inside," she says. "Send her these pictures she wants."

Tom reaches over before Cindy can get out of the car. He places a hand on her arm. "Cindy," he says.

She looks at him, expectant.

"Try not to get your hopes up too high," he says. "Don't put all your eggs in this one basket. Whatever she tells us, chances are we're still gonna have to find other ways to bring them down."

Cindy looks at him, chewing her lip. She takes a deep breath. Calms herself. Settles back in her seat. She looks at Tom. Reaches out and places a hand on his thigh. "I get it. I really do. My hopes might be a little high right now, but I'm still a realist. This is the closest I've gotten since they killed Erica. I can't let that slip away."

Tom nods. "If tomorrow is a bust, we'll find another way."

"I know we will," Cindy says, opening her door. "I didn't come this far to only come this far."

21

Cameron wakes as early as he always does. He doesn't get straight out of bed, though. He lies in the dark and stares at the ceiling. He didn't sleep well last night. He's still annoyed about the incident at the strip club.

Amy lies next to him, sleeping. She'd looked unimpressed when he got back. She didn't say anything, but she didn't need to. Her silence spoke volumes. She got into bed without a word. Cameron didn't attempt to engage her.

He supposes anger and self-pity aren't going to get him anywhere, so he drags himself out of bed. He doesn't feel like working out, or meditating, so instead he just has a quick shower, then gets dressed. He wears a simple grey suit with a white shirt – the same outfit he always wears when he's going to the office. He opens the refrigerator and stares long and hard at the half grapefruit waiting for him. He imagines its acidic bitterness on his tongue. He sighs, grabs the carton of milk instead and pours himself a bowl of cereal. The cereal is sweet and very sugary, and doesn't belong to either him or Amy. It could be Hugh's, though he keeps most of his own food over at the pool house. It could also belong to one of the security guards. Cameron takes a seat at the breakfast counter and looks up to the camera in the corner of the ceiling, raises the box of cereal in its direction.

A couple of moments later, while he's eating, Stephen joins him in the kitchen. He wonders if Stephen was manning the surveillance, and if he misinterpreted the waving of the cereal box as a summons.

"I'll replace the cereal," Cameron says. "I just couldn't bear the thought of another fucking grapefruit this morning."

Stephen looks confused. "Uh, okay."

Cameron watches him while chewing. He realizes he's carrying a laptop under his arm, pressed up against his side. "What do you want, Stephen?"

Stephen starts to smile. "I have news," he says. "Good news."

"Oh really?" A thought occurs to Cameron. His eyes narrow. "Kylie?"

"Maybe," Stephen says. "We hope so."

"You hope so? Well, it either is or it isn't. Spit it out, damn it." Cameron pushes the unfinished bowl of cereal away, no interest in eating any more of it. His attention is thoroughly engrossed now on his head of security.

"We might have a lead," Stephen says, taking the laptop out from under his arm and placing it on the breakfast counter near Cameron. He opens it up and turns it on. "Last night, while we were at the strip club, we got a hit."

Cameron sits closer, though the laptop is on its home screen and has nothing to show him yet. Stephen starts typing, pulling up a file. He hits play. The footage is dark, filmed at night. It's a suburban house. Cameron doesn't recognize it. "What am I looking at?" he says.

"Do you remember Catherine Massey?" Stephen says. "She used to work for you. She was a researcher."

"I don't remember her," Cameron says, shaking his head. He looks up at Stephen. "But if she was a researcher, I can imagine what became of her."

Stephen nods. "She quit after Kylie disappeared. She signed an NDA, took a pay-off. She's stayed quiet, but we keep an eye on her." Stephen indicates the screen. "We've got cameras on her house."

"In case she talks?" Cameron says.

"In case Kylie turns up," Stephen says. "They were friends. Now, Kylie hasn't turned up yet, but look who did last night." Stephen starts fast-forwarding the footage. In high speed, Cameron sees who he assumes to be Catherine's family leaving the house in one vehicle. She closes the door, and then shortly after, another car pulls up in front of her home. As the occupant of the car gets out, Stephen hits pause. He points to the driver. "I've triple-checked," he says. "That's our man from Los Tierras Bajas."

Cameron leans closer, getting a good look at the man's face. "Do we know who he is yet?"

"We do," Stephen says. "Tom Rollins. Ex-Army. Most recently employed as a forest ranger in Northern California, a place called Oak Hills. You heard of it? It was in the news."

Cameron shrugs. He doesn't pay much attention to the news, unless it has anything to do with him, his company, or his rivals.

"They had a problem with drug dealers and cartel, and then to top it all off there was a forest fire. Anyway, shortly after that, this guy Rollins disappeared. It's not clear what he's been doing the last few months. Doesn't matter too much, because he's *here*."

"Yeah, he's here, and what the fuck's he *doing* here?" Cameron says. "Does he go up to the house and talk to – to – *her*?"

"Catherine," Stephen says. "And yes, he does."

"*And?* Do you know what they were talking about?"

"We don't."

Considering Stephen doesn't seem to have any of the answers Cameron wants, Cameron thinks how he's still looking very pleased with things. "Then why the hell have you got that stupid look on your face?"

Stephen's smile falters momentarily, but he quickly regroups. "We got the details of the car," Stephen says. "I've sent men out to follow them, using ANPR technology to find their vehicle. We can't know for sure that they were asking Catherine Massey about Kylie, but if they *were,* there's a chance they could lead us to her."

Cameron feels a cold chill run through him. He thinks of Kylie Hood, and of Los Tierras Bajas. He's managed to suppress everything she's tried to spill so far – but she *is* still trying. He needs to ensure her silence, before she's able to find someone who he can't buy off, or before she's able to get something online. They've managed to scrub everything so far, but she's persistent. She's careful, though. Never uploads near where she is, for fear of leading them to her. Of course, that care is what's preventing her from actually getting her story out. She needs time, and so long as they maintain their pressure, she never gets that kind of time. "What's his interest in all this? What has any of it got to do with him?"

Stephen doesn't answer, because he can't. "I believe we'll find out soon enough," he says. "My men are following them, and they'll report back to me as soon as they have anything worthwhile to—"

Cameron frowns, seizes on a word. "*Them?*"

Stephen blinks, then turns back to the screen. He plays a little more of the footage, until the passenger has gotten out the car. It's a woman. She's short, with bleached hair. Cameron feels a dryness in his throat. She looks familiar. His heart is pounding. He can't think why her face is eliciting such a response.

And then it hits him.

"Oh," he says. "Oh, *shit*."

He hasn't seen her picture in years. She's older now, but he knows exactly who she is.

"Cindy," he says, clicking his fingers and trying to remember her last name. "Cindy *Vaughan*."

Stephen doesn't understand.

"Erica Vaughan's sister," Cameron says, talking to himself, feeling sick. "Damn it, Hugh. God fucking damn it, what have you done?"

"Who?" Stephen says. "Sir?"

Cameron wheels on him. "Circulate their pictures among your men," he says. "Make sure they know what they *both* look like. Tom Rollins and *Cindy Vaughan*. Have you got that?"

He turns away, shaking his head. "She's coming for him," he says to himself, his mind racing, not realizing he's speaking out loud. "She's coming for him – is she coming for *me*? Does she know? Is she coming for him *through* me? If she – if she – she could tear it down, tear it all down..."

"Mr Brewer, are you okay?" Stephen says.

Cameron snaps back to attention with a start. "What are you still doing here? Didn't you hear what I said? Get after them! Stop them!"

22

K ylie Hood sent the location for their meet-up. Cindy checked it online before getting into bed: the site of an old office block demolished five years ago. It was supposed to be turned into a parking lot, but the project managers ran out of money and it had been sitting abandoned ever since, strewn with rubble and rusted metalwork. It was surrounded by trees. There were a couple of walking bridges nearby. Plenty of spots for Kylie to get a good look at them while she decided whether she was going to approach or not.

Tom stayed awake a while longer, though he didn't need to. Cindy had set up a security camera out in the hall, linked up to her laptop. The footage played live on her screen. He watched it for a little while. No one passed by. The only other people he'd ever seen appear were occupants of the other rooms. The occasional hotel employee, but these were rare. No one came near their door. Cindy had set up a laser alarm just outside – two small projectors embedded in the wall either side of the corridor, a foot away from their door. If anyone got too close, it would set off an alarm. It would be loud enough to wake Tom. Still, old habits die hard. He couldn't bring himself to get straight into bed and relax. He needed to check things over first, see them with his own eyes, make sure they were secure. He watched the street below, the cars going by. There were only a few people, passing on the sidewalks.

Finally convinced they were secure, Tom got into the bed next to Cindy. They got a room with a double bed, figuring a request for two singles might raise an eyebrow. Easier to pass as a couple. Cindy rolled over in her sleep, nestled into him. Tom put his arm around her and felt himself gradually slip into sleep.

They get an early start in the morning. Cindy is raring to go. She wants to meet Kylie Hood. To find out what she can give them, if she can help them.

They step over the laser as they leave the room, but they leave it turned on. It's connected to Cindy's laptop and her phone. If anyone approaches, it will sound an alarm and Cindy will be able to check who it is. They don't want anyone getting the drop on them while they're out. They called reception about an hour ago, told them they won't require any housekeeping for the duration of their stay. The last thing they want is for the cleaner to set the alarm off. They've hung the Do Not Disturb sign on the door, too.

Tom drives. Cindy gives directions. Tom watches the mirrors. Checks the vehicles behind. They get onto a freeway. The road is busy. It's rush hour. People are going to work. It doesn't take long before they're caught in a gridlock. Tom can sense Cindy getting antsy.

"Don't worry about it," he says. "We've given ourselves plenty of time."

"If we're too late, she might not hang around. You heard her when we spoke. She's cautious. *Real* cautious."

"We'll get there," Tom says.

In his side mirror, he spots a vehicle three cars back, to their right. A dark green Ford. The passenger is wearing sunglasses, but his face is turned in their direction. It could be nothing, but Tom marks it.

Eventually, the traffic starts moving freely again. Tom keeps an eye on the car he spotted watching them. It holds back, but it doesn't disappear. It doesn't turn off. It maintains its speed – matching theirs. It feels off. Not a single other vehicle has matched them. The others speed up and slow down. They change lanes. They overtake and drop back. This one doesn't move. It's a Ford, a generic vehicle. It's supposed to blend in with all the others. If they *are* sent by Cameron, it would be too obvious for them to use one of the vehicles he manufactures.

As they enter downtown, the green Ford follows. Tom turns off the route Cindy has put him on. It's not an abrupt turn. He signals. He takes it nice and calm, just as he would if he didn't think they were being pursued. The Ford follows.

"I'm gonna circle around," Tom says. "Keep an eye on where we're going. Find us an alternative route. Somewhere not obvious."

Cindy frowns, but she's already checking. "Are we being followed?"

"It looks like it."

Tom keeps the pace leisurely. He sticks to the limit. The green Ford tries to hold back, so as not to make what they're doing obvious. It's a quiet road, though, and their distance gives them away.

The road starts to fill up again. They reach a busier spot. A stretch with cafes and boutiques. Up ahead, Tom spots an intersection. The light is on green, but it's about to change. There are cars to the right, lined up, ready to come through.

"Hold on," Tom says.

Cindy braces herself.

Tom puts his foot down. He speeds through the light as it changes. Behind, he sees the green Ford suddenly lurch into life, but too late. The vehicles from the right are flooding through, cutting the Ford off. Tom gets across the intersection, then speeds to the next left. He takes an immediate right after it, goes along to the next left and takes that.

"All right," he says, slowing a little, getting back to the limit. "We've lost them. Get us back on course."

23

Tom and Cindy decide to park the car down the road, away from the meeting place. They hide it from the road behind a bush, but this is a quiet place, and it doesn't look like many people or vehicles come down this way.

"Take anything you don't wanna lose," Tom says as they get out.

Cindy doesn't ask why. She understands. If they come back from meeting up with Kylie and the people who were following them have found the car, are lying in wait to ambush them, they can't go back to it. They'll have to find another means of travel. Cindy stuffs her laptop into its case and slings it over her shoulder.

Tom has his Beretta tucked into the waistband of his jeans, pressing into his lower back. His shirt and jacket conceal it. They stay off the road as they walk to the meeting place, passing through some trees to keep themselves concealed.

They're ten minutes early. They reach the former

construction site. It's a wasteland. There's no one present. No sign of Kylie.

There's an overpass opposite them, in the distance. Tom can see cars passing by on it. He sees something else, too. A flashing of light, like lenses catching the sun. He almost panics. Almost grabs Cindy and dives back into the trees, thinking it could be the lens of a sniper's rifle. It's not, though. It's too bright, too wide. Like there are two lenses, and they'd be too close together for a sniper's scope. Binoculars. It could be Kylie, watching them from afar, making sure they've come alone. Making sure she's safe.

She keeps them waiting another twenty minutes. "Do you think she's gonna show?" Cindy says. "Maybe she got cold feet."

Tom can still see the reflecting light on the overpass. He doesn't draw attention to it. Doesn't let the person know he's spotted it. "I think she'll come," Tom says. "She's just being cautious."

"Should I try calling her?"

"I wouldn't," Tom says. "If she has anything to say, she'll call us."

The reflective lenses on the overpass disappear. It's too far for Tom to make out what the person walking away looks like, to see if it's Kylie. He just sees an outline, disappearing from view.

Another ten minutes pass. Cindy's phone rings. It's Kylie. "I'm here," Cindy answers.

Tom leans close and Cindy tilts her body and holds the phone out so he can hear. "Walk north," Kylie says. "You'll reach a tunnel. Go through it and keep going. I'll tell you when to stop." She hangs up.

Tom and Cindy look at each other, then shrug. They start walking. They head north, as Kylie said. They're heading toward the overpass.

When they get to the edge of the abandoned site, they spot the tunnel. They go through it. One of its lights is flickering. The walls are covered in graffiti and what look like gang tags. The tunnel is about thirty feet long. It doesn't take them long to get through it. They don't pass anyone else on the way. This whole area is quiet, almost abandoned. Tom can see why Kylie would want to meet here.

They walk on. The slopes on either side of them are covered in overgrown grass. The path stretches as far as Tom can see.

Then he spots movement, to their right. Someone steps out. There are tunnels, or caverns, in the slope. The person looks at them both. It's a woman. It takes a moment to realize it's Kylie Hood.

"All right," she says. "That's far enough."

Tom and Cindy stop walking. There's a distance between them, as if Kylie might bolt at any moment and she wants to make sure she gets a good head start.

She doesn't look like she could run far, though. She looks tired. She looks like she's been living rough. She could pass as any one of the many homeless in LA. Her body is cloaked in a long, scuffed overcoat that hangs down to her knees. Below that, she's wearing boots. It's clear she's wearing dark jeans. Her hands are shoved into the deep pockets of the coat. Her dark hair is tied back, but strands of it hang loose and wisps of it fly freely. She's wearing glasses with big circle lenses. One of them, the left, is cracked. There is dirt smeared on her cheek and along her jaw.

She's looking them both over. "All right," she says, "what do you want?"

"I think we want the same thing you do," Cindy says. "We want to bring down Cameron Brewer. For different reasons, maybe, but that doesn't mean we can't help each other out."

Kylie snorts. She barks a quick laugh without any humor

behind it. "Bring him down?" she says. She shakes her head. "Look, I get that you're here on some mission of vengeance—"

"Justice," Cindy says.

"Whatever. I'm really sorry about your sister, but you're not going to *take down* Cameron Brewer. He's a fucking billionaire, for Christ's sake. Do you know how many people he has in his pocket? Cops, politicians – so many powerful people he can pay off to either look the other way or help him out. People like him, and his family, they think they can do whatever they want and get away with it – because they *can*. Because they *have*. And because they always *will*."

"Maybe," Cindy says. "But I'm still going to try. I have to. For Erica."

"Y'know," Kylie says, "after you called the first time, I looked into you. I read about your sister, and what happened to her. I reckon you've probably read the news reports too, right?"

Cindy nods, grimly. "They were bullshit."

Kylie nods back. "They figured it was a secret lover. You know why they figured that? Because that's what Cameron would've told them to write, and to say. He wouldn't have told them directly, of course – that would raise too many eyebrows. Always the risk of one enterprising, moral young reporter on the team. He would've fed it to them through the cops. Why would they doubt the cops, right? Now, look. I know you've come a long way from Texas, and I can see you've brought your muscle here, but I'm telling you, you're not gonna make a difference. I'm sorry about your sister, but you can go back to your life and live it."

"Why are you in hiding?" Tom says.

Kylie looks at him, an 'Are you kidding me?' expression on her face.

"Can *you* just go back to your life and live it?" he says.

"No, of course not. Don't be ridiculous."

"Because they're after you?"

"Exactly."

"They're after Cindy. They're probably after me, too. But they know where Cindy lives. They went to her home. We're in this now. Until the end."

Kylie looks at Cindy. "Is that true?"

Cindy nods. "The men that killed my sister, they were in my apartment just recently. And they had help. They'll have a lot of help because of Cameron, like you said."

Kylie thinks, running her tongue around the inside of her mouth, her brow furrowed.

"We get that you're scared," Cindy says, "and that it took a lot for you to agree to meet with us today. We know you just want to hide and be safe. But we need your help. You don't need to do anything. All we need from you is for you to tell us what Cameron is doing. Why he's looking for you – what you tried to share that was suppressed. If you give us that information, we might be able to do something with it."

Kylie shifts her weight from foot to foot, looking like she wants the ground to swallow her up. She closes her eyes tight. "Even when I'm hiding, I'm not safe," she says, her voice small. She opens her eyes. "It's not safe for a woman on the streets, but I didn't know what else to do." She takes a deep breath. "Do you know what I did when I worked at Zeus Conglomerates?"

"You researched rare earth minerals," Cindy says. "Same as Catherine."

Kylie nods. "That's right. Do you know what they're used for?"

"The batteries in electric cars," Cindy says. "I did *my* research."

Kylie nods again. "And did your research tell you there's a dearth of them coming into the country at the moment?"

Cindy shakes her head.

"They usually come from China. Just over a year ago, there started to be some supply issues. Nothing serious at first, but enough that Cameron Brewer became cautious. He needs those minerals for his cars or else he can't manufacture them. If he can't manufacture them, his factory stands useless, costing him hundreds of thousands of dollars every day. Tens of millions of dollars a month."

"We've seen it," Tom says. "It's real quiet."

"That doesn't surprise me," Kylie says. "I figured the lines would have to be running *very* low right about now. So, a year ago, he starts to get worried, and he hires a team of us to either find him more or an alternative. We got to work. I know for me, and for Catherine, we thought we were doing something worthwhile, y'know? Getting more electric vehicles onto the road, that's a good thing, right? We're environmentalists – I think we all were – that's why we worked for a company like Zeus Conglomerates, one of the top suppliers of renewable energy sources in the country. We were ready to give this job our all.

"But then time passes, and we started to pick up on some things. Like Cameron, for a start. We didn't see much of him – didn't expect to. We knew he was busy. But when we did, he was always very impatient. He's results-driven – he wants results, and he wants them yesterday. So when we're sitting in his lab without any results for him, he starts getting angry. When one of us tried to offer up an explanation, Cameron fired them.

"I mean, you hear about people like him. They're not easy to get along with, or work for. You expect it to go with the territory. But what soon became clear was that he wasn't an environmentalist. Not at all. He didn't give a shit about what he was doing, or how it would benefit mankind or the planet.

He cared about the money he could make off the back of it. That's all."

She sighs, looking to the side, her face twisted bitterly at the memories. "He started putting more pressure on us. He was getting desperate. He knew his supplies were running out. He needed a replacement, and fast. In turn, his pressure made us start to panic. We were working sixteen-hour days. Even when we were able to eventually go home, we weren't sleeping. We started getting desperate. Catherine and I, we were part of a group that was checking soil deposits in the local area. We didn't expect any kind of results, but, like I said, we were getting desperate. We couldn't take him coming down and screaming at us again. At least if we had some research to show him, some results, he eased off a little. If he could see that you'd been trying everything you could.

"But then something happened. We actually *found* something. We couldn't believe it. We triple-checked. Our minds were blown. It didn't seem possible. In local soil, we'd found trace elements of rare earth minerals. We tracked down where the sample came from."

"Where was it?" Cindy says.

Kylie smirks. "It came from some ground just outside of a low-income housing estate on the outskirts of LA. When we probed deeper, we found out the vast majority of the deposits were underneath it."

"Los Tierras Bajas," Tom says.

Kylie's eyes narrow. "You know it?"

"We've seen what they're doing there," Cindy says. "That's why? For the minerals under their streets?"

Kylie takes a deep breath. "When Cameron found out – his reaction – I didn't know how to take it. I didn't like the look I saw in his eye when we explained the situation, and the problem. I remember what he said. He looked at us all, and he said, *I'll deal with them*. It was like – it was like he was talking about *bugs*. Like he was gonna crush them, or sweep them aside. It wasn't like he was talking about people, or their homes. And it became clear pretty soon why it sounded that way – because that's how he meant it. He didn't see them as people. Didn't see their homes as having worth. He just saw them as something that was in his way."

"So he's trying to force these people out of their homes so he can, what, buy the land?" Cindy says. "Then mine it for the minerals?"

"That's right," Kylie says. "And he's put his brother in charge of getting them out. I never met his brother; I just saw him around a couple of times. He always looked like he'd rather be somewhere else. I've heard stories about him, though. I'd never heard he was a killer until today, and yet somehow it doesn't surprise me. It doesn't surprise me about either of them."

Cindy doesn't correct her, saying she believes Lenny was the actual killer. It doesn't matter. "If he's so rich," she says, "why doesn't he just buy the occupants out? He could afford it, easily."

"He didn't become a billionaire by just giving his money away," Kylie says. "No one does. I'm sure all those payouts he's had to make to cover up his brother's messes just eat away at him. I'd always heard there was some tension between the two of them. But you're right, he *could* buy the people of Los Tierras Bajas out of their homes. But if he did that, his competitors – the same people who are *also* short on rare earth minerals right now – could become aware of what he's doing. They could try to outbid him, which would jack the price way higher than he'd be willing to pay. Then what about the person who actually owns the land? If they knew what it was suddenly worth, do you think they'd be willing to part with it without getting *their* billion first?"

"Why don't the residents try to defend themselves,

though?" Cindy says. "I've wondered that from the first night. Why don't they get guns, fight back?"

"If they start shooting, it goes either one of two ways. They either end up in court, battling a legal case they can't hope to win against Cameron's lawyers – or they pull one gun and Cameron's men pull ten. They pull twenty, they pull fifty, however many it takes to retain dominance. Whatever the people of Los Tierras Bajas choose, they can't hope to win."

"What did you try to leak exactly?" Tom says. "Did you take this information to his competitors?"

"No, screw them," Kylie says. "I was trying to help the people of Los Tierras Bajas. I found myself a young, idealistic, moral reporter and I told them everything. And then their boss found out the story, told Cameron in exchange for him coughing up a pretty payment, and the story got quashed. I tried to take it to others, but no one will talk to me. Cameron's influence reaches far. No one was willing to put their careers or their necks on the line for a bunch of residents of a low-income estate they'd never even heard of before. I've tried to get the story out since. I try all the damn time. I try to put it online. I don't know if anyone will care, but so long as it's out there, *someone* who gives a damn might see it. But it's hard for me to even *get* online – I have a burner phone, for Christ's sake. If I go into a café or a library to use their computer or their internet, I can't stay there long. Cameron has people searching for me online, around the clock.."

"Why didn't he just try and pay you off?" Tom says. "Get you to sign an NDA in return for money?"

"I don't know that he would have done that," Kylie says, shaking his head. "I'd betrayed him. He wouldn't have been happy with that. And I wouldn't have taken his money anyway. I should never have gone to work for him." She bites her lip. "Once the story got killed, I knew he'd come looking for me. He'd send men. His head of security, Stephen Hawke,

keeps his men in line – but Cameron knows that. So
Cameron finds men who *will* do his dirty work, no problem.
Those are the kind of men he would have sent after me, and I
wasn't gonna wait around for them to turn up. So I ran. It's
been three months now."

"You think he would have had you killed?" Tom says.

Kylie takes a deep breath. "I didn't find out about what
was happening at Los Tierras Bajas right away. It was
Catherine who told me. She'd been working late one night,
and as she was leaving she saw a van of guys, all dressed in
black, heading out. She says she doesn't know what possessed
her, but something didn't feel right, so she followed them.
Followed them to Los Tierras Bajas, and that's how she found
out. Then she told me. And the more we looked into it, the
less we liked what we were hearing. We even spoke to some
of the residents. They told us that they'd seen a lot of their
neighbors move out, but some of them, the more belligerent
ones who were standing up to the hassling, who were fighting
back, they disappeared. The neighbors didn't *see* them move
out, but they didn't live in their houses any more. So, yes, I
think it's a distinct possibility that Cameron would attempt to
have me killed."

Tom and Cindy look at each other. Cindy turns back to
Kylie. "You should come with us," she says. "We can keep you
safe."

Kylie is already shaking her head. "Look, I don't know
either of you, and I've already put myself at too much risk just
talking to you both." She's looking around, checking in the
distance. "I'm not going anywhere with you. I've kept myself
safe so far, and that's what I'm gonna keep doing."

"Until when?" Tom says. "What's your end goal here?"

"Survival," she says, looking him in the eye. "Every day
they can't get their hands on me is another day I spit in their
eye. I'll keep going. Maybe one day someone will be ready to

hear the story I've just told you, and maybe one day people might care. Until then, I stay alive. Listen, I hope what I've told you can help you in some way. But if I'm honest, I don't see how it can. But good luck to you both. I hope you're successful." She's already backing up, toward the tunnel from where she first appeared. "But I'm not gonna hold my breath."

24

Cameron can tell from the look on Stephen's face that he's not bringing good news.

Cameron is in his office when Stephen sheepishly enters. He's at his desk, going over payroll. Thinking how he wants to fire most, if not all, of Zeus Motors before they can cost him another wasteful fucking penny. He knows he can't, though. It would raise too many eyebrows. It would make national news. The sharks would smell the blood. And hopefully, soon, he'll have the minerals he needs anyway – if Hugh hurries up and gets the last few stragglers out of Los Tierras Bajas. Once he has the minerals, he'll need the staff. If he fired them all now, he'd just have to rehire them all back later, or else find new employees.

He looks at Stephen. "What is it?" he says. He doesn't have the patience for Stephen to draw things out.

Stephen clears his throat. "My men, they were following Rollins and Cindy, but they, uh, they lost them."

Cameron stares at him, unblinking. "They lost them?"

"Rollins was driving, he must've spotted them. He took evasive maneuvers and—"

"Jesus Christ!" He interrupts Stephen, shaking his head, his voice coarse. Cameron doesn't want to hear it. He's not interested. It's just another excuse. "Can you ever do anything fucking right?"

Stephen doesn't respond. He blinks at this outburst, though. He shuffles from side to side.

Cameron throws up his hands. "How can I be expected to get any work done when all I keep hearing is how you and your men can't do your own fucking jobs? I give you *simple* tasks, Stephen, and they're still not complete. I ask you to find Kylie Hood, and three months later I'm still waiting. I tell you to follow Rollins and Cindy, and you fucking lose them!"

Stephen opens his mouth, perhaps to protest that he wasn't actually following them himself, but he decides against it. Purses his lips. It's not an excuse. They're his men. He's in charge. The buck stops with him.

"Get out of my sight," Cameron says, turning his head, unable to look at him any longer. "You're such a disappointment, Stephen. Next time I see you, you'd better be bringing me good news."

Stephen leaves without a sound, chastised. He clicks the door carefully into place behind him.

Cameron sits and seethes alone. He runs a hand down his face. Incompetents. He's surrounded by incompetents. It's a wonder he's ever able to get anything done.

He returns to the payroll. Now he *really* wants to fire someone.

25

The car is clear when Tom and Cindy return to it. They watch from a distance for a while before they approach. To make sure no one is nearby, or monitoring it from afar. Waiting for them. When they're satisfied there isn't, they go to it. They get inside but don't set off right away.

"If they were following us," Cindy says, "is the hotel safe?"

Tom considers this question for a while. "They didn't follow us from outside the hotel," he says. "They appeared later. Could be they knew the car. In which case, we need to change it. If they were Cameron's men, and it's likely they were, as I can't imagine why anyone else would be after us, they could be into CCTV, like how you do. They could have found us that way, on the move, and got behind us in transit. I don't think they know where we're staying. All the while we've been out, the alarm on our room hasn't gone off. After they lost us, that should've been the first place they went."

"So, we change the car and then we risk going back?" Cindy says. "Work out our next move?"

"I already know our next move," Tom says. "We wait for dark and then we go to Los Tierras Bajas. If the attacks there are nightly, we wait until they get started and then we capture one of the heavies."

"All right," Cindy says, intrigued. "And what do we do with him?"

"We get him to talk."

"On camera," Cindy says, lighting up.

"Exactly."

"And if we have someone from Cameron's payroll," Cindy continues, "and we've got footage of him confessing to everything, then maybe Kylie will talk, too. That would be two sources, confirming what Cameron is doing. People would have to listen. And...and if Hugh and Lenny..."

Tom nods. He knows what she wants to say. "If I have the opportunity to capture either of them, I will."

Cindy looks grateful.

"In the meantime, after we've switched vehicles, we'll go back to the hotel. I think it's the safest place – we're high enough I can watch the street, and we have your security set-up. If they come, we'll see them. We can get free before they get anywhere near us. Out the window, down the fire escape."

"Then it sounds like we've got a plan," Cindy says. "It sounds like we've got things moving."

"Yeah," Tom says. He waits a moment, then continues. "We could get justice on Cameron, Hugh, and Lenny, for what they're doing at Los Tierras Bajas, but unless I capture Hugh or Lenny, we're not going to get them for what they did to your sister. Any of the other heavies – it's doubtful they're going to know anything about that."

"If I can't get justice for Erica directly, then so be it," Cindy says. "It's been a long time, and I always knew getting them for what they did to my sister was a longshot. But they'll know that *I* did it, and because of that they'll know *why*. They'll know it was for Erica. That'll have to be enough."

Tom starts the engine. He nods at her laptop. "Find me somewhere I can trade this in."

26

Stephen's face is burning after the admonishment from Cameron. He leaves the building and goes out to his car. He doesn't want to be seen by anyone, not right now. He needs to calm down. He's always prided himself on keeping a level head, no matter what is thrown at him. Lately, it feels like he's had a *lot* thrown at him. It didn't used to be like this. Ever since Hugh's abrupt two-week vacation, Cameron has been on edge. Stephen wishes he knew why.

It's hot in his car. He keeps the windows up. Trying to sweat the fury out. Being called a disappointment is eating at him. Lately, the insults, the embarrassment, the abuse – it's all built up and built up. Molehills have become mountains. Today he may have reached his limit. It may be the straw that breaks his back.

He closes his eyes and takes deep, meditative breaths. In through his nose, filling his lungs, then out through his mouth. He feels a bead of sweat trickle down the side of his face.

Stephen used to be a cop. He was a good cop. He didn't get anywhere near as much constant abuse on the streets of

LA as he has recently in the employ of Cameron Brewer. Sure, he got shot at a few times, but the sudden vitriol with which he's spoken to is unlike anything he's experienced before. When he applied for the head of Cameron's security team, he thought he was getting an easy job. How hard could it be to protect a billionaire? He's had this job for six years, and up until now it *has* been easy. Save for a few lapses in patience and temperament – and who *doesn't* have an occasional lapse? – Cameron has been a delight to work for. He's been a good boss, and he's paid well. Sure, Cameron is probably involved in a few things less than legal, but no one is getting hurt, and everyone is getting rich.

Well, except for maybe at Los Tierras Bajas. Stephen isn't proud of it, but he turns a blind eye to what's happening out there. His men keep an eye on the place via surveillance, but they never go out there. Hugh takes his own hired thugs, and Stephen doesn't want anything to do with *them*, either.

The last time Stephen saw Cameron worked up like this was a few months back when Kylie suddenly disappeared. Stephen isn't sure what happened there, but he knows a lot of people – Catherine Massey among them – needed to sign NDAs. He knows it was to do with Los Tierras Bajas, too. The thing is, Stephen knows that if he could find Kylie, just talk to her, he could persuade her to sign an NDA too. He knows Cameron would be willing to pay her a substantial amount to ensure her compliance. Money can numb any kind of sting, whether it's a case of pride or empathy. He knows it does for him.

And then there's Hugh. Jesus Christ, Hugh... It feels like he's getting worse all the time. The latest incident at the strip club is just another in a long line of escalating issues. In the past, Stephen has seen Cameron's fury directed at his brother on a regular basis. All those times, Stephen was glad it wasn't pointed at him.

That's another thing he tries not to think about – the men that Hugh hires to go out to Los Tierras Bajas. Who knows what else he might get them to do? Stephen trusts his own men. Vernon, his second-in-command, is primary among them. They were cops together. After Stephen had worked for Cameron a couple of years, he got a call from Vernon asking if there was a place on the team for him. Stephen had told him of course. Had told him it was an easy gig, and the best money he'd ever make.

Stephen sighs. He hates to admit it, but he's become a slave to the dollar. He wouldn't get anywhere near as much anywhere else. He never thought he'd become like this, but once he got a little money, he wanted more, and more. It's easy to see how men like Cameron can become what they are.

His meditative breaths are not helping. Neither is being in a hot car. He's sweating harder, and it's agitating him now. He turns on the engine and blasts himself with the a/c. He runs his hands down his face, wipes the sweat from his eyes and from his mouth. He stares up at the reflective surface of the building. He can't stand the thought of going back in there. What was it Cameron said to him? The last thing he said: *Next time bring me good news.*

He pulls out his phone and calls Vernon. For the most part, Stephen has been able to shield his men from Cameron's temper. He knows he can't do this forever, though, and he knows they're not blind. They're not stupid, either. He's heard whisperings among them, talking of how Cameron's temper has gotten worse, and how they walk on eggshells around him. "Vern, I'm leaving you in charge for the day," he says. "If anyone needs me, tell them I had to go deal with something."

"Sure thing," Vernon says. "Everything all right?"

Stephen wonders if Vernon has heard yet about the

telling-off he received from Cameron. If Cameron's secretary overheard everything through the door and she's already spread the word. It's only a matter of time. "I'm fine," he says. "Just something I need to go do."

He leaves the parking lot. He goes to the street where Catherine Massey lives. He parks down the road and he watches her house.

He makes sure to park in the shade, so when he turns off the engine, and the air conditioning with it, he doesn't get too hot. He winds his window down. There's enough of a breeze. It feels good on his skin, but it's not enough to calm him yet. He's still tightly wound. Still angry.

He stares at the house. He knows Catherine is in there. It's early afternoon. Her children are probably still at school. Her husband will be at work. Catherine doesn't work. Not since she left Zeus Conglomerates. Stephen wonders if she's looking for a new job, or if she's content with the payoff she received as part of her NDA.

Does she know where Kylie Hood is? Is that what Rollins and Cindy came to see her about, and did she tell them? Has she known this whole time?

Stephen was the one averse to hassling her. She'd left the company, he was content to just let her live in peace. Cameron insisted on putting the camera on her home, in case Kylie ever turned up. "If they were friends, there's a chance," he'd said. He wasn't taking any chances when it came to Kylie.

He promptly forgot Catherine's name, though. She didn't matter as much – he'd paid her off, and she'd signed her name. Now that he didn't have to worry about Catherine, he forgot all about her. Only Kylie matters. Kylie is who he's desperate to get his hands on. He can't forget her name. Not until Stephen can get her to sign the NDA. Not until they've guaranteed her silence.

Stephen drums his fingers on the steering wheel, watching. Something is happening, within himself. He's cooling off. He's not so angry as he was before. He's calming. Things are becoming clearer. His thoughts are less muddled.

After another hour, Catherine's kids return home. Stephen sinks lower in his seat. He starts questioning what he's doing here. Watching a home with kids in it. A family.

Another hour goes by. Catherine's husband comes home. They're all home together, all four of them.

Stephen asks himself, again, what he's doing here. What's his plan? Is he going to go up to the door, like Rollins and Cindy did, and politely ask Catherine what the two of them were doing at her house? And then what – if they *were* looking for Kylie, does he ask directions to where she's hiding out?

And if Catherine refuses to answer, what then? Does he drag her in, give her to Cameron, let him question her?

Stephen has calmed down since he first arrived. He feels more like himself. If he goes up to Catherine's house, if he knocks on her door, if he ends up dragging her from her home, he's crossing a line. He'll be casting what morals he has left to the wind.

So Stephen asks himself, one last time, if he's willing to cross that line.

It's evening now. The day has gotten so much cooler than it was. He closes his eyes, and he takes a deep breath. He shakes his head.

"No," he says, starting the engine. "Not yet."

He hopes not ever.

The hotel remains secure. Cindy takes a nap from the afternoon into the evening, and while she rests Tom stays by the window. He watches the street below. Makes mental notes of the cars that pass by, and the people he sees. No one keeps coming by. No one hangs around longer than he's comfortable with.

On the table near him, Cindy's laptop sits open, showing the feed from the hall. Tom keeps one eye on it. No one hangs around out there, either. No one gets remotely close enough to the lasers to set off the alarm. He sees only two people in all the while he's watching. They appear hours apart from each other, and both of them go straight to their separate rooms.

Tom doesn't know how the men who were tailing them found them, but it's not clear whether they know about the hotel or not. He goes back to the theory he posited earlier – they've got an alert out on security cameras on their vehicle, and once they spotted it they put the pedal to the floor and caught up to them. Maybe they were already in the area – they *are* close to Cameron's home, after all.

If the car was all they had to go off, Tom and Cindy should be safe, going forward. They traded it in shortly after meeting with Kylie. The new vehicle, a Ford, is parked around the back of the hotel building, off the road.

When Cindy wakes, she sits up on the bed and pushes her hair back from her forehead. She blinks around the room, looks to her laptop. "Are we still clear?" she says.

"It looks that way," Tom says.

She checks the time. "When are we going to go?"

"Soon," Tom says. "I wanna get there early. Give us plenty of time to get into position, get set up."

"All right. Let me go take a shower, wake myself up."

Tom cleans his Beretta while she washes. He's going equipped – handgun and KA-BAR. Can't be sure what kind of situation it might become. If it devolves, he wants to be prepared. Cindy won't be in any danger. She'll be up on the ridge.

She comes out of the shower with her short hair wet and scraped back. She's wearing clean clothes – black jeans and a plain black T-shirt. Tom doesn't think he's seen her wear a T-shirt before that didn't have a band name on it. Cindy sees him looking. She guesses his thoughts. "We're being covert, right? I figured I should dress as plain as you are."

Tom grins. "Good. Except you'll be so far out of the way we shouldn't have to worry about how covert you're being. But I appreciate the effort."

"I'm glad to hear it," Cindy says, propping herself on the edge of the bed and slipping into her boots.

They head out and drive to Los Tierras Bajas in the waning light. The sun is going down, and on the horizon the sky is orange. Tom makes sure to check the mirrors. Cindy sees what he's doing. She's doing the same, though she doesn't have his experience. "Do you see anything?" she says. "Anyone following us?"

"No," Tom says. "You?"

"I don't think so."

By the time they turn off for Los Tierras Bajas, there isn't anything behind them at all. Tom stops the car about a mile away from the estate and gets out. It's dark now, and he'll continue on foot. Cindy takes the car and heads to the ridge. They'll keep in touch through earpieces and microphones. "Just like old times," Cindy says, as they separate.

Tom passes over scrubland. In the distance, he can see the dim glow of the streetlamps – the ones still in working order – and from the homes of the half a dozen or so remaining residents of Los Tierras Bajas. He makes his way toward them. When he gets close, he goes to one of the houses without lights on. One of the abandoned ones. He climbs over the rear fence and goes to the back door. He doesn't have to break it open, or pick the lock. It's already off its hinges. All the windows at the back of the house are smashed. Hugh and the rest have done a number on this property.

Tom heads inside, holding a penlight to look around. Whoever lived here before left in a hurry. They've taken most of their valuables with them, but they've left the bigger items behind. The things that were too big to transport easily. He checks all the rooms of the house are clear before he settles in, makes sure no one homeless has decided to squat for the night. It's empty.

The windows in the living room, looking out onto the street, are smashed. They've been covered with wooden boards. The boards have just been thrown up, though. There are gaps between them. Tom has a clear view of the street. Of the road leading into it.

He speaks into the microphone on his collar. "I'm inside," he says. "You in position?"

"Been here a while," Cindy says. "Which house are you in?"

"You remember the house of the guy who got knocked out the other night? John?"

"I remember it."

"I'm four over, to your left."

"With all the boarded windows?"

"That's the one."

"Can you see out?"

"There are gaps. Any sign?"

"Not yet, but it's still early. I can't even see any vehicles approaching yet. I reckon we'll have a wait, first."

"Yeah," Tom says. He goes to one of the sofas and takes a seat. "Let me know when they're coming."

28

L enny drives. Hugh sits in the passenger seat and yawns.

He's getting bored with this routine. Every night, to Los Tierras Bajas. They got a night's reprieve last night, after what happened at Titty City, but that's not the worst thing. Sometimes expecting something, and then it not coming, can be worse. It'll have the residents on edge. Hugh's men will just have to be extra effective tonight. A total smash run. A fucking *blitzkrieg*.

In fact, Hugh thinks it's time to start ramping things up. It's getting tedious. "We need to get these motherfuckers out, Lenny," he says. "Enough is enough." He's thinking of last night again. The strip club. The dressing-down Cameron gave him after. The longer this takes, the less patience his brother is showing him.

Lenny grunts.

Hugh sits up. "We're gonna have to get serious with them. *Real* fucking serious. Busting heads and smashing up property isn't enough. We're gonna have to start breaking bones."

"Cameron said not to take things too far," Lenny says. "He

said there's only so much he can get the cops to turn a blind eye to."

Hugh remembers. It was back when Cameron told him to stop making certain residents disappear. It would raise too many questions. If the law got wind of it, they'd *have* to ask about it.

"I know what he said. But we've gotta do *something*. We keep going on like this, we're gonna be a dog that's all bark, no bite. And you know what? I think these fuckers left behind, I think they *know* that. They're not scared of us. Nowhere near as scared as they should be. We could be doing this for months more – fucking *years*, maybe." Hugh sits up straight. He clicks his fingers. He's had an idea.

Out the corner of his eye, Lenny has noticed. "What are you thinking?"

"We burn them out," Hugh says.

Lenny turns his head, but keeps one eye no the road,

"We smoke these fuckers out," Hugh says. "Burn down these houses that are so precious to them."

"Will Cameron be all right with that? It's the ground under them he's interested in. Could fire harm what he's after?"

Hugh shrugs. "How should I know? I mean, I think those minerals are supposed to be pretty deep, right?" Hugh considers. "I guess I should probably run it past him...just to be sure..."

"So, no fire tonight?"

"Not tonight. But we're still gonna ramp things up." He looks into the mirror, at the headlights of the vehicles following them to Los Tierras Bajas. "I'm getting tired, Lenny. I wanna move on from this shit. Every damn night. It's getting too much. I'm bored of it. It was never supposed to take this long."

Lenny nods.

"We smash them tonight. We smash their houses, and we smash *them*. I don't care what we break. I don't care if we give them broken bones and concussions, that clear? We're getting them out. I want them gone. And if Cameron wants to complain about it, he can. Whatever. But then it'll be done, and long-term he'll thank me. *And*, if tonight doesn't finally get them out, I talk to Cameron and we burn the whole fucking place down. That's what we're gonna do. I've had enough of these fucking ants. They've made me look too bad for too long. You remember what I told Cameron when he first put me in charge of this?"

"You said you'd have them out in a week. Two, tops."

"That's right. And now it's been three fucking months." He sits back, sighing. He's not tired any more, though. He feels rejuvenated. Ready for tonight. Ready to get the residents of Los Tierras Bajas out once and for all. He pulls out his phone. "I'll call the others, tell them we're taking it to extremes tonight. I want them ready."

29

"They're on their way."

Tom gets up from the sofa at the sound of Cindy's voice. He goes to the boarded window, peers out into the street. After a moment, he can see their headlights approaching, stretching out before them into the street.

"They've stopped," she says. "Do you see them?"

Tom can hear their engines idling. "They're just out of view," he says. "How many cars?"

"Six. They're starting to get out." She pauses a beat. Tom hears her take a breath. "Hugh and Lenny are here."

"Let me know their movements."

"Got it. Nothing's happening yet. They're all standing together. Hugh is talking, same as the other night. Giving them a pep talk, I guess. All right, okay, they're on the move now. Hugh is still at the cars, but Lenny is with another guy. It looks like he's going to a house near you."

Tom sees them come into view. They walk by the house he's in. Tom noticed, on the way here, that there was a house with lights two down from this one. He waits until they're past before he speaks. "Two down?"

"Yeah," Cindy says.

"I'm going for them. Bring the car down and try to get a little closer than where you dropped me off. Lenny's a big guy, and if I get him I don't wanna have to travel so far with him on my back."

"Got it."

"Keep the engine running."

"Will do."

Tom goes through the house and out the back door. He moves along the abandoned back yards to the house two doors down. The curtains at the back are drawn, but light spills out from around them. Tom can hear commotion inside. The door has been broken down. People are screaming. Lenny and the other heavy are inside. It sounds like they're smashing things up.

The back door is thrown open, and a woman stumbles out. It's late, but she's dressed like she's ready to be outside. She's more than likely been prepared for this attack. Prepares for it every night. She falls as she flees, though. She hits the ground and looks back. She sees Tom. She probably assumes he's another of the men who smash up their homes. Before she can react to him, the rest of her family are coming out after her. Her husband, and a teenage son. They're all dressed to flee, too. The two men stop to help the woman up.

Tom goes to the open door and steps inside the house. He's in the kitchen. He goes through to the living room. He sees Lenny picking up the television from the stand it rests on in the corner. He raises it up high and then smashes it against the wall. Sparks fly briefly. Lenny is a big guy, and he's strong. Tom wants to get the drop on him while his back is still turned. To keep the element of surprise.

The other heavy is nearer. He looks up as Tom enters.

They're close to each other. This man is a lot smaller than Lenny. He doesn't look like he could lift up a television with such ease. He's busy smashing up family portraits on a nearby sideboard. Tom grabs him by the throat to prevent him from making a sound and drags him back into the kitchen. The man's eyes are bulging. Veins pop in his temple. Tom drives the point of his elbow into the bridge of his nose, breaking it. The pain will bring tears to the man's eyes – will blind and incapacitate him. Tom follows up with a hard forearm across his jaw, knocking him down, subduing him.

He peers back into the living room. Lenny's back is still turned. He throws the remnants of the destroyed television through the window.

Tom moves on him fast. He drills a fist into his kidney, catching him by surprise and dropping him to a knee. With him down, Tom wraps an arm around his throat and begins to squeeze.

In his ear, he hears Cindy. "I'm in place."

Tom can't respond. Lenny struggles against him. He's trying to get back to his feet.

Then someone appears in the doorway to the house. Tom's head snaps around, expecting another heavy he's going to have to deal with. It's Hugh.

"Shit," Hugh says, looking back at him.

Hugh turns and runs from the house, calling to the others.

"*Fuck.*" Tom wonders, for a brief moment, what brought Hugh here. What made him come investigate. They haven't made any noise – none more than what was already being made, anyway. And yet he turned up like he knew something unexpected was going on.

Tom doesn't have long to think about it. He increases his pressure on Lenny's neck, pressing down hard on his carotid artery, then drags him back so his feet go out from under him.

If Lenny had managed to stand, Tom would have been stuck here on his back. He drags him to the wall and twists his body, slams the top of Lenny's head into the wall while maintaining the pressure on his neck.

Eventually, Lenny goes limp. Limp enough that Tom is able to sling him over his shoulder and carry him out the back door. The heavy in the kitchen is trying to get to his feet as they pass. Tom kicks him across the jaw, knocks him back down.

Outside, in the garden, hiding in the shadows, is the family whose house they were in. Tom goes to the fence and heaves Lenny up and over, dropping him in a heap down the other side. He follows him over, then scoops him back up again. He's heavy. He's not easy to carry. Tom runs as fast as he's able across the ground, toward the road where Cindy is.

"I'm on my way," he says into the microphone.

"I'm flashing the lights," Cindy says. "Do you see me?"

Tom does. "I'm coming."

Behind him, he hears raised voices. Hugh and the others, trying to work out where they've gone. He hears them start to scale the fence, to follow. Tom has the head start, but already he can feel himself faltering. He flashes back to basic training, when he first joined the army. Running for miles on end with his pack and his weapon. But he was a younger man then, and his pack didn't weigh anywhere near as much as Lenny does. His thighs are burning. His breath is ragged. His heart is pounding in his chest, and his lungs are straining with the effort. But he's getting closer to the car. Closer to Cindy.

She sees him coming. Likely they appear as a misshapen shadow coming out of the darkness. She gets out the car and opens the trunk. She pulls out a roll of tape.

Tom reaches the rear of the car and drops Lenny into the trunk. He's starting to stir, blinking himself back into full consciousness. Cindy makes to cover his mouth with the tape, but she's trembling. The trembles turn into shakes. She's frozen. She can't follow through. She stares at Lenny. So close to one of her sister's killers.

The others are coming up behind them. They probably see the lights of the car as a beacon, whether they know this is where Tom and Lenny have come or not.

Tom takes the tape from Cindy. "Get in the car," he says. He quickly covers Lenny's mouth, then binds his wrists and his ankles. He slams the trunk lid. As he turns, he sees one of the other heavies gaining on them. The fastest of the bunch. Far behind, he hears Hugh's voice calling. "Stop them!" he says. "Get them!"

Tom cuts down the first of the heavies short with a raised leg, burying his boot into his sternum and driving all the air out of him. The heavy crumples. Tom places a hand on his head and shoves him, rolling him off the road and back toward the others. Tom spins, dives into the car, into the driver's seat, and he drives away, leaving Hugh and the others behind.

30

They don't take Lenny back to the hotel. They scoped out a place earlier, an abandoned warehouse downtown. They go there. Before they stop the car, they make sure there's no one else around. No one that might see them, and be curious of what they're doing. No one that might see them haul a bound man out the trunk of their car and think maybe they should call the police and let them know what they've seen.

There's no one.

Tom pulls the car to a stop close to the entrance of the warehouse. He kills the engine, but doesn't get straight out. Cindy still appears shaken after being so close to Lenny. "Are you all right?" he says. "Can you do this?"

She nods, but doesn't speak. She looks paler than usual.

"You don't need to come in," Tom says.

"No," she says, her voice just above a whisper. She clears her throat. "I *do* need to come in," she says, firmer now.

Tom holds out his hand. She takes it, squeezes it, then they get out the car. She goes straight inside the building. Tom goes to the trunk. He uses his KA-BAR to cut the tape binding Lenny's ankles. "You try anything," Tom says, hauling him out by his elbow, "and I'll stick this knife straight through your heart."

Lenny looks back at him. His eyes are empty. There's nothing behind them.

Tom is sure this dead-eyed stare is very effective to the uninitiated, but he's seen it all before. It doesn't affect him. He drags Lenny into the warehouse, the KA-BAR pressed to his already bruised carotid.

There's a chair in the center of the empty building. Tom forces Lenny into it and wraps tape around his torso and legs, binding him to the chair. He pulls the tape from his mouth, then puts the KA-BAR away and takes a step back. "You can make any amount of noise you want," Tom says. "No one's gonna hear you around here."

Lenny doesn't make a sound. He looks them both over.

Cindy has to clear her throat before she speaks. She swallows. She sets her jaw. "Do you remember me?" she says. Her voice is firm. It's loud and clear.

Lenny looks at her. His face doesn't change. It's impossible to gauge what he's thinking, or feeling.

But then he speaks.

"Long time no see, Cindy," he says. Tom thinks he sees the flicker of a smirk at the corner of his mouth, but it's fleeting. Lenny flicks his head toward Tom. "This is the Tom Rollins I've been hearing so much about?" He looks at Tom. "I'm not impressed."

"You don't need to be impressed," Tom says. "I got you here."

"The worst place you want me," Lenny says. He cracks a smile. "For you." He looks back at Cindy. "And for you."

"Not from where I'm standing," Tom says.

Cindy's eyes narrow. She balls her fists. Her arms are shaking. "You killed my sister," she says.

"Is that what you think?" Lenny smirks again. It's more unnerving than when his face is blank.

"*You killed my sister,*" Cindy repeats. "You, and Hugh, and Cameron. And you're going to admit to it. On camera. And you're going to admit to what you're all doing at Los Tierras Bajas. You're going to admit to every little damn thing you know about."

Lenny looks amused. "Is that what you think I'm going to do?" he says. "As simple as that?" He looks at Tom. "Do you think you've got what it takes, Rollins? Do you think you can make me talk?"

For the first time, Tom sees a gleam in his eye. He looks like he'd like to see Tom try. "Bigger men than you have wondered that," Tom says. "And they've all talked."

Lenny's smirk is almost permanent now. "You want me to admit to everything on camera," he says. "For what? To give to the public? Are the public going to take seriously a video of a bloodied and beaten man coerced into a potentially false confession?"

"There won't be anything false about it," Tom says. "And they won't be able to see your blood. You think I'm going to bust up your face? You think I'd risk breaking my hands on that thick skull of yours? Why would I do that, when there are nerves so much more sensitive in your hands and in your feet. Under your fingernails and toenails. There are so many ways I can hurt you, Lenny. There are so many ways I can make you talk, and none of them will show up on camera."

Lenny's smirk doesn't falter. "If only you had the time," he says. "You won't make me talk, Rollins. You might as well kill me now, because I'm not going to be tied to this chair forever. And once I'm free, I'll be coming for you." He takes in Cindy. "I'll be coming for both of you."

"We're not going to kill you," Cindy says, defiant. "We're going to bring you to justice. You and Hugh and Cameron.

I'm going to get justice for Erica. She's had to wait so long for it already."

"Justice?" Lenny says. He starts to laugh. From his mouth, clearly unaccustomed to mirth, it's a hideous sound. "There's no justice here," he says. "If only you knew, Cindy. You think you know what you're chasing, but you don't. You think you know what you want, but you don't have a clue. You're going to end up just like Erica. And there's nothing *he* can do to help you." He tilts his head toward Tom.

And then he laughs some more.

31

Hugh races back to the house. Cameron isn't happy to hear about what has happened.

He's in the kitchen when Hugh comes rushing through to find him. He's drinking orange juice from the carton, standing by the open fridge. There's no sign of Amy.

Cameron listens with narrowed eyes. He slams the juice carton down on the edge of the counter. It bursts. Juice flies everywhere. It drips from the ceiling. Some of it splashes into Cameron's face, and onto the front of his shirt, but it doesn't cool him. He's red in the face. "What the hell are you telling me right now?" he says, his voice on the verge of a scream.

Hugh doesn't answer. He knows his brother heard exactly what he's told him. Rollins and Cindy have captured Lenny.

Hugh glances around the kitchen. He and his brother are alone. Hugh can't help but notice how all the other men who were at Los Tierras Bajas, who came back to the house with him, have left him alone to bear Cameron's wrath. Hugh holds up his hands in a feeble attempt to calm his brother.

Cameron isn't interested in being calmed. "Don't you think I have enough to deal with right now?" he says, his voice already growing hoarse. He finally wipes orange pulp from under his right eye. "And this is on *you*, Hugh – the only reason these two assholes are here, and causing more hassle than I need right now, is because of *you*."

"Cameron, if you just give me a minute to explain, if you just listen to—"

"I've got no interest in listening to *anything* you've got to say."

Cameron's shouting brings Stephen. "What's happened?" he says.

Cameron explains with more shouting. Stephen already looks like he regrets coming and asking.

"Jesus Christ, yeah, it's a problem," Hugh says, raising his voice to match Cameron's volume so that everyone has to listen to him, "but if you'll all hear what I have to say, you'll see it's not so bad as it appears. In fact, this might not be such a bad thing at all. It's good for us."

Cameron runs both hands down his face, wiping off the last of the juice. "How can this *possibly* become a positive situation?"

Stephen looks intrigued by this, too.

"I don't let Lenny out my sight," Hugh says.

"I know that," Cameron says.

"I've got a camera on him," Hugh says.

"What?"

"And a tracker. The tracker's in his boot. And the camera, it's fucking tiny, and it's in the collar of his shirt. So when Tom Rollins got the drop on him at Los Tierras Bajas, I saw it happen. They've taken him away, but I know *exactly* where they have him."

Stephen is frowning. "Does Lenny know about this?"

"Of course he knows about it," Hugh says. "He's not just my employee – he's my friend. If I tell him I want him to do something, he'll do it. He's loyal – and he understands what that word means. And he *changes* his shirts, Stephen – I'm not gonna put a camera in every single one."

Cameron blinks. "So, you know where he is right now? And you have a *camera* on him? Then what the fuck are we doing in here talking?"

Hugh rolls his eyes. Nothing is ever good enough for Cameron. "Let me go get my computer," he says. He leaves the house and rushes out to the pool house. There's no one outside, around the pool. There's no sign of Amy. He wonders, briefly, where she is. She must be out. Nightclubbing, probably. He grabs his laptop and goes back to the house, to the kitchen, turning it on and activating the software. He accesses the camera footage. He's in the kitchen, now. He sets the laptop down on the counter near where Cameron burst the orange juice carton.

Cameron watches him with his arms folded. "So if there's a camera on him at all times," he says, "I assume there's footage of him wrecking the strip club last night?"

Hugh doesn't look up, but he freezes in his work. "Uh," he says. "It's not set to record."

"Uh-huh," Cameron says, doubtfully. He knows it's a lie, but he doesn't push it.

Hugh continues quickly. "I've got it going – take a look."

Cameron and Stephen lean in to watch. "Where are they?" Stephen says. "It looks like a warehouse."

Hugh pulls out his phone, checks the tracker. "Downtown," he says. "I've got the coordinates."

"Is there volume on this?" Stephen says.

Cameron reaches closer, turns it up. They hear Cindy's voice. Cameron looks at Hugh. "So this is the bitch you couldn't deal with? She's tiny. She's *nothing.*"

Stephen looks like he's pretending he doesn't hear what Cameron is saying.

"I've found her, haven't I?" Hugh says. "She's not gonna get away this time. They don't even know we can see them."

Cameron is nodding at this, at least. "All right, gather everyone up. Let's go get them."

"Whoa, whoa, let's wait a minute," Stephen says, taking a step back and holding up his hands. "Everyone calm down and think this through for a moment."

"Now's not the time for your soft-touch bullshit, Stephen," Cameron says.

Stephen blinks at this. He stammers for a moment before he's able to speak clearly again. "Just listen to me first, okay? Before we go rushing in."

"I'll listen," Cameron says. "But you better make it quick."

"All right." Stephen points to the screen, to Rollins and Cindy. "These two, they're wild cards. Sending men in after them, well, that might do more harm than good."

"How do you mean?" Cameron says.

"You think he's not armed?" Stephen says, pointing at Rollins. "You think he managed to take out Lenny, and keep him captive, without some weaponry?"

"I didn't see any weaponry," Hugh says. "He was trying to choke him out when I caught up to them."

Cameron's eyes narrow. "You caught up to them? In Los Tierras Bajas, you caught up to them? You saw him trying to choke out Lenny and you didn't intervene?"

Hugh bristles. "You're looking at the same guy I am, right? And *Lenny* was having trouble with him. The fuck do you think I could've done?"

Stephen motions for them to calm down. "We're getting off topic here," he says. He points back at the laptop screen. "He was probably trying to keep things quiet when you saw him. We don't know what kind of weaponry they could be toting. Do you really want to send men in there after him? We have no real idea of what he's capable of, or what he's willing to do. But you heard what the girl said, right? She said she's looking for *justice*. So, why don't we give it to her?"

Hugh notices how Cameron's face moves from confusion to elation. He starts to smile. "We call the law?" he says.

Stephen nods. "Exactly. Will they so readily fight back against cops, as they will against our men?"

"We send in the cops," Cameron says, "and then we let Malcolm deal with them."

Stephen's reaction makes it clear that this is not what he had in mind. He's frowning. "Who's Malcolm?"

Cameron ignores him. He's already pulled out his phone. He's putting things in motion. He's leaving the kitchen. He pauses on his way out, next to Hugh. He motions to the exploded juice. "Clean that up." Then he continues on, out of the room, making calls.

Hugh pats Stephen on the arm. Stephen flinches away from him. "That's some good thinking, Stevie," Hugh says. "Fucking genius idea. Why should we get our hands dirty, when Malcolm can arrange it for us?" He winks at Stephen, then leaves him alone in the kitchen, looking lost.

"But *who* is Malcolm?" he hears Stephen asking.

32

Tom and Cindy look at each other. They hear sirens approaching. They're distant, to begin with, but they're getting closer.

"Are they coming this way?" Cindy says.

"There's nothing else out here," Tom says.

Lenny begins to laugh. It's as horrible, coarse, and unexpected as it sounded earlier. There's no getting used to the sound. "Of course they're coming this way," he says. "They're coming for you."

Cindy talks to Tom. "How do they know we're here?"

Tom looks at Lenny. Lenny is looking back. "There's a tracker on him," Tom says.

Lenny laughs. "And more besides."

The sirens are getting louder. The cops are getting closer. Tom wonders what kind of cops these are. "The people coming, they friends of yours?" he says. "They on Cameron's payroll?"

Lenny shrugs. "Could be."

Tom turns to Cindy. "We need to get out of here. They're too close. We need to go now. Head out the back."

"Okay," Cindy says, breathing deep, preparing herself for the running they're about to do.

"Let me ask you something," Lenny says.

"Ignore him," Tom says.

Cindy can't.

"Who do you think killed your sister?" Lenny says. "Now, I get that it doesn't matter. You hold us both responsible, right? But who do you think it was actually beat her to death with his own two hands?" He watches her expectantly.

Cindy stares at him.

"Do you think it was me?" Lenny says.

"He's trying to distract you," Tom says. "Stop us from getting away." He can't leave Cindy behind. He reaches for her, but she pulls her arm away from him.

"Do you think it was these two bound hands that did it?" Lenny says.

"It was Hugh," Cindy says. She can see what Lenny is getting at. "Hugh beat her to death. I always thought you did it, at his command…"

"Of course you did. Everyone always thinks that's the case, when it comes to the women Hugh likes to assert himself with. But women are about the only people Hugh believes he *can* have his way with. Sometimes he's wrong, and I have to step in, restrain them for him. But that didn't happen with your sister. That was all him."

Lenny is grinning. He sees how his words affect Cindy. He doesn't stop. "I don't think he meant to kill her, but who can be sure? It was just supposed to be a beating. She started letting her mouth run, she insulted him – she insulted both of us – and Hugh wanted to put her in her place. It was a warning to her. But Hugh – he gets carried away sometimes. It wasn't the first time it happened. Wasn't the last, either. Sometimes, he just—"

Tom strikes Lenny across the face with the barrel of the

Beretta, shuts him up. He wheels on Cindy. The sirens are almost on top of them now. "Get out of here. We can't bring them down from a jail cell."

Cindy can't tear herself away from Lenny. "You motherfucker," she says, leaning close to him, speaking through gritted teeth. "You son of a bitch. Did you watch him do it?"

Lenny grins. He nods.

"You're just as bad as he is," Cindy says. "And so is Cameron. You all did it. You're all responsible."

Tom can hear the cop cars outside; they're surrounding the building now. He curses under his breath. It's too late. They can't get away. His mind races.

"You pieces of shit, all of you," Cindy says. "I'm gonna get you – all of you. I'm gonna bring you all down – everyone involved with killing my sister, and everyone who knew about it and helped to cover it up. I'm gonna tear you all the way down."

Lenny is still grinning. "Like your friend said, you can't do that from a jail cell." His eyes remain empty, but he manages to look pleased with himself.

It's too late to get away. "Out the back," Tom says, grabbing Cindy by the arm now and dragging her away. "Come on."

They leave Lenny behind, still bound to his chair. Further behind him, cops burst into the building. Tom hears them calling, telling them to freeze. No doubt their weapons are out – FN 509s, if he recalls correctly.

"Don't stop," Tom says, pushing Cindy ahead.

They reach the back door. It's rusted into place. Tom has to force it open.

There are cops waiting outside for them. Two of them, next to their cruiser. One makes a dive for Cindy. Tom brings up his knee, cuts him off, driving it under his chin. Likely knocking him out cold – he's not in a rush to get back up, anyway. The other attempts to pull his gun, but Tom is on him, grabbing the wrist that reaches for his holster. Before he can pull the weapon out, Tom flips him over his shoulder, then kicks him in the back of the head. Tom pulls his blows as much as he's able. They're still cops, doing their job. He doesn't want to maim them.

"Tom!" Cindy calls.

More cops are attempting to get out the back of the rusted warehouse door. Tom can see their guns, already drawn. He throws himself at the door, forcing it shut. He knows more men will be coming from down the side of the building. They're trapped. He bites his lip and curses, looking at Cindy. All he can hope to do now is hold them up, give Cindy a chance to escape. He throws her his Beretta and KA-BAR. He's going down, and the last thing he needs is to be arrested with deadly weapons.

Cindy doesn't like it, but she understands. She quickly gathers up the weapons, and then she runs, escaping into the darkness.

Tom watches her go. She promptly disappears, swallowed up by the dark. Tom keeps his back pressed up against the door. The cops on the other side are pushing hard against it. He hears footsteps nearing, racing toward his position. Tom jumps away from the door and laces his fingers atop his head, dropping down to his knees.

Out the corner of his eye, he sees the cops appear at the corner of the building. They halt when they see him, guns pointed his way. "Freeze!" one of them shouts, redundantly.

The next thing Tom knows, he feels a weight slamming into the back of him, flattening him to the ground, a couple of bodies pinning him. The side of his face is pressed down into the dirt while his arms are wrenched from his head and twisted behind his back. They slap cuffs on him.

He's under arrest.

33

C indy curses.

She curses the cops for showing up. She curses Lenny for distracting her. Most of all, she curses herself for allowing him to distract her.

She runs as fast as she can through the darkness, her breathing loud and harsh in her ears, drowning out all else. She has her laptop bag slung over her back, her laptop thudding against her with each stride.

She curses herself, too, for not staying in better shape. She's doing well, she thinks, and going fast, but that's probably more to do with adrenaline than any past attempts at aerobic self-care.

Tom's gun and knife are in her hands. She can almost envision herself tripping on some unseen rubble and landing on top of the blade. An ignoble end. She stops running and looks back to check if she's being followed. She can't see anyone. She holds her breath, and can't hear anything, either. In the distance, at the warehouse, she sees the headlights from the police cruisers, and their red-and-blue lights on top.

She puts the gun and the knife into her laptop bag, then keeps going. A jog this time, rather than an all-out sprint.

They'll have Tom now, she's sure. She circles around in the dark, looking back over her shoulder all the while, and keeping an eye on the warehouse to see if the cruisers leave. Her breath comes easier now. It's not so ragged, or deafening. She's exhausted, though. Despite this, she pushes herself on, realizing that tears are rolling down her cheeks.

All this time, it never mattered which of them specifically killed her sister. Until now, they'd both been equally responsible. This is still the case, but something about knowing Hugh did it, that Hugh beat her to death – pathetic, weakling, misogynist Hugh. Something about this gets to her. Something about this, knowing for sure after all this time, it stabs at her.

And she *does* believe what Lenny said. He was taunting her, mocking her with it. The cops had arrived and he knew he was no longer in any danger – if *he* had been the one who killed Erica, he would have told her right then and there.

Cindy thinks, now. She thought she came here looking for justice. For the law to do its job. She's always believed that's what Erica would have wanted. But now she can see the cops, and they're not here to help *them*. They're here to assist the ones Cindy and Tom are fighting against. The cops are helping the ones they should be locking up. The law cannot be trusted, not when there's a billionaire involved. She's seen that at Los Tierras Bajas, and she's heard it from Kylie, and now she's seeing it, first-hand.

But, more than that, is seeing up close how little they care about what they did. Lenny laughs about it. No doubt Cameron does, too. Hugh maybe brags about it. It could be the proudest moment of his life, when he killed a woman and got away with it. But from what Lenny was saying, perhaps Erica is not the only woman he's ever hurt, or killed, and he's gotten away with it all. He'll keep doing it, and he'll keep getting away with it, until someone can stop him.

Cindy feels her breaths hitching, great sobs tearing themselves free from her chest and throat. They don't care about what they did. Erica was nothing to them. She was Cindy's whole world, but to them she didn't matter. Not even to Cameron. He had no idea who she was, but still he covered for his disgusting brother. Still he paid whatever needed to be paid, to keep him from justice.

Justice might not be enough.

Cindy needs to marshal her thoughts. Needs to straighten out her mind. Needs to deal with everything, one step at a time. She knows she cannot stay in this area. They'll search it soon enough, looking for her. She needs to get clear. Before she does, though, she finds herself close to the entrance of the warehouse. Without thinking, she's circled back behind another of the nearby abandoned buildings. She creeps close, up to the corner, and she peers out. The front of the warehouse is well-lit from all the cop cars. She notices other vehicles there, too. A couple of cars without any markings. She wonders if they're with the police. All together, she counts eight cruisers.

She sees Tom. They drag him down the side of the building and into the light. They have him in cuffs. They're pointing guns at him. They bundle him into the back of a cruiser, which promptly turns around and speeds off. Cindy feels herself deflate. Part of her had hoped he would emerge from the darkness, having managed to escape.

Cindy can see their own car. It'll be impounded. It's worthless to them now. She'll need to get a new set of wheels. She'll need to find out where they've taken Tom, and find a way to get him out.

She's about to turn, to leave, when she spots further movement. It's Lenny, emerging from the warehouse. He's rubbing at where his wrists were taped. Then someone gets out of one of the unmarked cars. It's Hugh. Maybe it's from the running, or maybe it's the sight of him, but Cindy's heart leaps into her throat. He goes to Lenny, arms wide, laughing. He embraces the big man. Lenny doesn't hug him back, but he accepts the show of affection. Cindy stares, grinding her teeth. She wishes she had a gun that could shoot far enough. A sniper rifle, something like that. She wishes she knew how to use it.

She slips away into the dark. She needs to regroup. Needs to find a new car.

And, most importantly, she needs to help Tom.

34

The cruiser takes Tom further than he expected. It doesn't take him close to where he was captured. Part of him wonders if this is because they were so far out of the way. Another part of him knows it's because they're working for Cameron, and they're likely taking him somewhere very specific.

If they're taking him anywhere at all. They could be driving him to the middle of nowhere, to drag him out and put a bullet in the back of his head. It wouldn't be the first time someone has attempted this. Tom keeps himself prepared for whatever comes next.

They drive for an hour. By the time they get where they're going, the sun is coming up. It's not quite the middle of nowhere, but it's close. There's only one building to be seen. It's a jail. A small jail, by the looks of it, probably only containing a couple of dozen inmates at max.

Neither of the cops has said a word all the way here. Now, the passenger turns in his seat. "You hurt a couple of my buddies back there," he says. "You know not to fight a cop, right? You should never raise a finger to a cop, because you'll get fucked up tenfold." He stares at Tom with disgust, his tongue rolling over his front teeth like a shining slug. "If we weren't taking you to Malcolm, you can guarantee we'd have pulled over miles ago and paid you back. But you're gonna get yours."

"And then some," the driver agrees.

There are three men standing in front of the building. Two of them are in uniform, and the one in the middle – a short, squat man with a mustache, wearing a tan suit – is who Tom assumes to be Malcolm.

"You don't need to take me for booking first?" Tom says. He can already see how shady this whole thing is, no doubt arranged by Cameron. He's just trying to annoy them.

"Man, shut the fuck up," the passenger says, turning back around.

The cruiser comes to a stop. Malcolm and his two men come forward. The cops in the front get out. They close the doors, so Tom can't overhear while they talk to Malcolm. Soon after, the two guards with Malcolm come and get Tom out the back of the cruiser. They each take an arm and drag him toward the building.

The two cops are standing nearby as they pass. They have their arms folded, glaring at him like he's killed one of their own, rather than just beat a couple up and wounded their pride.

"Enjoy your stay," the passenger says, sneering.

"I'll be sure to send you a card," Tom says.

Malcolm is smiling as his guards pass by with Tom between them. "You know where to take him, boys," he says.

The guards take Tom into the building, through the entrance where a couple of other guards are hanging around the female receptionist at her desk. They take him past the lobby, into the main part of the building. Down past rows of the other cells. The other inmates hoot and holler as he passes by. He hears excitable calls of *Fresh meat!*

The guards take him down to the end, then down a flight of stairs into the bowels of the building. It's quiet here, and clean. It looks like this area doesn't get much use. The cells, four of them, are all empty. The guards push Tom in one of them and slide the door shut. Tom puts his wrists through for them to take the cuffs off.

Malcolm has followed them. "Heard a lot about you, Rollins," he says. He's smiling. "My name's Malcolm Graves. I'm the warden here, and I've been curious to see you for myself."

"I hope I match up to your expectations." Tom could reach him through the bars. He's standing close. The two guards he's brought with him are standing close by, like they expect him to attempt something. "I appreciate the escort all the way down here, and from the warden himself. That certainly wasn't expected."

Malcolm grins. "Just a little service I offer to our special guests."

"Guests, huh?"

"I like to think so." Malcolm scratches his jaw. "Five stars. Excellent service. I'm sure you'll leave us a glowing review."

Tom grunts. "What's the deal here, Malcolm? What kind of place are you running? This where all the dregs get sent while they're awaiting their trials? And if men like Cameron Brewer have some people they need to get out of the way, you don't mind burying them under your building for a reasonable payoff? That sound about right?"

Malcolm strokes his jaw, then smooths out his mustache. He grins. "I'll be sure to let Mr Brewer know that you're settling in comfortably." He chuckles, and then he leaves, motioning for the two guards to follow him.

Tom is left alone. He leaves the bars and goes to the bed.

It's not a single. It's a bunk bed. Tom is the only person in the cell. He takes a seat on the bottom bunk and laces his fingers. He needs to think. Needs to work out how he's going to get out of here. He's not being held legally, and therefore he doesn't have to worry about making too much noise during a jailbreak. He wonders, too, if Cindy got away. Something tells him that if she'd been caught she'd probably be here in the jail with him, if not necessarily in the same cell.

Tom looks up at the empty top bunk. He looks across at the cell opposite. It has a single bed. If they planned on him staying alone, Tom can't help but feel they would have put him in there. He doesn't think he's going to be alone for too long.

And whoever they put in with him, Tom doesn't think they'll be interested in being friends.

35

Cameron is finally smiling.

Well, it's more of a half-smile.

The police were able to capture Rollins, but Cindy got away. Still, he can't blame this latter on Stephen, who stands warily nearby, like he's expecting exactly this kind of reaction. Stephen was nowhere near the scene.

He turns to Stephen now. "Where is my brother?"

They're in the living room. Cameron is reclining on the sofa, allowing himself a rare day away from the office. There's so much else going on, he figured he was best suited staying at home, in case there were any new fires that suddenly needed to be put out. Stephen is not sitting. He stands by the door, like he's ready to be sent out at any moment. He clears his throat before he speaks. "I spoke to him earlier," he says. "After Rollins was captured. He said he was taking Lenny out for breakfast as a treat."

"A treat?" Cameron says, raising his eyebrows, already feeling his smile begin to falter.

"That's what he said."

"Keep in touch with them," Cameron says. "Make sure

breakfast is *all* they treat themselves to. I don't want a repeat of the other night."

Stephen nods. "Yes, sir."

"Speaking of the capture," Cameron says, "has there been any update on Cindy?"

"The LAPD searched the area, but there was no sign of her. She managed to slip away. But there's enough of them on your payroll, and they know what she looks like. They'll keep looking."

Cameron grunts at this. He knows how unlikely it is that they'll actually manage to find her. He's annoyed they let her get away. It's doubtful they'll get another opportunity like the one they had in the early hours of this morning.

Cameron looks at Stephen. "Did *you* know he has a camera and a tracker on Lenny?"

Stephen shakes his head. "I didn't."

"I suppose it shouldn't surprise me too much," Cameron says. "Hugh's always been clingy. When we were young, he used to follow me around all the time. Dad used to refer to him as my shadow." Cameron shakes his head, remembering. He looks around the room, then back at Stephen. "Where's Amy?"

"She's in bed," Stephen says. "Sleeping. She came home late."

"I didn't see her."

"She slipped in while you were following the raid's progress."

Cameron frowns. And she didn't stop by, didn't think to say hello or let him know she was home? He forgets about her for now. Let her sleep. He can deal with her later. Bring up the subject of her increasingly bad attitude. Right now, though, he needs to make a call. "Go find yourself something to do, Stephen," he says. "I need to call Malcolm, and I'm sure the contents of our conversation won't agree with your sensitive disposition."

A sour expression creeps onto Stephen's face, but he does as he's told, leaving the living room and disappearing into the house. Stephen doesn't know who Malcolm is, or how he's helped some of their problems disappear over the years. Cameron keeps him deliberately in the dark about this. It's better he doesn't know. He wouldn't agree with it.

"Find Cindy," Cameron calls after him. "And then we can put this all behind us."

Stephen doesn't give any indication whether he hears or not.

Cameron pulls out his cell phone and puts a call through to Malcolm Graves. It doesn't take him long to answer. "Hello, Mr Brewer."

"Hello, Malcolm," Cameron says, his tone cheerful. "It's been a while. I hope you're doing well?"

"All the better for hearing your voice, Mr Brewer," he says. "I'm sorry I wasn't here when you called last night."

"That's all right. I trust all the information was relayed to you?"

"It was, Mr Brewer. And I'm at the jail now. I got here to welcome Mr Rollins to his cell personally."

"I'm sure he appreciated that."

"Everyone appreciates my charm." Malcolm chuckles his dirty laugh.

"Indeed," Cameron says. He doesn't care much for Malcolm. He's a goblin-like man of poor hygiene – and deviant tastes – but he has his uses. Cameron has found himself doing business with far worse specimens than Malcolm in the past. "Now listen, Malcolm, and listen closely, because there's a bonus in this for you."

"My ears are perked," Malcolm says.

"This Rollins, he's caused me some trouble," Cameron

says. "And there's a risk that he may know too much about certain of my operations."

"You want to know he's not going to cause you any more trouble," Malcolm says. "And that he can't tell anyone about what you've got going on."

"Exactly," Cameron says.

"You got it. Don't worry about it. I figured this is probably how you'd want things to go. I'm already making moves. Everything's in hand."

Cameron settles back, feeling his smile return. As vile as he finds Malcolm on a personal level, on a professional level he can always be relied upon. "That's excellent. And do us all a favor, and save us some extra trouble – make sure it looks like an accident."

He hears Malcolm's dirty chuckle again. "Don't worry, Mr Brewer," he says. "I know exactly what I'm doing, especially with a troublemaker like Rollins."

36

Cindy needs to find where Tom has been taken.

First things first, though – she has to get another car. She doesn't have any cash and has to pay for it digitally. She knows Cameron's people will be looking for her. A digital payment, especially for something as big as a car, will be like a mushroom cloud to them, will lead them right to her. But it's fine. Ever since Erica, she's always been careful. She has dummy accounts under fake names already set up. Cindy Vaughan isn't buying a second-hand car today – Linda Greenwood is. Cameron's people don't give a shit about Linda Greenwood.

She doesn't go back to the hotel. She needs to stay active. She finds a quiet place to park under a bridge and then scours databases for any sign of where Tom may have been taken. She's not having much luck so far. She's checked the departments closest to where he was captured, but there's no record of him being logged. This, of course, raises a concern – maybe he hasn't *been* logged. If this is the case, Cindy is going to have a *very* difficult time tracking him down.

There's a bad feeling deep in the pit of her stomach. Tom is in danger. She's quite sure of this. But, even when she finds him, she's not sure how she's going to free him.

She can cross that bridge when she comes to it. For now, she needs to focus on one thing at a time, and the priority is knowing where he's been taken.

Her fingers fly over her keys, trying everything she can think of to track him down. She accesses security footage, follows the cruiser that took him away from the warehouse. It travels through a couple of neighborhoods without any cameras, though, and she promptly loses them. She curses and slams the side of her fist into the door. She manages to track their license plate, but, looking at the time stamp on the footage, it's a few hours later before she picks them back up. By now, it doesn't look like Tom is in the back. They're on patrol. They've taken him wherever they were going and gone on with their shift.

The bad feeling deepens. Cindy feels like she might throw up.

Dark thoughts try to edge their way in. What if he's already dead? What if they've killed him? What if she's never going to find him because there's nothing *to* find?

She has to push these thoughts aside. To ignore them.

She closes her eyes and pushes her head back into the headrest. Her hands cover her face. She pushes them into her eyes until she's seeing stars behind her closed lids. There's no time for this. No time for exhaustion, or desperation. She has work to do.

She takes a deep breath. Calms herself. Focuses. One thing at a time.

For now, she needs to exhaust all possibilities as to where Tom could be. It's too early to give up. She can't give up. She knows Tom wouldn't. She knows he'd keep looking until he found her and then he'd figure some way to break her out.

Cindy sets her jaw. She cracks her knuckles. There's a long struggle ahead of her, she knows. She needs to get on with it.

37

Tom spends the day alone.

The guards bring him food on a tray they push through a space in the bottom of the bars, then they promptly leave him alone. They don't talk to him, not that Tom attempts to initiate any conversation. Tom checks the food over before he eats it. It's not in his nature to be trusting, especially in such circumstances. He makes sure there isn't a razor blade in the apple, or any residual powder that could be poison in or around the sandwich. Makes sure the seal on the water bottle is still intact.

It's hard to kill time. He lies on the bottom bunk with his fingers laced behind his head, and he waits. There's nothing else for him to do. They have him buried under this building on the outskirts of LA. He wonders if they're planning on keeping him here indefinitely. Locking him up and keeping him from the world, forgetting all about him, leaving him to waste away into dust.

It's late evening when Tom is finally brought a roommate.

He's a big guy. A skinhead who looks like he's been subsisting on a steady diet of smuggled steroids. Has probably been in and out of prison all his life. He's yawning, like he's just woke up, or he's bored. He grins when he sees Tom, though. His teeth are chipped. His lips are scarred. He's a fighter. Maybe not a good one, judging from all the damage around his mouth. Tom has dealt with bigger.

Malcolm has returned, too. "This here's Terry," he says, leaning through the bars as Terry is unshackled by the two guards who have transported him down here. They're different guards than the ones who brought Tom here. "Big one, isn't he? It was getting a little noisy upstairs and he was having trouble getting to sleep, so I figured why not bring him down here, where it's nice and quiet?" Malcolm is smiling. It's the kind of smile Tom could spend hours punching and still not get bored. "As I'm sure you can see, Terry here needs his beauty sleep."

"I can see you're short on space," Tom says, pointedly looking at the empty cell opposite, knowing there are two more nearby.

"Terry's a friendly guy," Malcolm says. "We wouldn't want him to be all on his own now, would we? And you've been on your own down here a while, Rollins. Thought you might like some company. Like I say, Terry's a *real* friendly guy."

Tom looks Terry up and down. He's got about six inches in height on Tom, and he's about double Tom's width. Could be about fifty to sixty pounds heavier. Terry grins, showing off all his cracked and broken teeth. He runs his tongue over them, then moves past Tom to the beds. He climbs onto the top bunk.

Tom remains standing in the middle of the cell. He looks toward Malcolm and the two guards he has with him.

"We'll leave you two to get acquainted," Malcolm says, with a wink. "Enjoy your first night together." Then Malcolm and the two guards leave.

In the silence, it turns out that Terry is a heavy mouth-breather. Tom turns back around. Terry is propped up on the top bunk, grinning back at him. "Didn't know if you have a preference," he says, "but I always like to be on top."

"Good for you," Tom says, then goes to the bottom bunk and lies down. He hears Terry settling above him. He lies very still. The mattress ceases, rocking from side to side as Terry makes himself comfortable. His heavy breaths become calmer, shallower, like he's drifting off to sleep. Tom doesn't believe he's sleeping. He's wide awake. Creating a false sense of security.

Tom lies still in turn, but does not close his eyes. He keeps them focused on the bunk above. Neither man moves. Hours pass. They're waiting each other out. Tom knows neither of them will sleep this night.

It gets late. The lights are switched out. The cells, the whole area, is plunged into darkness. Tom freezes, holds his breath, waits to see if Terry makes his move. He doesn't. He's waiting. He's patient. Continues pretending to sleep.

Terry isn't sleeping. Terry is a predator, waiting for the perfect opportunity to strike. He's waiting for Tom to sleep. Tom knows this. There's no other reason why Terry would be brought here, to this cell, with him. This is what Tom has been waiting for, expecting.

The hours tick by. Tom's eyes adjusted to the darkness long ago. It must be after midnight, now. It's probably after one. Tom has been focusing on staying awake, not tracking the time. Tracking the time would be a good way to unwittingly doze off. Terry doesn't move. His breathing doesn't change.

Then, Terry *does* move.

Slowly, at first. He pushes himself up. He leans over the edge of the bunk. He whispers. "You awake?"

Tom doesn't respond. He half-closes his eyes. He can only see the top of Terry's shaved head.

"How about we have some fun?" Terry says. "You ever had fun like this before, boy? You know what's coming, don't you?" His voice never rises above a whisper. "I'm gonna spread you wide, boy. If I like you, I might spit on it a bit first. Help ease it in. You give me any trouble, it's gonna be dry."

Tom stays quiet. Keeps his breathing regular, like he's sleeping. He doesn't think Terry means what he says. He thinks Terry is just trying to get a rise out of him. To see if he's still awake. Trying to panic him into giving himself away.

"How's that sound to you, boy?"

One final check. Tom doesn't move. Terry waits a moment longer, leaning out further to watch him. Through his half-closed lids Tom can see the full outline of his head now.

Satisfied, Terry gets down off the top bunk. He starts pulling the sheets off. He's careful. Making as little noise as he can. He starts knotting them up. Tom wonders what he's doing. Then he sees what he's made – a noose. He's going to choke Tom out. Hang him. Make it look like a suicide.

Tom wonders why they'll bother. They haven't booked him in – unless they're planning on doing that later, when he's already dead, and compliant. Then they'll start spinning the story – he attacked some cops, then hanged himself in his cell. Maybe they'll pump some drugs into his system, make it look like he wasn't in his right mind.

Terry is finished with his noose. He reaches for Tom on the bed. His hands are big and rough. He drags Tom off the bottom bunk. Tom acts like he's still half-asleep. He mumbles incoherently.

"Up you get," Terry says. He's raising the noose, intending to wrap it around Tom's neck.

Tom makes his move, catching Terry off guard. Striking fast, he grabs at Terry's right hand from where it rests on his left shoulder. He grabs his thumb and yanks it back, snapping it. Terry cries out, pained and surprised. Before he can back up, Tom lashes out with a kick, catching him in the side of the knee. His hope was to blow Terry's knee out, but Terry manages to twist his body a little, and the blow succeeds in bending his leg, lowering him to a kneeling position. He roars and grabs at Tom's face. Tom bites a finger as it comes near his mouth. With his other hand, Terry drags Tom forward, rolling onto his own back.

Tom releases the finger and rolls through. Terry is strong. Even with one thumb broken and one finger being bit, he was still able to throw Tom around like he was nothing. Terry's still on the ground, rolling over and pushing himself up. Tom can't let him get up all the way.

He kicks Terry in the center of the face. He needs to subdue him. To make sure he's not going to be a further risk. He stomps down hard on the back of his right arm. Terry screams. Bloodied bone bursts through his skin. Tom places a knee in his lower back, then presses a hand to the back of his skull and hooks his left arm. Tom puts his mouth close to Terry's ear.

"I heard what you said before," he says. "I didn't appreciate all your threats of rape. I appreciated what you were planning on doing with that noose even less."

Terry tries begging off. Tom ignores him. He snaps his left arm. Terry screams again. Screams himself hoarse. Tom takes the sheets he'd knotted into a noose and uses them to hogtie Terry in the middle of the cell. Terry's crying as his broken arms are wrenched back to be tied into place.

As Tom straightens, he notices a camera out in the hall. It's pointing into the cell. Tom looks down the lens. He doesn't know if they'll be able to hear, but he speaks anyway. "You'll have to do better than that."

He takes a seat on the bottom bunk as he hears a door being thrown open and the rushing of many feet coming his way.

38

Cameron has woken early, and he's getting ready to go to the office. He took yesterday off to make sure things were getting back on track, and he's confident they're getting there. Now it's time to get to work.

But then his cell phone starts to ring. He's in the bathroom brushing his teeth. The phone is on his bedside table. It wakes Amy. She comes through holding it out to him, looking unimpressed. She's wearing the underwear and T-shirt that she sleeps in, and her hair is dishevelled, but she still looks as amazing as she does when she's dressed up and has her makeup on, despite the fact she looks like she wants to beat him with his own phone. "It woke me," she says.

"I can see that," Cameron says, taking the phone from her. He feels a mixture of hope and anticipation as he checks the caller ID and sees that it's Malcolm.

Amy looks like she's ready to collapse back onto the bed and slip instantly into sleep, but she doesn't leave the bathroom doorway. She must see the look on his face, and she hangs around, curious.

Cameron doesn't chase her away. He answers the phone, expecting good news.

That's not what he receives.

Malcolm tells him what has happened. Cameron listens, squeezing the phone. He can feel his face dropping, twisting. Amy looks alarmed. More than that, she looks scared.

"Listen, we'll deal with it," Malcolm says. "I'm on it, don't worry. I just thought I should give you an update – better you hear it from me than from anywhere else, right?"

"It sounds like I need to worry, Malcolm," Cameron says, speaking through his teeth.

"What's that?" Malcolm says.

"You said I shouldn't worry," Cameron repeats, feeling his temper fraying. He doesn't care what Amy hears. "But I think I should. Because it seems no matter where I turn, I'm surrounded by incompetents." He lets loose. Amy flinches. "How could you fuck this up? God*dammit*! You *have* him! He's in a fucking *cell*!"

Malcolm stammers, trying to make excuses, but he can't form any coherent sentences.

"Save it! I don't wanna fucking hear it. Here's what you're going to do – I don't care if you make it look like an accident any more. Make it messy as hell, for all I care. Make it look like he's upset someone in a gang or something. But I want him *dead*, Malcolm. He's a dangerous problem and I need him out of the way, do you understand me? I want him dead by the end of the fucking day, and don't call me again unless it's to tell me *exactly* what I want to hear!"

He hangs up before Malcolm can respond. Amy is still in the bathroom doorway, watching him. She's wide awake now. She swallows, then takes a step forward and strokes his arm. He notices her hand is shaking.

She's like Stephen, Cameron thinks. Always turning a

blind eye and a deaf ear to anything she doesn't want to know about. This isn't the first time.

"It's all right," she says, attempting to soothe him. "Whatever it is, it'll get dealt with. It's not so bad. You don't mean what you say. Don't stress yourself out about it. You're going to give yourself a stomach ache."

Cameron watches her face. Without makeup, her cheeks and eyes a little bloated from sleep, she's still beautiful. He sniffs. She smells sweet.

"You take too much on," she says, still stroking his arm. "You need to let others deal with things sometimes. It makes you say crazy things, Cameron. You don't want anyone dead. You don't really mean that."

Cameron catches her stroking hand. "Everyone else lets me down," he says. He lowers her hand. Slips it into his boxer shorts, where he already feels a stirring in proximity to her.

She looks at him, raising an eyebrow.

Cameron holds her hand in place. She can take the hint.

39

indy hasn't slept.

She's worked through the night, powering herself with coffee and energy drinks. It's getting toward midday now, and she's feeling wired, jittery. She hasn't kept the car in the same place. She's moved it around. A few hours ago, she came out to Zeus Conglomerates. She needs to exhaust all avenues in her search for Tom. A little while ago, she had a breakthrough. She was able to get through their security.

She took a moment to sit back and breathe a sigh of relief, but just a moment. She had to get straight back into her search. That buzz has kept her going since.

On the internal cameras, she can see Hugh and Lenny. Hugh sits back in his office, feet up on the desk, filing his fingernails. He looks bored. Lenny sits in the corner of the room, reading a magazine. Cindy feels herself staring. She has to tear herself away. There's no answers there. She can see Cameron in his office, too. He's working on his computer, and taking calls. Every so often, he stands and paces the floor, lacing his fingers atop his head. He stands by a window and stares out. He looks like he keeps sighing. Cindy wonders if, from his view at the window, he's looking right at her. Staring right at her car, without a clue she's inside. After every brief pacing, he promptly returns to his desk, to his work.

Cindy stares at his computer through the screen. It could have all the answers she's searching for. She can't get on it from here, though. It's running on its own network, separate from the building's WiFi. Cameron isn't taking any chances on anyone piggybacking into his computer through the building's primary WiFi. Smart. Cindy would need to be at the computer, physically, to get into it.

She stares out the car window, at the building, biting her lip. It's so close. The building, the laptop, the *answers* – they're all so close.

A delivery truck pulls up. Cindy feels herself getting an idea. It's a ballsy idea. A stupid idea. It makes her heart pound and her breath come faster. She feels herself beginning to shake, psyching herself up.

"Oh, fuck," she says, muttering under her breath over and over, because she knows she's going to do this. The idea has settled itself, it's taken root, and she knows it's going to happen.

She checks the security cameras. Hugh and Lenny are still in their office, and Cameron is still in his. None of them look like they're going to move any time soon. She checks the foyer. Gets an idea of the layout. Spots where the fire alarm is.

Cindy accesses the live footage through her phone, so she can keep an eye on them, and then she gets out of the car. Before she can think about it too hard, she's already walking toward the building.

One side of her brain tells her this is a terrible idea. The other side tells her it's the *only* idea. She watches the delivery truck up ahead, its driver already leaving the entrance. He gets in the truck and he's driving away. Cindy speeds up. She goes down the side of the building, to where the dumpsters are. There's no one around. She takes a box out of the recycling, reshapes it, then starts heading to the entrance. She's dressed all in black still, from the night they grabbed Lenny from Los Tierras Bajas, and she's glad. She's not sure this would work if she was wearing her ripped jeans and a band T-shirt. As it is, she's not sure how believable she's going to be not in the uniform of a delivery company. That doesn't matter, though – this can be a private delivery.

Before she goes inside, she reminds herself of the name of Cameron's girlfriend. Amy Pernier, the socialite. Then she checks they're all still in their offices.

She enters the foyer, carrying the empty box up to the receptionist. The receptionist is the snooty type that doesn't look up as Cindy approaches, and deliberately ignores her for longer than is necessary. Cindy slams the box down on the counter so the receptionist gives a start and has to look up. Cindy smiles. The receptionist frowns at her bleached hair. She looks her up and down – what she can see of her that isn't obscured by the counter at least – and then makes sure to peer down her nose as she says, "*Yes?*"

Cindy keeps her broad smile plastered on her face. "Hi there," she says, making her voice as plain as she can, disguising her Texas accent. "I've got a delivery here for Mr Cameron Brewer."

The receptionist's top lip curls. "Okay," she says. "I can take that for you."

She reaches for it, but Cindy moves it out of reach. Cindy can't let her touch the empty box. "I'm sorry, but it's coming from Amy Pernier. She gave strict instructions to ensure I hand it to him directly."

The receptionist doesn't look at all doubtful. Cindy wonders if this is something that happens often.

"I can take it up to him myself, if that's easiest," Cindy

says. "If you don't want to disturb him. I'll just need directions."

The receptionist considers her offer. She looks Cindy over again, judging her. "Okay," she says, finally, slipping on a fake smile. "If you wouldn't mind." It's clear she doesn't want to have to disturb Cameron directly. She gives Cindy directions to Cameron's office. Cindy doesn't listen. She doesn't need them. She already knows the way from the security footage. She nods her gratitude when the receptionist finishes, then leaves the lobby, heading to an elevator to the side.

Cameron's office is on the top floor. So is Hugh's. Cindy pulls out her phone and keeps an eye on them on her way up. None of them move. The elevator doors open. Someone walks by, glancing at her as she steps out. They frown, but then they see the box she's carrying and they stop caring.

Cindy makes her way down the corridor, being careful not to look around too much. She already knows where the security cameras are, and the fire alarms. Her back is to the camera. To her left is another corridor. She slips down it, out of sight. A little further down this corridor, there's a fire alarm. She pulls it on her way past, keeps walking. A shrill alarm sounds. Cindy reaches the bathroom and slips inside, pulling out her phone.

She watches Cameron. He looks up at the sound, frowning. He doesn't leave his office, not straight away. Instead, he stands and goes to the window, looks out and down, as if the answers to the alarm's cause could be found there. He hesitates. He goes back to his desk. For a moment, it looks like he's going to close his laptop, take it with him. Cindy's breath catches. Instead, he reaches for the phone on his desk. He presses a button and makes a call. It's probably to reception, asking them if they know what's going on.

"*Come on, come on,*" Cindy mutters, willing him to just hurry up and leave his office.

He talks on the phone for a little while, then he puts it down, looking annoyed. He leaves his office, shaking his head. The laptop is left behind.

Cindy breathes a sigh of relief. She leaves the bathroom. As she does, she realizes she's left too fast. She should have checked the rest of the cameras on this floor – she should have checked Hugh's office. She can see him, now, in person, off to her left, coming down the corridor.

She spots Lenny first. He's taller than the other people making their way to the fire exits. Hugh is beside him, looking up at him, saying something.

Cindy almost freezes at the sight of them, but she can't. If she freezes, she's caught. She's dead. She turns to the right and she starts walking, burying herself in the middle of everyone else. She lowers her head and keeps going. No one calls after her. No one hurries to catch up with her.

Ahead, she spots Cameron. People are talking to him, asking him questions, but he's just as in the dark as they are. Cindy slips by him, cuts to the left. Toward his office. The corridor is thinning out. Soon, there's no one else around.

She gets to his office and looks back before she slips inside. No one is following her. His office is huge, bigger in person than it appears on screen. She rushes to his desk, grabs his laptop and places it inside the box she's been carrying. She checks the security cameras. The building's workers are filing out, taking the stairs at the back of the building down to the fire exit. They're gathering out in the parking lot. Cindy heads back out the office. She goes to the stairs, too. There's no one else around by the time she reaches them. When she gets to the bottom, she doesn't go out the back door to join the others. She goes through the lobby, out the front door. She walks fast and confident, and doesn't look back.

By the time she gets back to the car, she's breathing hard.

She throws the box into the back, then jumps in the front. Her heart is pounding. She starts the engine. She can't hang around here, not now. Soon, when they realize there's no fire, they'll all go back inside. It shouldn't take them long. Cameron will get to his office and find his computer gone. They'll check the security footage, and they'll see her entering, taking it. Hugh and Lenny will recognize her. They'll know it was her.

She thinks about deleting the footage. Erasing her presence. They'd never know who took the computer. She knows if Tom were here, he'd insist on it.

She doesn't do it.

She doesn't delete the security footage. She won't.

For better or worse, she wants them to know it was her. Wants them to know just how close she got to them, and they didn't even see her. Wants them to know that, with Tom or without, she's still coming for them.

She grits her teeth and speeds away from the building.

40

Tom has been alone in the cell since the guards took Terry away. Five guards rushed in after the fight. Three of them carried Terry away, not bothering to loosen him from his hogtied bindings. Terry screamed as they hauled him out. The other two guards pulled their truncheons and left Tom with something to think about. Tom managed to block the worst of the blows aimed at his head with his forearms, but his ribs weren't so lucky. When he shifts and presses his palm to them, he can feel the bruises. He grunts and concentrates on his breathing. It hurts when he fills his lungs. He fights through it, blocks out the pain, numbs himself to it.

He lies back on the bottom bunk and naps. He didn't sleep last night while monitoring Terry. It comes fast. Then, seemingly just as fast, the guards are waking him.

"Get up, Rollins." It's Malcolm, at the bars. He has a couple of men at his back. Every time Tom has seen him, he's come with backup.

Tom raises his head. He feels a twinge in his ribs as he

moves, but doesn't let it register on his face. "Do all wardens make personal visits? Or do you just like coming to see me?"

Malcolm doesn't respond to this. His face is pinched. "Get off the bed," he says, his voice clipped. "Lunch time."

Tom rolls to the side, sits up. He resists grimacing as his ribs twinge again. Doesn't want to show Malcolm or the guards any weakness. "I'm used to having my meals brought to me," he says, standing. "I'm used to that first-class service now. It makes me feel special."

Malcolm shakes his head. "I'm not interested in quips, Rollins. Get a move on. Let's go."

Tom stands. The guards slide the door open. One of them is holding up cuffs. Tom shakes his head. "I'm not wearing those," he says. He looks at Malcolm. "Not when I'm just going for lunch, right?"

Malcolm bristles.

"You always try to cuff inmates when they're about to eat?" Tom says. "We need our hands for the utensils. I can't speak for everyone here, but I'm not an animal."

Malcolm throws up a hand. "Just grab him," he says to the guards. "Let's go."

The two men do as they're told. They each take an arm and transport him from the cell. They go upstairs. Malcolm leads the way. Tom doesn't fight back, not yet. The building is full of other guards. He waits to see where they take him first, what their angle is. He's ready to fight if and when necessary, but it won't hurt to get a better look at the rest of the building first. If he's going to have to fight his way out, he needs an escape route in mind.

They take him to the canteen. Its double doors are shut. Malcolm pulls keys. They must be locked, too. He pushes the doors open, and Tom is shoved inside.

"Enjoy your fucking lunch," Malcolm says, as the doors are pulled shut. Tom hears him relock them.

Tom looks around. He's not alone in the canteen. There are four other guys, and they all look like carbon copies of his former cellmate, Terry.

The canteen isn't big, but it has a dozen tables. The four men are all seated around one. There's no one behind the counter where food is served. There's no food available. The shutters are down. The four men all turn at Tom's arrival.

"Let me guess," Tom says, looking over the four shaved heads. "You're friends of Terry's?"

The four men begin to stand. None of them says a word. Tom knows how this is going to go. He's been in this situation enough times before. The four men come toward him. They spread out, to surround him. Tom stays close to the nearest wall, keeps his back to it. The men are all big, and they're all mean. They probably spend all of their time here working out.

Tom can't reason with these men. They aren't interested in being reasoned with. They can't be warned off, either. They won't listen. These men are used to violence. They're built for it. They want to hurt him. In turn, he's going to have to hurt them worse. He's going to have to strike first, fast, and hardest. It's the only way he'll survive. They're coming for blood. Coming for his life.

The two to his left are practically identical. All four look alike, but these two could be twins. The only difference between them is that one of them has a scar beneath his right eye.

The man coming at Tom, directly opposite, is older than the rest. His midsection is a little softer, too. The man to Tom's right has a goatee beard. Tom attacks him first, looking to open up a little space for maneuvering.

He jabs into the center of his face, right on the bridge of his nose. It'll tear up his eyes, momentarily blind him. The sharp pain will resound through his skull. As Goatee stumbles back, holding his face, the older guy lunges at Tom. Tom lashes out with a back kick, drilling it hard into his soft midsection, driving the air up and out of his lungs. The older guy goes down, gasping.

The unscarred twin moves fast. He gets to Tom and throws his weight at him, drives him back and down to the ground. Tom manages to keep hold of the front of his shirt with both hands and drags the man down with him, then flips him over and rolls through with him, coming up on his feet. Before he has a chance to strike the unscarred twin, the scarred twin is attacking. He forces Tom back. He's throwing punches. He doesn't have a boxer's finesse, but his blows are heavy. Tom covers up, protecting his head, but then Goatee joins the fray and tags him in the bruised ribs with a rabbit punch.

Tom feels pain explode there, but he does his best to ignore it. To swallow it down. He can't afford to be defeated by it. If he goes down, they won't let him get back up. It's important he remains on his feet. So he backs up, out of range of their shots. He doesn't rub at his ribs where the blow landed, or attempt to protect them more than anything else. Doing that, he might as well paint these four men a bullseye.

He manages to put a table between himself, Goatee, and the twins. The older guy is still on his hands and knees, gasping like an asthmatic. The table is bolted to the ground. The stools are built into it. The twins come at him, round either side of it. Goatee makes a mistake, though. He lunges over the top. Tom laces his hands together on the back of the guy's skull and drives his knee up into the center of his face, to the bridge of his nose again. He breaks it this time. Feels it crunch, and the wetness as blood soaks into his jeans. He dives to his right then, past the slower, scarred twin. He rolls through and runs to the older guy, who's still not up. He drives a boot into his midsection, looking to incapacitate him for the rest of the fight.

The older guy is lifted almost a foot off the ground with the impact. He comes back down vomiting. Tom kicks an arm out from under him, and he collapses into it.

The twins are in pursuit. Tom keeps out of reach of them. He goes back to Goatee, who has rolled onto his back on the table. Tom kicks him in the side of the head, snapping it to the side and knocking him off the top. He hits the ground with a grunt, looking unconscious.

Just the twins left. Everyone is breathing hard. The unscarred one, the fast one, gets to Tom first. He dives at his waist, wrapping his arms around and raising him up, slamming him down onto the ground. Tom keeps his head up, avoids a concussion. The scarred twin slides along the ground, close to him, grabbing at his throat. Tom manages to sink his teeth into the web of skin between the index finger and thumb of his grabbing right hand. He sinks it in deep, trying to get his teeth to meet in the middle. The scarred twin screams at the pain and strikes at Tom's face with his left hand. His knuckles catch Tom on the corner of the right eyebrow, drawing blood. He throws another punch and Tom angles his face down, so the fist connects with the hard bone of his skull. He feels a crunch, similar to Goatee's breaking nose. The scarred twin has broken at least one finger on impact with Tom's skull. The blow will leave Tom with a bruise, but it's worth it. Tom bites down harder on the web of flesh, his mouth filling with blood. He tears the flesh loose, spits it out.

As the scarred twin falls back, his bloodied and broken hands clutched to his chest, the unscarred twin slams his foot into the middle of Tom's face. This time, the back of Tom's head hits the hard ground. He's dazed. He can taste blood and can feel it running from his nose and his mouth. Then there's pressure on his chest, and hands wrap around his throat.

Tom does his best to shake the cobwebs loose, but it's difficult to do when he can't breathe. The fingers squeeze tight, constricting his throat. They dig in deep, almost deep enough to draw blood.

Through the fog, Tom can see the unscarred twin's snarling face, his bared teeth. The veins in his arms are popping. He's made a mistake, though – Tom realizes his limbs are free. The unscarred twin hasn't made any effort to pin his arms. As the edges of his vision darken, Tom grabs at the side of the unscarred twin's face. He's aiming for an eye. He misses – catches an ear instead. He doesn't let go. He holds it tight and begins to squeeze.

Instantly, he feels the pressure on his neck loosen. The unscarred twin's expression turns from snarling to pained, though there isn't much difference between the two. His body falls to the left as Tom begins to twist on his ear. The twin is crying out. Tom twists harder, and he pulls. The man's ear comes away from the side of his head in a burst of blood. The twin is screaming now. His hands are gone from Tom's neck. His weight falls from Tom's chest. Tom can breathe freely again, though it hurts to do so.

He's coughing. His vision clears. He lets go of the ear, throws it away. He looks around. The unscarred twin isn't done. He's in pain, but he's still coming. He's trying to push himself up. He's reaching for Tom again, no doubt looking to finish the job he started on his throat. He crawls close, but his legs are either side of Tom's right shin. With all the strength he has left, Tom brings that leg up, buries it into the twin's crotch. The twin is paralyzed with pain. His eyes are watering. Tom pushes him away before he can throw up, like the older guy did.

Tom rolls onto his side, pushes himself up, still trying to

refill his lungs. His head is swimming. He spits blood. He looks around. The four men are down, and moaning. There is vomit, and blood, and bits of flesh scattered across the floor. The pain in Tom's ribs isn't so bad any more. It's been surpassed by everything else that has been done to him.

The scarred twin sees him looking. He grimaces, then pushes himself back, presses himself against the wall and forces himself up. His hands are useless to him, but he looks determined to continue.

"Are you fucking kidding me?" Tom says, his voice hoarse.

The scarred twin comes at him. Tom is angry, and impatient. He grabs the scarred twin by the throat and drives him back into the wall he'd used to prop himself up, then presses a hand to his forehead and drives the back of his skull into it. This puts the twin down. There's a bloodied print on the wall where his head made impact. He slides to the ground.

Tom limps to a table near the locked doors, and waits for them to be unlocked.

41

Cindy knows where Tom is.

She races to the jail on the outskirts of LA. She was able to get into Cameron's laptop a couple of hours ago, but it took her a while to find a clue that could lead her to Tom. Finally it came, in the form of some payments. A recent payment, in fact, made to a man named Malcolm Graves. Cindy looked deeper, and found a record of them. Clandestine payments made to Malcolm, the warden of a small jail.

It didn't take much to access their security cameras, using a simple spoofing attack. She saw Tom on them. Saw him arriving, being taken to his cell. She scanned through, to make sure he was still alive. She saw the big man taken to Tom's cell, and then their fight in the early hours of the morning. Saw Tom break both of his arms. She winced at this, but she's sure he deserved it, whoever he was.

She couldn't leave straight away, despite knowing where Tom was. She needed a plan. She looked into Malcolm Graves. Going in and telling him she knew about Cameron's payments to him, which are no doubt to make problems disappear, wouldn't be enough. He'd probably laugh at this. She needed something more. Hopefully, something she could scare him with.

Hacking into his computer, she got everything she hoped for, though it made her sick to her stomach.

She reaches the jail, throwing the car into a space, and then runs inside. If the big man Tom had to incapacitate was any indication, then they're planning on killing Tom in this building. To make it look like he got himself into some trouble while in custody. She needs to get him out, fast. She gets inside and goes to the desk. She takes a deep breath before she speaks.

The desk clerk looks up at her. He raises an eyebrow. "It's not visiting hours," he says.

"I'm not here for a visit," Cindy says. "I'm here to see the warden. Malcolm Graves."

"I know who the warden is," the clerk says, looking at his computer screen.

"Then get him for me," Cindy says. She hasn't got the patience for the clerk's disinterest, or his patronizing judgement.

"He's busy," the clerk says, without looking up.

Cindy slams her hands down on the counter to get his attention. "Then tell him this is an emergency."

The clerk looks up now, unimpressed. "Who are you?"

"Tell him I'm his therapist, and I'm here to see him about his affliction."

The clerk raises an eyebrow. "You don't look like a therapist. And I doubt Malcolm's ever seen the inside of a therapist's office in his life."

Cindy leans over the counter. "Fucking *tell him*."

The clerk stares at her, then turns and picks up the phone. He taps a button, pressing the receiver to his ear.

"I'm not going anywhere until I see him," Cindy says. "Be sure to tell him that, too."

The clerk turns away from her, lowers his voice when he talks into the phone. It's a brief conversation. Towards the end, he raises his voice a little. "Yeah, no problem. I'll tell her." He starts to turn.

Cindy understands the tone. It's not positive. The warden has turned her down. Before the clerk can put the phone down, she says, "I'm here about Rollins."

The clerk hesitates. He turns away again, resumes speaking in his lower voice. He puts the phone down and addresses Cindy. "He's coming through," he says. He avoids looking at her.

Cindy stays by the counter. A couple of minutes later, a short man comes into the lobby. Cindy already knows it's Malcolm. She knows what he looks like. She's seen pictures of him already. The thought of them, of what he's doing in them, turns her stomach. He's smoothing out his mustache. He looks flustered. He looks around the lobby. Cindy is the only person he doesn't recognize. He looks past her, to the clerk. "This her?"

The clerk nods.

Before he can address Cindy, she cuts him off. "You're gonna want us to talk in private."

He looks taken aback. "What?"

"We should go to your office," she says.

Malcolm starts waving his hands. "I don't got time for this," he says. "I'm busy."

"Then you're gonna make time for what I have to talk to you about." Cindy isn't moving. She steps closer to him. She lowers her voice. "I know your secret," she says, sneering.

Malcolm flinches. He doesn't ask what she means. He sees the look on her face, and he understands. "All right," he says. "Okay, follow me."

He leaves the lobby, and Cindy follows. They go to his office. Malcolm takes a seat behind his desk and motions for her to do the same opposite. "What's this about?" he says.

Cindy sits. "You're holding my friend here," she says. "Tom Rollins. I want him back. And I know there's no record of him being booked in here, so letting him go shouldn't be any kind of problem, should it?"

"I'm not going to just—"

"Did you hear me out there?' Cindy cuts him off. 'I know your secret, Malcolm. I know the filthy, disgusting things that you do. I have the images. They're ready to go public. Soon *everyone* will know the filthy, disgusting things that you do. Unless you give me Rollins."

Malcolm looks shaken. He can't speak. He knows what she's talking about. He knows *exactly* what she's talking about.

"I have a post ready to go public," Cindy says. "Only I can turn it off, and I'm not doing that unless you give me what I want."

"How—" He has to clear his throat before he can continue. "How – how do I know you're telling the truth? That you...that you won't post it anyway, if I give you what you want?"

Cindy looks him dead in the eye. "You don't," she says. She doesn't blink. She stares a hole through him. She sees how he squirms. He makes her sick. "But the only hope you have is if you give me Rollins."

"You're – you're lying," Malcolm says. "You don't know anything about me."

Cindy expected him to call her bluff. She pulls out her phone, shows him an image. Malcolm turns very pale. He can see she's not bluffing.

"Not even Cameron's money could protect you from this," she says. "Do you think even a man like Cameron would *want* to?"

Malcolm is sweating. He hesitates, but not for long. He picks up his phone and presses a button. "Is Rollins still alive?"

Cindy feels her heart skip a beat. She notices how Malcolm's eyes flicker in her direction. He looks relieved, then says, "Okay. Okay, good. Free him. Don't worry yourself about that – just bring him through. He's free. Cut him loose." He puts the phone down. He looks at Cindy, holds out his hands. "You heard. It's done. They'll bring him outside."

Cindy gets to her feet. "How long?"

"I don't know, maybe five minutes..."

"Two minutes." Cindy checks the time. "I'll be outside. Two minutes, or I post and tell all the world about you."

She turns away and leaves his office, makes her way back outside and waits by the car. She watches the time. At one minute and forty-five seconds, Tom is outside. Two guards drag him out, one either side of him. They let go of him, then they go back inside. There's no further sign of Malcolm.

Cindy goes to Tom. She wraps her arms around him, squeezes him tight. She notices how he flinches, but he doesn't tell her to let go. He hugs her back. She looks up at him. There's dried blood on his face and a bruise at the top of his forehead. "Let's get out of here," she says.

"What happened?" Tom says, following her to the car. "How'd you get me out?"

"I'll tell you on the road," Cindy says. They get in, and she starts driving. "Your weapons are in the glove compartment."

Tom opens it up, takes out his gun and his knife. "Thanks for keeping them safe." He looks in the mirror. The jail is disappearing behind them. "How'd you get me out?"

"I found the skeletons in Malcolm's closet."

"And what were they?"

Cindy hesitates telling him, because she knows how he'll

react. She looks in the mirror. The jail is gone from view. They've left it far behind. "The warden has a predilection for underage boys and girls."

Tom reacts exactly how she expected. His face goes cold, and hard. "Turn this car around."

"Not yet," Cindy says. "But we will. We'll go back for him. We won't let him get away."

"He's going to run."

"I know he will, but wherever he goes I'll find him. But we can't go back now – we've only just got you out. Malcolm can wait. He knows we know. I saw his face. He's terrified."

Tom shakes his head. "If I'd known, I would've found a way to kill him while I was in there."

"I know." Cindy reaches over, places a hand on his leg. "We'll get him, Tom. We won't let him get away."

42

Stephen stands in the corner of the room and waits for the fury to be turned his way.

Cameron finds out what has happened at the jail, though whatever it is, he doesn't share it with the room. Stephen has tried to ask a few times already what they've tried to do with Rollins, and who Malcolm is, but each time he has been ignored. Cameron tries to get in touch with Malcolm, but can't.

Someone else at the jail finally answers. They're on speakerphone, and Stephen can hear them. They say Malcolm has disappeared. He didn't tell anyone anything. Just up and left without a word. He's not answering his home phone. Cameron asks about his cell and is told that he left it behind. Cameron frowns at this.

Cameron was already angry before he received this news. He's screaming at his brother and Lenny. Cindy came to their building and stole his laptop. They caught her on camera, brazen, like she wanted them to see.

"So how the *fuck* did you miss her?" he says, jabbing a finger in his brother's face.

"How was I supposed to know she was there?" Hugh says.

"You're supposed to be looking for her!"

"And I am! But I didn't expect her to be right under our fucking noses!"

They're all gathered in the living room. There is no sign of Amy. The pit of Stephen's stomach is filled with dread.

Sure enough, Cameron turns on him. He explodes. He screams. It's nothing Stephen hasn't already heard lately. He – and everyone else – is called incompetent. Stephen isn't sure how it's his fault Rollins was able to get out of the jail, except for that it was his idea to have him arrested. He didn't want him sent to Malcolm, though, whoever Malcolm may be. He wanted it done lawfully, properly. If they'd done it the way he wanted, Rollins would still be behind bars.

Cameron throws up his hands and circles the room. "So what the *fuck* do we do now?"

Nobody says anything for a while. Cameron looks at them all expectantly. Stephen avoids his glare. Hugh looks back at his brother, grinning, like he enjoys seeing him so worked up. Lenny stares straight ahead, as stoic as ever.

"*Well?*" Cameron says. "I'm willing to hear some ideas, or do I have to do everything myself, as usual?"

Stephen swallows. "There's no reason why we can't call the cops on them again—"

"I don't want the fucking cops!" Cameron says, wheeling on him. "I want them *dead!*"

"I've got an idea," Hugh says.

Cameron looks like he isn't sure he wants to hear it. "All right," he says, sounding doubtful. "Spit it out."

"We've tried doing it his way," Hugh says, nodding at Stephen. "The lawful way, right? Sticking to the straight and narrow. But we called the cops, and they were no fucking good. So why don't we go the other way?"

"Do you have something *specific* in mind?" Cameron says.

"I'm not sure I want to hear this," Stephen says.

Hugh smirks at him. "Then don't listen."

The two brothers look at him expectantly. Stephen looks between them both. He doesn't want to hear whatever Hugh's idea is. No doubt it'll be stupid, and reckless, and probably will follow through on Cameron's wishes for Rollins and Cindy's deaths.

Stephen takes a deep breath. He just wants this all over with. To end it. To wrap it up, before anyone else can get hurt. He clenches his jaw. He knows what he has to do. He doesn't like it, but it's the only way to stop all this chaos. He's going to have to cross a line. He can suffer the consequences later. If it saves some lives, then so be it.

He turns and leaves the room. No one tries to stop him.

43

Tom and Cindy are at the hotel. Tom has had a shower. He's taped up his bruised ribs. He's sitting on the edge of the bed, trying not to wince. They're making plans for their next step. What they hope is their final step.

"Cameron has too many powerful people in his pocket," Tom says. "We need to end this."Cindy nods. She sits cross-legged in the chair by the window. She's had a shower, too, and her wet hair is combed back from her face. She's back in torn jeans and a band T-shirt – Ministry, this time. "I got into the Zeus Conglomerates system," she says. "I'm confident I can get into his household security. If I do that, we can record them – maybe catch them saying something they don't want getting out. We get that, we put it online – we put it *everywhere*."

Tom paces the floor. "That might work," he says. "But is it enough?" He presses at the scab on his eyebrow, but stops himself before he makes it bleed again. "We can't guarantee they'll talk about what we need them to talk about it," he says. He stops pacing. "We might need to find a way to prompt them into saying what we need. But still, is *that* enough? Can we guarantee that they won't just instantly pull it down and scrub it? And if it even gets through them, can we guarantee that enough people will care?"

Cindy sucks her teeth, thinking. She opens her mouth, but before she can say anything, there's a sound from her laptop.

She frowns. It's on the desk near her. She grabs at it, places it in her lap, starts tapping at the keys.

"What's happening?" Tom says. "What does that mean?"

"Oh, shit," Cindy says. "Oh, *shit.*"

"*What?*"

Cindy types some more. She reads, leaning closer to the screen. "This isn't good," she says. "Cameron has put a hit out on us on the dark web. Five million dollars, *each.*"

"How long ago?" Tom says.

"Right now. I've got alerts set up for our names. He's got our pictures on there, too."

"Any way of knowing how many people have seen that post?"

Cindy shakes her head. "No, but there's already a *lot* of people responding to it. And a lot of them look like they're nearby..."

"So what does this mean, exactly? How many people have access to this?"

"Everyone who knows how to get on the dark web has access to it. And what it *means*, is that every hit man, gangster, crooked cop, and petty criminal in the city, and perhaps from beyond, will be coming for us. Anyone who's *seen* us could be coming for us. We can't trust anyone right now."

This is what Tom feared. "Can you take his post down?"

She looks at him. "I'm gonna fucking *try.*"

"Then you'll have to do it on the move," Tom says, standing. "Gather up your things. We need to go. We can't stay here. Too much chance it's already been compromised."

Cindy nods, starts gathering up her things. They've kept their stuff packed neatly in their bags, ready to flee at a moment's notice. There's not much else to take. Cindy goes to close her laptop last. She bags it up. Another alarm sounds, from Cindy's pocket. They look at each other. Cindy pulls out her phone. She mouths to Tom, "*It's the door.*"

She turns the alarm off. Tom comes closer, and they check the camera they have out in the hall. Someone is at their door, has set off the lasers. Someone has their ear pressed to the wood, checking if they're inside. Tom and Cindy look at each other.

"I recognize him," Tom says, keeping his voice low.

Cindy nods. She does, too. "It's the receptionist."

44

Stephen goes to Catherine's house. He doesn't go alone. He takes two men with him. Vernon is one of them. He trusts Vernon to help keep things under control.

They're still in the car. "Her husband is at work and her kids are at school," Stephen says, speaking to his two men. "We go inside, and we get her to talk, but we keep it clean. No mess, and no one gets hurt. Understood?"

Both men nod.

"Let's go. Follow my lead."

The three men get out of the car and go to Catherine's house. Stephen is in front. He rings the doorbell. Catherine takes her time answering. They haven't been parked outside for long, and he doesn't know for sure that she's home, but the camera footage never showed her leaving. He *needs* her to be home, though. He rings the doorbell again, over and over.

Stephen is getting desperate. He knows it, and he doesn't like it. But the longer this whole thing takes, the messier it gets. The more people that can get hurt, or worse.

And the more likely Cameron is to listen to his psychotic younger brother.

Already, Cameron is listening to him – Stephen – less and less. His temper's getting worse. He's losing control. It's affecting everyone around him. It's affecting Stephen himself.

This isn't him. This isn't what he's like. Coming to a woman's house in the middle of the day, prepared to do what he's about to do. He's never done anything like this before. He grits his teeth and swallows down bile. He doesn't like who he's becoming.

Catherine answers the door, frowning at the doorbell having been rung so incessantly. She sees Stephen. Her frown turns to confusion. "Stephen? What are you doing here?"

"Rollins and Cindy," Stephen says. He steps forward, backs her up inside her own house. He pushes her door wider. His men follow him inside. "Why did they come here? What did they ask you?"

Catherine can't speak. Her eyes are wide, popping out of her skull.

Stephen grabs both of her arms, holding her tighter than he should. She flinches at his grip, looks pained. "*Why did they come see you?*"

"I don't – I don't know who you're talking about—"

"Don't fucking lie to me!" Stephen says. He's shouting. He never wanted to shout. God, this isn't him...This isn't what he's like...They've made him so *desperate*...

"It was about Kylie, wasn't it?" he says, pushing on. "They came to ask about her, didn't they? They wanted to know if you could put them in touch with her, isn't that right?"

"Stephen, you're hurting me!"

"A lot of people are getting hurt, Catherine. This needs to end, goddamm it! Do you understand what I've done for you? For *her*? I *promised* him you didn't know anything about her – I promised Cameron you didn't know where Kylie was. I kept him away from your goddamn door. I've done everything I can, and it's not enough! Tell me what they wanted!"

Catherine struggles against him. Stephen slams her up against a wall, stops her wriggling. Something falls nearby. He looks. It's a picture frame. Her two kids. Stephen feels sick. He feels himself deflate. He looks at his two hands holding her.

He lets go of her. "*Please*," he says, "just tell me where she is."

Catherine doesn't speak.

"Don't get soft, Stephen," Vernon says behind him. "We've come this far. No going back now."

"Get out of my house," Catherine says.

She sees how Stephen has faltered. She hasn't told him anything. She's not going to.

"Get out, or I'll call the police," she says.

Stephen looks at her. "What good do you think that'll do?" he says. "You think Cameron won't just pay them off? You think he hasn't already?" He goes to that dark place again. The frustrated, browbeaten, defeated place. He ignores the framed pictures of her kids. He grabs her by the arms again, shakes her. "Don't you understand? I'm still trying to help you," he says. "Right now, I'm all that stands between you and *them*." He tilts his head back toward his two men. "They have no qualms about doing whatever they have to to get information out of you. Do you understand? Once I give them the word, it's done. I can't stop them. I won't be able to call them off. They're like wild dogs."

It's not true. Vernon and the other guy aren't like this. If they were, Stephen wouldn't have brought them with him. Nevertheless, Catherine's eyes flicker in their direction, and he can see the alarm, and the fear, in them. He presses on, sensing an advantage.

"Rollins and Cindy," he says, softening his voice. "They were looking for Kylie, weren't they?"

Catherine closes her eyes. She hesitates. She looks like she's about to cry. Finally, she nods. Just once.

"And did you tell them where she was?"

Again, the hesitation. Then she nods, again just the once.

Stephen lets go of her arms. Catherine takes a hitching breath. "Can you still get in touch with her?" he says.

"Yes." Her voice is a whisper. Her face is lowered. She can't look at him.

"Then you're going to arrange to meet up with her, Catherine." This isn't what he wants. He wants to apologize. To beg her forgiveness. He can't. It's too late. He needs to follow through. "And then you're going to come with us, to see her. So don't do anything you're going to regret later."

45

"He's armed," Tom says, pointing to the screen at the bulge at the back of the receptionist's jeans, hidden under his shirt.

"What do we do?" Cindy says. "Out the fire escape?"

"Not yet." Tom presses a finger to his lips and moves silently across the room to the door. He places a hand on the handle, then looks back at Cindy. Motions to the door, asking if the man outside has moved. Cindy shakes her head.

Tom pulls the door open. He grabs the receptionist and pulls him inside, spins him around and twists his arm halfway up his back. He pulls his gun out from his waistband and presses it into the base of his skull. "What do you want?" Tom says.

The receptionist is just a kid. Early twenties, barely. Tears are already streaming down his cheeks from the pain in his arm, and the cold, hard feeling of his own gun against his head. "I – I –"

Tom spins him around, pins him against the wall with an arm across his chest, the barrel of the gun pressed into his cheek now. It's a revolver, a Smith & Wesson model 686, a .357

Magnum. "You wanna find out the kind of damage this thing can do up close?" Tom says. The kid looks terrified. "Start talking."

"I was just – I was just checking you were still here," he says.

"That's not part of the service," Cindy says, standing and coming closer. "I've seen you, down in the lobby. You're always on your computer. You saw the post, didn't you? You saw the bounty."

The kid closes his eyes tight, and that's answer enough.

"Who else knows?" Tom says.

"I told – I told my cousin," the kid says.

"And who's your cousin?" Tom says. "He coming alone?"

He has to push the barrel of the gun in a little deeper to get an answer out of the kid. "He's coming with his boys," the kid says. "Coming with his crew."

"His crew? What is he – a gangbanger?"

The kid opens one eye, and that answers Tom's question. "How far out are they?"

"Not far," the kid says. "They might even be here now. I was just checking to make sure you were both still here."

Tom looks at Cindy. Cindy checks her phone, the cameras out in the hall. Her eyes widen. She holds it out to Tom. He can see men approaching, half a dozen of them. They're armed, and not lightly. They're carrying assault rifles as they creep along.

The kid spots it, too. "In here!"

Tom pistol-whips him, striking him hard in the temple, putting him down. He doesn't need to check the camera; he can hear the men outside rushing down the hall toward them. He spins to Cindy, dropping the kid. "Out the window!"

Bodies strike the locked door. An alarm goes off as they cross the lasers. Tom dives over the bed. Bullets blast through the door, tearing up the room. Cindy is halfway out the window when it happens. She flinches, covers herself up. Tom grabs his bag, pulls it onto his back. He reaches Cindy. "Keep moving," he says, placing his hands on her shoulders and easing her out the window, the rest of the way. "Don't stop, and don't look back." He has to shout to be heard over the gunfire.

Cindy gets moving, keeping her head low. Tom takes her place, half in and half out of the window, looking back toward the door. He points the kid's gun toward it. The shooting stops, and the door is kicked open. Tom looses two rounds and puts down the first man through the door. He wonders if it's the kid's cousin. His blood sprays back into the face of the man behind him and he falls also, blinded. Tom keeps firing, emptying the rounds. The others behind fall back as his bullets tear chunks out of the wall and frame. With the revolver empty, Tom follows Cindy down. They move fast.

In his mind, he tries to work out where the gangbangers could be at, what they're doing. At what point they reach the window and look down. Maybe fire on them. They'll hesitate after Tom stops shooting, thinking it's a fake-out, that Tom is waiting for one of them to poke their head around so he can take it off their shoulders. Then, cautiously, they *will* look in. They'll see the room is empty. The window is wide open. Maybe, if he and Cindy are lucky, the gangbangers check their fallen friends. They check the receptionist, fallen and bleeding. They have to cross the room. If they're smart, they take their time about it. They've gotta be careful, gotta think about anywhere Tom could be lying in wait, ready to ambush them. They should check the bathroom first, make sure it's clear. Even when they reach the window, they need to be cautious. Tom could be waiting right beneath, waiting to pick them off. They can't be sure he's trying to escape. He could be setting traps. He could refuse to leave until they're all dead. They don't know who he is.

They don't know what he's like. He's already killed one of them.

All the while these thoughts are running through his head, he and Cindy are descending the fire escape. They're near the bottom when the gangbangers start shooting. Tom hears the bullets raining down above them, pinging off the steel frame and floor of the fire escape. Cindy freezes at the sound. Tom wraps his arms around her, covers her. He picks her up and keeps moving. The more floors they put between themselves and the gangbangers, the harder it's going to be for them to hit them.

The shooting stops. They're following. Tom can hear the footsteps pounding down on the grating above.

Tom and Cindy reach the bottom. They run to the back of the building, to the parking lot. Someone emerges from the corner of the building, wielding an M16. He's just a kid. Not much older than the receptionist. Tom and Cindy have come up on him too fast, and he can't get his bearings. Tom grabs the rifle by its barrel and slams it up and back into the kid's face. It bloodies him, but doesn't put him down. His grip has loosened, though. Tom yanks the gun out of his hand, spins it around and slams him in the jaw with its stock. He hits him so hard his jaw breaks. Tom drops the rifle.

Cindy has continued running, on to the car. She starts the engine as Tom approaches and turns it around so it's pointing toward the exit. Tom dives into the passenger seat. They speed out of the parking lot, out onto the road. Tom looks back. He sees the gangbangers reach the bottom of the fire escape.

46

"Take the wheel!" Cindy says. "You need to drive!"

Cindy climbs into the back as Tom takes her place behind the wheel. She then climbs back over and into the front, taking his place in the passenger seat. She pulls out her laptop, boots it up. "I need to get that post down," she says.

The road is busy. They're surrounded by cars. Tom looks around, checks the mirrors. They reach a traffic light at an intersection. They're second from the front. Tom doesn't like being stopped, but it's hard to tell if anyone is in pursuit.

"Shit," Cindy says.

"What is it?"

"It's not just the original post," Cindy says. "The one that Cameron has posted. The post has spread – the receptionist back at the hotel, when he sent the info to his cousin's gang, it looks like they've spread it further afield, and it's been hijacked by other gangs in turn. It's widespread, now. I'm gonna have to take it down fucking *everywhere*."

Tom can't think about this too long. Out of the corner of his eye, in the mirror, he sees movement. Three cars back, someone gets out of their car. They look ahead. Tom thinks he's looking toward them. Someone gets out of the back of the car, too.

"Get my gun out of my bag," Tom says.

Cindy doesn't ask any questions. She does as he says, reaching into it for the Beretta. Tom looks to the left, then to the right, over the top of her. There's someone on the sidewalk, raising a gun. "Stay down!"

Tom hits the accelerator and spins the wheel. The person on the sidewalk fires. The window above Cindy shatters. The glass falls down onto her back. The car lurches forward, clipping the back lights of the car in front as Tom squeezes past them. Behind, he sees that the men from the car, the men he was watching, are firing back at the man on the sidewalk. They hit him multiple times, his body performing a St Vitus dance before it hits the ground. They dive back into their car and start pushing through the traffic in pursuit. Tom notices a couple of other cars are doing the same.

He can't think about how many people are in pursuit of them right now – they're in the middle of the intersection, vehicles speeding by them from left and right. Cindy raises her head as they plough through it. "Oh, shit!"

Tom doesn't hesitate. He can't. If he hesitates, they're dead. He speeds faster, gets through to the other side. Glancing in the mirror, he sees a long-haul truck smash into the side of the vehicle that shot down the man on the sidewalk. It wipes them out.

Cindy is gasping once they get to the other side. "Jesus Christ, did they catch up with us?"

"I don't think it was the same guys from the hotel," Tom says. "Maybe they were back there somewhere, but I don't know what they were driving."

"They've already caught up to us."

"Like you said – every gangbanger in the city is gonna come looking. Did Cameron post our details?"

"What we look like, and our car."

"Shit." Tom thinks of the man dead on the sidewalk, as well as the vehicle that just got smashed by the truck. He wonders who they were in their everyday lives, if they're in gangs, too. Or if they aren't – if they were just desperate and they saw an opportunity. "He's got a lot of people hurt, and a lot more still to come."

Tom can make out three cars that look as though they're still in pursuit. A bit of reckless driving and speeding is typical LA behavior, but once Tom sees drivers trying to ram each other, to run each other off the road, he knows for sure they're assassins trying to eliminate the competition. He speeds up again, takes a tight left.

Cindy braces herself. "Jesus," she says, trying to look back. The wind blows in through the shattered window, waving through her short hair. "We need to get somewhere quiet. Tear-assing around like this, I can't get anything done!"

Tom's going to have to lose their pursuers before they can find anywhere quiet. The cars have stopped bumping into each other, now they've realized their target is getting further and further away. They ignore each other for the time being, and concentrate on catching up.

A cop car pulls in front of them up ahead, its siren blaring. It tries to block the road.

"They could be corrupt," Cindy says, bracing herself.

Tom is already aware. He had no intention of stopping for them. He spins the wheel and pulls on the handbrake, skidding around them. Two of the cars following manage to get around the cruiser, too, but the third smashes into it. The cruiser begins to roll.

In the confusion, Tom swings the car to the right, down a

quieter road. "Can you get the post down?" he says. "Can you get these people off our backs?"

"I can do it," Cindy says. "But we'll have to lie low for a few hours after – we'll need to give people a chance to see it, for the word to spread. I'm not gonna change it, and then all of a sudden they're gonna pull back like a switch has been flicked."

"What if Cameron tries to repost it?"

"Then I'll take it back down," Cindy says. "Over and over again, until it's diluted, and no one knows what to believe any more. No one will trust it."

Tom checks the mirror. The two cars have turned the corner. "We might need to get out at some point," he says. "Dump the car and find somewhere to hide out, so you can do your thing."

Tom drives on. He's looking for a quiet area. Somewhere rundown, perhaps, full of abandoned buildings. Somewhere they can lay low, hide out.

Up ahead, a car pulls across the road, like the cop cruiser did not so long ago. Someone gets out of the back. He has a shotgun.

"Fuck!" Cindy ducks down again.

The shotgun fires. The windshield cracks. The glass doesn't shatter completely, but Tom feels a small shard cut his right cheek, just under his eye. Blood runs down to the corner of his mouth. "Give me the gun!"

Cindy has held it in her hand since she got it out of the bag. She holds it out to Tom. He takes the Beretta. He can't see through the shattered windshield. He shoots blindly through it, knocking a hole through the already-damaged glass at eye level. They're coming up on the car. The shooter has the shotgun levelled. Tom shoots him before he can fire on the car again. As he goes down, his shotgun goes off, over his shoulder. It blows off the side of the passenger's skull. He slumps down in his seat, leaning out the open window, his blood running down the door.

Tom skids around the front of the car.

"Where did they come from?" Cindy says.

"The cars behind," Tom says. "They must be in communication with them. Friends of theirs, and they're telling them where we're going." He keeps an eye up ahead, at every junction and alleyway, at every vehicle.

Tom checks the mirrors. He sees the cars behind sticking close. "I need to get rid of these two," he says. He can barely see where he's going through the small hole he's made in the windshield. He finds a quiet road, then pulls the handbrake again and skids to a one-eighty halt. He leans out the window and shoots at the closest pursuing car, aiming for the windshield. The glass cracks, blinding them, as the shotgun has done to Tom and Cindy. The car swerves to the side, crashes into a streetlight. The driver behind it slams on his brakes at both the sight of the gun, and of what happened to the car in front of him. The car starts to reverse. Tom shoots out their front tires, then spins back around and speeds away from the scene.

"We need to get somewhere, fast," he says. "There's gonna be more coming."

Cindy looks around, sees no one is currently in pursuit, and pulls out her laptop again. Tom makes sure to take a few turns, to lose anyone who could be following. They pass people and other cars. The shattered windshield is getting too much attention.

Finally, he finds the kind of area he's looking for. Not all of the buildings look empty, but he can see a few of them do. Tom drives further, finds somewhere to dump the car, then they walk back. They stay away from the road, out of view of anyone who might pass by. They stay close to the trees, then slip into the first abandoned building they reach. Tom makes sure it's empty, it's clear, then Cindy finds a place to sit and gets to work.

Tom leaves her to it. Doesn't agitate her with questions; does nothing to distract her. He goes to the windows, checks outside, makes sure no one is out there, looking for them. The road here is quiet. The whole area is quiet. Tom stands for a while, looking out. The only sound is of a breeze rustling the branches of a nearby tree, and the clicking of Cindy's fingers on the keys behind him.

Eventually, Cindy's typing begins to slow. He hears her breathe out in relief. Tom glances back. She smiles at him, but she looks tired, like her brain is fried.

"It's done," she says. "It wasn't easy, but I got through. I've wiped everything I could find."

"What did you do?"

"I assume you don't want to hear every technical in and out?"

"No, I just want to know what you said."

"I got into Cameron's account, and I deleted the old post and put out a new message that said we were dead, and the prize has already been claimed. Then I did the same on the others. I got into the hotel receptionist's account and sent new messages from it, updating everyone on 'Cameron's' new post."

Tom nods. He doesn't leave the window. "So now we wait a few hours, give the word a chance to spread?"

"Yeah," Cindy says. "And if anyone comes looking for us, I guess we treat them as still hostile."

"Yeah," Tom says. He turns back to the window and watches the road.

47

Cameron takes the realization of what Cindy has done better than Hugh expected. He doesn't rage and scream, doesn't flail his arms around in the air. Doesn't turn red in the face. Hugh supposes he's probably tired himself out from doing all that so much already.

Instead, he steps away from the computer and paces the floor with his fingers laced atop his head. He takes deep breaths. They're in the living room. He looks around, at Hugh and Lenny, the only two present with him. "Do either of you know where Stephen has gone?"

Neither of them do. Hugh motions to the computer. "What do you want me to do about this?" he says. "Should I put another post up? Tell people the last one wasn't true – Rollins and Cindy are still alive, that we never called the hunt off?"

Cameron shakes his head. "If we change it, they'll just change it back. No one's going to know what to believe. They'll stop paying any attention."

"Then what do we do?" Hugh says. "We have to do *something*. They'll be coming here next."

Cameron lowers his hands from his head. He strokes his chin and stares off to the side while he thinks. "They probably *will* come here next," he says. "You're right. And they've done so much harm already." He drops his hand from his chin, walks to a window. It looks out over his pool. Amy is out there, swimming laps. Hugh noticed her earlier, but then he was distracted by the stuff with Rollins and Cindy. For a brief while, they were getting updates on the chase. They were convinced it was about to be over. Rollins and Cindy wouldn't be a problem any more. And then the updates stopped coming in. Everything went silent for a while – and then Cindy put out the fake report that they were dead.

They knew it was Cindy. She hacked into Cameron's account on the dark web, and made the post from the source. When they first saw it, they'd thought it was someone claiming the kills. It didn't take them long to realize what had actually happened.

It doesn't look to Hugh like Cameron is watching Amy swimming. He's not distracted by her. He's staring off into the distance.

"Here's what I want you to do," he says, turning back around, facing his brother. "There were some nasty people out there looking for Rollins and Cindy, right? Go through, pick out the worst of them – but find the ones you think will listen. Reach out to them. Offer them temporary jobs. Here, as security, at the house. They'll bolster the security I already have, but they're less likely to be swayed by Stephen's bleeding heart. He won't have any influence with them. And tell them, there's a bonus for whoever takes out Rollins or Cindy. And then, once we've dealt with Rollins and Cindy and the colossal pain in the ass they've proven to be, then our new recruits will help clean out what's left of Los Tierras Bajas. Get that dealt with once and for all. Get things back on track around here."

"Speaking of," Hugh says, "there was something about that that I wanted to raise with you. Now, listen, I know the clearing of Los Tierras Bajas has taken longer than I thought it would, but I've got an idea for the next time we go – we burn them out. Burn them right out of those homes they're clinging to so desperately."

Cameron looks at him like he's an idiot. "I told you," he says, clapping his hands for punctuation, "*no fires.*" He shakes his head. "The police I can pay off, get them to keep things quiet, but the fire department is another matter altogether. Fires spread. People see them from far and wide. You can't keep them quiet. Fires draw too much attention. You got that?"

Hugh nods solemnly, his idea shot down. "I got it."

Cameron claps his hands again. "*Good.* I'm gonna go get something to eat."

Cameron leaves the room. Hugh looks back at Lenny, standing stoic in the corner. "I thought he might've at least hung around and helped," Hugh says. "This is gonna take a while."

Lenny grunts.

Hugh sighs, then sits at the computer and gets to work. He calls back to Lenny over his shoulder. "Go and get us something to eat too, will you?"

Lenny grunts again, but he leaves his corner and follows Cameron out of the room.

48

It turns out, Cameron went out for food. He's been gone a couple of hours. Hugh has just finishing up reaching out to some of the people that went after Rollins and Cindy, and their affiliates. He hasn't heard back from them all yet, but the ones who have responded have all agreed to the offer.

Lenny got food from the kitchen. He made sandwiches. They finished eating a while ago. Hugh pushes the laptop away and looks up. "I'm done here," he says. "I'm gonna go lie down. My brain's fried." He stands and stretches his back, twisting side to side. Lenny stands, too, ready to accompany him.

Hugh passes by the window and looks outside. The same window Cameron was thoughtfully staring out of earlier. Amy was in the pool then. She's not now. There's no sign of her. The loungers are all empty. Hugh wonders if she came back inside. He never heard her. He glances back at Lenny, waiting expectantly. "Is Cameron still out?"

Lenny nods.

"Okay," Hugh says. "You go on out to the pool house. I'll meet you there."

Lenny gives him a questioning look, but he doesn't voice anything.

"I've just gotta take a piss," Hugh says.

Lenny's expression is blank. It's impossible to tell if he believes this story. It doesn't matter, though. Lenny does as he's told. He heads out to the pool house.

Hugh thinks about the footage from when Lenny was captured by Rollins and Cindy. The way he ran off at the mouth. He chuckles, remembering. He's never heard Lenny talk like that before. He gets it, though – Lenny was keeping them distracted. Giving the cops a chance to turn up, capture them. As soon as he was cut loose, he went back to his largely silent, stoic ways.

Hugh goes deeper into the house. He looks around. Some of the security are hanging around, but they mostly stay out the way. Hugh goes upstairs. He creeps down the long hall to Cameron and Amy's room. The door is closed. He knocks on the door.

There's a pause, then Amy's voice. "Who is it?"

Hugh grins to himself. He knocks again.

"Who is it?" Amy says again, louder this time.

Hugh waits a moment longer, long enough for Amy to start wondering if she heard anything at all, or if someone's just fucking with her, and then he opens the door.

She's on the bed, wrapped in a gown. One long, tan leg is crossed over the other. Her hair is wrapped in a towel. She's filing her nails. She stops as Hugh enters, looks up at him. Her eyes narrow. She's not pleased to see him. She never is.

"What do you want?" she says. Her tone is curt. Whatever he's here for, she wants it over and done with as quickly as possible.

Hugh smirks. "What, you don't want to say my name? You know I love to hear you say it."

"That's exactly why I don't," she says. She returns her attention to filing her nails. A sneer plays over her lips, even when she's not looking at him.

Hugh doesn't leave. He steps further into the room, closes the door behind him.

Amy looks up at this sound, frowning. "What are you doing?"

Hugh looks at her legs. He stares at her chest through the gap in her gown. He doesn't try to hide what he's doing. Amy pulls the gown tight. "Get out," she says.

Hugh goes to her on the bed. He walks around it, to the side where she lies. He notices how she stiffens. She stares up at him. He presses the tip of one finger to her big toe, lets it trail up the length of her leg, to the bottom of her gown. Then he stops. He smirks at her.

"Get off me," she says through her teeth.

"Why?" Hugh says. "Are you scared you might like it?"

She spits at him. It hits Hugh in the face, under his eye. He blinks, surprised. He laughs. "It's lucky for you I'm into that kind of thing," he says. "Or did you know that already?"

"You're disgusting," Amy says.

With his other hand, the one not on her leg, Hugh wipes the spittle away. He sucks it from his fingers.

Amy makes to roll away, to cross the bed to the other side. Hugh grabs her by the shoulder, pulls her back. He pins her to the bed.

"What are you doing?" she shrieks.

Hugh puts his face close to hers. "You know," he says, speaking into her ear, "since the first moment I met you, I've wondered what you taste like." He nips her ear lobe with his teeth.

"Get off me! Get the fuck off me!"

"Make as much noise as you want," Hugh says. "Cameron isn't here. He's out. No one else cares." He squeezes his fingers deeper into her shoulders. He raises his head, his face inches from hers. "I don't know how much Cameron tells you, but there's a man coming here. He's probably going to try to kill me, and Lenny too. Maybe Cameron, I don't know. But I think that, if he gets here, it would be a *real* shame to die never knowing exactly how you taste."

"Get off me!" Amy shakes violently from side to side, trying to break free of his grip, to shove him off.

Hugh leans in. He bites her bottom lip.

And then he feels a hand on the back of his neck, dragging him away from Amy, throwing him across the room until he hits the wall.

He looks up as he makes impact, startled. It's Cameron. There's murder in his eyes. "What the *fuck* were you doing?"

Amy scurries across the bed, pulling her gown tight. "You saw what he was doing!" she says. "You know exactly what he was going to do!"

It's unclear whether Cameron has heard her. His eyes never leave Hugh's. He strides forward and grabs his brother. Hugh tries to push him off, but Cameron is too strong. "Get off me!" Hugh says, realizing how much he sounds like Amy did, just moments before.

Cameron doesn't let go of him. Instead, he punches him. His knuckles bury deep into Hugh's left eye. Hugh goes down. He's never been very good at taking a punch. When he's on the ground, Cameron starts kicking him. He doesn't hold anything back. Hugh feels the air driven out of his lungs. Feels bile forced up his throat, until the side of his face is resting in his own vomit.

Cameron gets down on his knees. He starts hitting Hugh in the face, bloodying him. He's speaking while he does this. Hugh can't make out much of what he's saying. *Fucking piece of shit. Scumbag.* These are the words that manage to get through, between blows.

Then the assault stops. Hugh pushes himself up. His entire skull is throbbing. He can taste blood, and can feel it running down his face. He looks up. Lenny has appeared. He's grabbed Cameron by the wrist and hoisted him from the ground. He holds him still, keeping him back. Keeping Hugh safe.

"What are you doing?" Amy says, kneeling on the bed. "Do you know what he was trying to do?"

Lenny doesn't look at her.

Cameron's eyes blaze as he stares up into Lenny's impassive face. "Let go of me *right now*," he says. "You're fired – you're fucking fired. How dare you lay a finger on me, you—"

Lenny cuts him off. "I don't work for you." He lets go of Cameron, pushing him back as he does so.

Hugh pushes himself up, wiping bile from his cheek. Lenny keeps the two brothers separated. Hugh looks at Amy, still kneeling on the bed. He winks at her.

"You motherfucker," she says, shaking her head.

Cameron stands to the side, seething. He has to lean around Lenny to see Hugh as they back out of the room. "This isn't over, Hugh," he says.

"If you say so," Hugh says, his cockiness returning.

"I should fucking hand you over to them myself," Cameron says.

Hugh knows he's referring to Rollins and Cindy. "If only you could," he says. "But they're coming after you now, too, aren't they?"

Cameron bristles, but he has nothing to say to this. He knows Hugh is right. "I'll deal with them," he says. "And then I'll deal with you, you son of a bitch."

"Imagine if Mom heard you say that."

"Shut up! Just shut up! Shut up and get out. When this is

done, you're out. You're out on your ass, the both of you. I'm gonna leave you with nothing, you piece of shit! You'll be on the street!"

"Fuck you, Cameron!" Hugh says, not holding back any more. "After everything I've done for you – you wouldn't have any of this if it wasn't for me! This should all be *mine*! You ungrateful fucking prick, you're nothing without me! *Nothing!*"

He sees the look on Amy's face. Her doubts – she thinks he's just blowing hot air. "Why don't you ask him, Amy? Why don't *you* tell her, Cameron? Tell her everything I've done for you – tell her all the dark things you haven't wanted to get your own hands dirty with. Why don't you tell her how all these troubles we're having right now came about. Tell her what you told me to do, Cameron."

Cameron glares. "I never told you to do *that*, asshole. You took it upon yourself."

Hugh laughs. "Sure, you tell yourself that." He shakes his head. Lenny is trying to get him to leave. They're in the doorway now. Hugh refuses to go. "Tell her the truth, Cameron! Tell her all about the blood that's on *your* hands! Maybe she won't want to fuck *you*, either!"

He laughs harder, seeing the look on Cameron's face. Hugh has had enough. He doesn't care any more. If Cameron says he's going to kick him out, then Hugh's not holding back.

Cameron has no response to this. His silence, the look on his face – it's all too delicious to Hugh. He didn't get what he came to this room for, but he got enough. He's ready to leave now. He lets Lenny lead him away.

49

"We must've spent a fortune on cars," Cindy says, as they drive away from the used car dealership. "I don't really wanna think about it."

"I never do," Tom says, getting himself accustomed to the way this vehicle handles. It's a Toyota Corolla. "It happens more often than I'd like."

Cindy laughs. "You're lucky I'm paid so well for what I do." She reaches out and squeezes his hand. "When this is over, I'll pay you back for whatever you've spent."

"You don't have to do that," Tom says. "And besides, you've paid for most things."

Cindy squeezes his hand again and looks in his eye. She doesn't say anything, but Tom understands. She's going to pay him back, and she won't hear otherwise.

She lets go of his hand. "We should keep in touch more often," she says. "It sounds like you keep busy in between the times I see you."

Tom laughs. "Like you wouldn't believe."

"Always looking for trouble," Cindy says.

"I wouldn't say I go looking for it," Tom says. "It just always has a habit of finding me."

"You really believe that?"

They reach a traffic stop. Tom turns to look at her. "What do you mean?"

"I mean – I know the situation you're in now is my fault..."

"It's not your *fault*," Tom interjects.

"I just mean, I asked you for help," Cindy says. "And I'm glad you're here. But what I'm saying is bigger than that." She pauses, thinking. "A time's gotta come when, if you keep finding yourself in scrapes, you've gotta admit to yourself that maybe *you're* the one actively looking for these scrapes to throw yourself into. I mean, when we first met, that was definitely the case. And then, when me and Zeke had to find you in Mexico, and then Arizona, you'd managed to get yourself into a hell of a lot of trouble then, too."

Tom looks straight ahead. This isn't the first time these thoughts have crossed his mind. Recently, he's started to wonder the same thing himself. He always thought he was looking for peace. But even when he was young, he never really knew peace. And then, as soon as he was old enough, he went off to war.

Sometimes he worries he'll never find peace, because he doesn't know what it's like. He doesn't know what it *is*. Peace would require a seismic change in who he is as a person, and even at just thirty-two he's not sure he can make those changes. He's not sure he wants to.

"I didn't – I didn't mean to hurt your feelings," Cindy says, as the light changes and they start rolling again.

"You didn't hurt my feelings," Tom says. "You just voiced something I've been questioning myself lately."

It's early evening. Not long ago, as they bought the car, the sky was golden. Now, it's turning bronze. Soon, it will darken. The streetlights are coming to life. The buildings are lighting up. They drive in silence for a while, heading to Los Tierras Bajas. They need to hide out while they plan their next move. Watching over Los Tierras Bajas feels like as good a place as any.

As they get near, Cindy reaches out. She places a hand on his thigh. "For what it's worth," she says, "I don't think you go looking to *make* trouble. I think you find people that need help, and you help them. And I think that's admirable, really. You're not causing harm to anyone who doesn't deserve it. I think you're a good man, Tom. That's why, when I reached out to you to help me with this, I knew you'd say yes. I never doubted that."

Tom places his hand over hers. She squeezes his fingertips. "Thank you," he says. He pauses, then adds, "I think maybe I needed to hear that."

They reach Los Tierras Bajas, go up the ridge where they can see over it. The darkness has settled in. They sit in the trees and eat food they picked up before they went to the dealership, looking toward the twinkling lights in the distance. Cindy checks her phone, the camera pointing at Cameron's house. Nothing's happening. She puts her phone away and rests her head on Tom's shoulder.

They watch Los Tierras Bajas. It's still too early to expect Hugh and his men. If – *when* – the crew turns up, as much as they dislike it, Tom and Cindy will wait until they finish and then follow them back to Cameron's home. After that, Cindy will start, once again, to attempt to get into the security system there. Tom will be watching what happens below closely, though. If things start to get out of hand, he'll move in. He'll have to. He can't just stand by and let it happen.

Truthfully, though, Tom isn't expecting them to turn up. Not tonight. They'll be regrouping, same as he and Cindy are. They talked earlier, before they left the abandoned warehouse where they were hiding out, and they decided to take tonight as an opportunity to rest, and then tomorrow they'll prepare to make their move. They're in the late stages now. Sooner or later, one way or another, this thing is ending. Cindy will get her justice. So will Kylie Hood, and Catherine Massey. So will the people of Los Tierras Bajas, the ones still down there, and the ones who were forced out of their homes.

But if Hugh and his men *do* turn up tonight, Tom's not going to let that opportunity go to waste.

The time ticks by. It gets later. Cindy's head is still resting on his shoulder. He hears her gently snoring. She's fallen asleep. He leaves her as she is. He could wake her, offer to walk her back to the car, but he's not sure the car would be much more comfortable.

A couple of hours later, Cindy wakes with a start. She blinks and looks down. "Have they come?"

"I don't think they're going to," Tom says.

Cindy wipes at her face, rubs at her eyes. "Why not?"

"They'll be locking down," he says. "All the moves we've made so far, they're expecting us to come to the house now. It's the only logical next step. We've tried to get them elsewhere. Now, the house is the only place left."

Cindy yawns. She stands. "If it doesn't look like they're coming," she says, "I'm going to go sleep in the car."

Tom nods.

Cindy hesitates before she goes. "They don't...they don't care about what they did to my sister," she says.

Tom looks back at her. He doesn't speak. He feels she has more to say.

"I think the only reason they remember her at all is because of me. Because I'm a loose end. But if they'd got rid of me long before now, they wouldn't remember me either. We don't matter to them. Right now, we're just a problem. Once they deal with the problem, they forget about it." She exhales, staring down at the ground. "I wanted justice," she says, looking back up. "I wanted them to think about what they did. I wanted them to suffer. I'm not sure any more...I'm not sure if they would."

Cindy trails off. They look at each other in silence. They can hear birds moving in the branches above them.

She runs her hands down her face. "Maybe you should try and get some rest, too," she says. "Since this thing started, I'm not sure you've had a full night's sleep."

"I'll sleep when it's over," Tom says. He looks up at her. "Not long now."

50

Kylie is cautious. They send Catherine to the meetup point alone, staying out of view. It's early in the morning. Kylie didn't respond to Catherine's message last night. Stephen and the others took Catherine, and they found a motel to stay in while they waited. It took so long for Kylie to respond that Stephen started to wonder if Catherine had perhaps sent her some kind of coded message. Vernon wondered the same, too. He berated her until she was crying, but still, she promised there was no code. She hadn't sent any secret message.

At dawn, Kylie responded.

Kylie has told Catherine to wait at an outside table of a café downtown. Catherine orders a coffee. She finishes it and sits staring out into the traffic. It takes another hour before Kylie sends Catherine details of where to meet next. Stephen and his men keep their distance, staying away from Catherine and hoping they're out of view. Catherine told them Kylie will be careful. She was probably thinking of her kids when she did. Vernon made some threats in the car. Said some things to make sure she plays ball. Stephen pretended

not to hear. He was grateful to Vernon for doing what he did
– what *he* couldn't – but he wasn't comfortable listening.

Vernon got Catherine to call her husband, too. He got her
to tell him she had to leave town in an emergency – to tell
him that her cousin is ill, and she needs to visit her in the
hospital. Vernon and Stephen don't make it clear to her, but
they don't know how long it's going to be until they can let
her go home again. More than likely Cameron is going to
have to get her to sign another NDA. Throw some more
money at her. He probably won't mind, though, not if it
means he doesn't have to worry about Kylie any more.

Stephen and his men take position as Catherine walks to
meet Kylie. It's a secluded area. They're near a multi-story
parking garage. Kylie told Catherine to go around the back.
Stephen is high, behind a tree. He's sent Vernon and the
other man around the building in a pincer formation. There's
no sign of Kylie yet. Stephen holds his breath, praying she
hasn't already spotted them and split in the other direction.
Catherine approaches the meet-up point. She reaches the
back of the building and she stands there, looking around.
Stephen watches her to see if she gives any indication that
Kylie is near, and that she might silently try to warn her
away.

Kylie comes from inside the parking garage. She
approaches cautiously. Stephen is on the line with Vernon. "I
have eyes – get her!"

Vernon and the other move around. Stephen comes out
from behind the tree, descends the hill.

Kylie sees them approach from all corners. Her eyes go
wide. She doesn't look back at Catherine. She starts to run.

Stephen is the closest, and the fastest. He runs her down.
Tackles her to the ground. She struggles. She manages to
wriggle free. She kicks Stephen in the face and gets loose, but
by now Vernon has caught up, and he wraps his arms around

her and keeps her down. She continues to struggle, but Vernon doesn't hold back like Stephen did.

The other guy takes Catherine by the arm and they all hustle back to the car. Stephen drives. Catherine sits up front with him, her wrists bound with plastic ties. Kylie is in the back with Vernon and the other guy. They've bound her wrists, too.

"Stephen," Kylie says, leaning forward to get his attention. Her voice is raised, trembling a little, but she's trying to control it. "Where are you taking me? Stephen, come on, speak to me – where are you taking me?"

Stephen doesn't answer. Out the corner of his eye, he notices how Catherine is silently crying.

Kylie clears her throat. "You know what they're going to do to me, Stephen."

Stephen stares straight ahead, driving back to Cameron's home. The traffic is bad. Because of it, they're still about an hour away.

"They're going to kill me, Stephen," Kylie says. "You know that. I know you don't want that to happen, Stephen. I remember you. I know what you're like. I know you're not a bad man. But you work for bad men. You can't turn a blind eye to this. You can't turn a blind eye forever. They're going to kill me, and my blood will be on your hands. If you give me to them, what happens next is on you. You can't hide from that. You have to live with it."

"Will someone shut her up?" Stephen says, barking over his shoulder.

"When are you going to stand up, Stephen?" Kylie says, speaking louder, faster. "The longer you wait, the more you become just like them! You're complicit! You're just as bad as they are!"

Then she's silenced, as Vernon puts his arm around her shoulder and clamps his hand over her mouth. Her voice is muffled. She struggles against him, but he's holding her tight. She soon gives up.

Stephen can feel Catherine's eyes on the side of his face. They reach a traffic signal on red. While stopped, he stares at her until she looks away. Stephen turns back to the road, his brow furrowed. He grits his teeth. Tries to ignore what Kylie has said. To forget her words. The light turns green.

He can't forget what she's said, though. Because he knows she's right.

51

Tom and Cindy check into a cheap hotel. They don't know how long they'll need to be here. It's a good place to lay low, to hide out while Cindy works her way into the security system in Cameron's house. She sets herself up at the desk at the foot of the bed. There's a mirror in front of her. Tom can see her face as her brow knits and she gets down to work.

Tom takes a walk around the area while Cindy gets started. He leaves her to it, gives her peace. She needs to concentrate. She told him in advance it wasn't going to be easy. "Probably take a while," she said. Tom makes sure they're secure. He finds a bench under a tree and watches the road for a little while. When he goes back to the hotel, Cindy is still hard at work. The tip of her tongue is poking out of the corner of her mouth in concentration. She doesn't look up, doesn't seem to notice he's returned.

He takes a shower. Stands for a while under the water, running it hot to ease the pain in his ribs and his head. Looking down, he sees the water turning pink as blood runs off him and swirls away down the drain. Before he gets out, he runs the water cold, to wake himself up, to keep him alert. He's running on not much sleep. He needs to keep himself sharp.

Cindy is still working. Tom looks out the windows, then lies down on the bed. An hour rolls by. Cindy slams her hands down on the desk either side of her laptop. Tom looks up. She leans back in her chair, letting her head roll back, the tension leaving her body. "Jesus Christ," she says. "I did it." She looks back at him, upside down. "It took a lot of brute force, but I hammered my way inside." She lets her head flop forward again, her eyes returning to the screen.

"How does it look?" Tom says.

"Let me take a look around, and then I'll get back to you."

Tom lets her work. He moves off the bed and sits at the edge of it. He can see her eyes darting around the screen in the mirror. Occasionally, she frowns. She does a lot of typing. Tom can see her opening new pages on her laptop, searching. She moves too fast for him to keep up.

"Hmm," she says, eventually.

"What's up?"

Cindy doesn't answer straight away. She types some more, does some more searching. Tom waits. She finally looks up, turns to him, answers him. "It looks like they have some new faces on the scene."

"How can you know?"

"Oh, I'll get to that. It looks like they've hired extra security, but it's a real mixed bunch. I've looked into it, and Cameron's gone ahead and found some guys off the dark web who were real intent on claiming that bounty on our heads. Gangbangers, for the most part."

"And I assume the bounty is still in place?"

"Looks that way. For these guys it is, at least." She looks back at the screen. "And they are *heavily* armed."

"They must think we're going to try and come in after them."

Cindy nods and turns back to the laptop. She pops her knuckles. "We're in now," she says. "All we have to do now is —" She falls suddenly silent and leans closer to the screen. "Oh, shit," she says.

"What is it?" Tom says.

"Oh, *fuck*," Cindy says.

Tom is about to push himself up, to leave the bed and join her at the laptop, to look over her shoulder and see for himself. She turns, now. Looks him in the eye.

"They have Catherine and Kylie."

52

As soon as Stephen sees Cameron's eyes settle on Kylie, the gravity of what he has done begins to settle on him.

Something feels off from the moment they reach the house. There are armed men roaming the grounds, and Stephen doesn't recognize them. Before he gets out of the car, he looks back at Vernon, who is just as confused as he is.

"Who the fuck are these guys?" Vernon says.

Stephen sees a couple of them up close as they pass by. They're rough-looking dudes. Heavy-set. They look like gang-bangers, but not like they're all from the same gang. He sees a mish-mash of tattoos. There are Nazi skinheads, and Latinos, some Black guys, too. A mixed group that does not look like they should be mingling. There's a tension in the air, like they might erupt on each other at any time.

Off to one side, he spots Hugh and Lenny. They're talking to a couple of the Nazis. Hugh's face is bruised and cut up. Stephen feels like he's missed a lot.

Cameron's face lights up when Kylie is brought to him. He looks like the cat who got the cream. He's in the kitchen, flanked by a couple of his new security. "Stephen," he says, almost purring like a cat, too. "Look what you've brought me. And to think I was about to have you replaced." He motions to the new men who surround him, who glare at Stephen and his own men.

"What's going on here?" Stephen says.

"Just taking precautions," Cameron says, but he's looking at Kylie. He steps closer to her, and she tries to shrink away, but Vernon is holding her from behind. "It's been a while, Kylie," he says.

Kylie's jaw is set. She stares back at him, defiant.

Stephen clears his throat. "Uh, maybe the two of you should go somewhere private, to talk. To discuss the terms of the NDA."

Cameron looks at him and barks a laugh. "An NDA? Are you fucking kidding me, Stephen? An NDA? She had her chance at an NDA." He looks at Catherine. "Who's this?" His eyes brighten suddenly. "Ah, I remember you, Catherine. It's all coming back now. *You* signed an NDA, didn't you? And we left you alone. You got to live your life in peace, with *my* money in your back pocket. And now, what's this? It looks like you've been holding out on us, Catherine. Why else would you be here right now? Something tells me you knew exactly where Kylie was, and you kept that information back."

Neither of the women answer him.

Cameron looks at Kylie and licks his lips. Stephen feels sick. Cameron looks like he's about to eat her. A cat, playing with its food.

"Did you think you could hurt me, Kylie?" he says. He shakes his head. "You can't hurt me. No one can."

"I need to take Catherine home," Stephen says. "Her family—"

"Fuck her family," Cameron says. "They stay here, the

both of them. Make excuses to the Masseys. I don't care what, just make it believable. They stay here until we've dealt with more pressing concerns. And then—"

"What pressing concerns?" Stephen says. He feels out of the loop.

"Rollins and Cindy."

Stephen looks around. "Is that why all these men are here? What are you expecting them to *do*? Cameron, this is insane. It's getting out of hand. You need to calm down and think about things."

"Stephen, you need to shut the fuck up before I get one of my new friends here to shut you up for me." Cameron stares at him, his face cold. He doesn't say anything for a while. He's thinking. He runs his tongue around the inside of his mouth while he does so and looks around at the people gathered. He looks at Catherine for a long time, and then he looks at Kylie. He smirks. "We've got time," he says to her. "You and me, we'll have plenty of time."

He smiles at her, and Stephen hates it. There are dark intentions in that smile. Stephen doesn't want to think about what Cameron might have in mind. He brought Kylie here to persuade her to take a pay-off and sign an NDA, and now Cameron is saying he has no interest in her signing an NDA.

"All right," Cameron says, clapping his hands together. "Find a room and lock them up. Both of them."

Stephen keeps his expression blank and nods, once. He motions for Vernon and the other guy to take Kylie and Catherine away. He makes to follow, but Cameron keeps him back, holding him by the arm. Stephen feels his blood run cold.

"Well done on finding her," Cameron says. "I meant what I said. Perhaps you still have some use after all. Perhaps you aren't the disappointment I was worried you were becoming."

Stephen isn't sure how to respond to this, so he says

something he thinks Cameron would like to hear. "Thank you, Mr Brewer."

Sure enough, Cameron looks pleased with this. "Go check in on them, make sure they're somewhere secure, and then come back here. I want you to meet the new additions to our security team."

Stephen looks at the two men that flank Cameron. They look back at Stephen. They have shaved heads, and there are many scars on their faces. They look like they're about to snarl at him. Stephen saw their kind often enough while he was working the streets as a cop. He thought he'd put that all behind him. He never thought he'd be working *with* men like these.

"Okay," Stephen says. "Will do." He hurries from the kitchen, pleased to leave it behind.

53

Tom is sitting on the edge of the bed. He straightens. "What?"

Cindy repeats, "They have Kylie and Catherine. A few guys just showed up with them. They're holding them in one of the rooms of the house."

"Do you know which one?"

"Yeah. Most of the bedrooms don't have cameras in them, but this one does. They've probably put them in there so they can keep an easy eye on them."

The parameters have changed. "Kylie was terrified for her life," Tom says. "We have to assume they're in danger right now."

Cindy nods. "They're not keeping them locked up for any *good* reason. We need to get them out."

"Tonight," Tom says. "We can't sit on this. How many extra security is there?"

"Hard to tell. People are coming and going. They're all over the grounds. Gotta be a couple of dozen, at least. And like I said, armed to the fucking *teeth*."

"Then it sounds like we need to be, too. We never planned

on making this a head-to-head fight, but it looks like it might to be. We go in careful, try to extract them that way, but if it comes down to a fight, we need to be ready for it. How do Catherine and Kylie look?"

Cindy presses some buttons, getting them back up on screen. "Scared, but unharmed. Kylie was pacing before, looked like she was trying to find a way out. Right now, the two of them are just holding each other."

Tom thinks about Catherine's family. He wonders what they've been told, where Cameron got her to say she is. He can't imagine this little detail would be left unattended.

"Keep an eye on them," Tom says. "Make sure they're unharmed. We're moving in tonight, when it's dark. In the meantime, we need to gear up."

54

Tom and Cindy don't want to go to a gun shop. They don't know how many people Cameron may have reached out to, or what he's monitoring. Instead, Cindy has found someone online who has all the stuff they're looking for, and is willing to do business.

They go to his apartment, but they don't enter the building straight away. Cindy says she found this guy on the dark web, and chances are he might have seen the bounty on their heads. They watch his building for a while first. They pick out which window is his. Cindy goes in first. Tom goes up the fire escape, to the apartment. Tom has his Beretta out. Tom can see through the window. The guy is watching television. He's laughing at a sitcom. The rest of his apartment is empty. Tom messages Cindy, tells her to knock. She does. The guy lets her in. Nothing further happens. They make small talk. Tom had remained on the outside so, in case of an ambush, he could have gotten Cindy out. He knocks on the window with the barrel of his gun to let her know it's clear. Cindy gets the guy to open the window and let Tom in.

"Whoa..." The guy is laughing. "You guys are pretty cautious, huh?"

Tom puts his gun away. The guy is younger than he was expecting. He's thin. He scratches his bony chest through his loose-fitting T-shirt. The skin around his eyes is dark, like he's been staying up late and waking early. "All right," Tom says. "Show us what you have."

"Not interested in pleasantries, huh?" the guy says, smiling. He coughs. "Sure. Follow me." He leads them through to his bedroom. Tom has already seen it from outside. It's neater than he would have anticipated. The bed is made. There are no clothes on the floor. There's no sign of any of the equipment they've come here to buy from this man.

"This is where the magic happens," the guy says, spreading his arms wide and laughing at his own joke. He goes down on his knees by the side of the bed, reaches under it. "I wish, anyway." He's still laughing. He pulls out a couple of cases and places them on the bed. He opens them up.

He has what they're looking for, and more besides. Automatic rifles, ammo, smoke grenades, explosives, gas masks, body armour, cameras. Cindy leans in closer to see beside Tom. She whistles low. "This is some heavy-grade stuff," she says. "Where'd you get it all from?"

The guy giggles. "You really wanna know?"

Cindy considers this. "Probably not." She points at the explosives. "You sleep on top of these?"

The guy shrugs. "I've got faith in my merchandise."

Cindy shakes her head. "There's not enough faith in the world..."

"I'll give you a few minutes to look everything over, pick out what you want," the guy says, then makes to leave the room.

Tom stops him, holding out an arm that bars his way. "No," he says. "You'll wait here with us. This won't take long."

The guy shrugs, then leans against a wall with his arms crossed. "You guys are *really* cautious, huh?"

Tom ignores him and picks out an M4 carbine, presses it into his shoulder and takes aim. He dismantles it, checks it over.

"I'm gonna assume you know what you're doing," the guy says. He doesn't sound concerned. He doesn't look like anything much ever concerns him.

Satisfied, Tom puts the weapon back together. He puts it to one side, along with some magazines. There's ammo for his Beretta, too. He adds it to the pile. He picks out a few smoke grenades, some body armor, explosives, and a gas mask. He stands aside while Cindy checks the cameras. The ones she picks out are tiny – micro cameras, the size of fiber-optics. When they're done, Tom turns to the guy. "Ring it up."

The guy sees their haul and whistles appreciatively. He gives them a figure. Cindy pulls out her laptop and pays it, transferring the money into an offshore account.

The guy puts it all into a sport bag for them. "I'll even throw the bag in for free," he says, winking. He hands it over to Tom. "You going out the regular way, or you leaving out the fire escape?"

"The regular way," Tom says. "And you're going to walk us out."

The guy rolls his eyes. "Jesus Christ, relax."

"Is that going to be a problem?" Tom stares at him.

The guy withers under his gaze. "No," he says. "No problem. Let me just grab my keys."

55

It's been hours since Stephen got back to the house, and his feelings of guilt grow worse. He's made a mistake. He's made a big fucking mistake. And if Cameron's words hadn't been proof enough of this fact, the kind of people he's hired for security in Stephen's absence further hammers it home.

"I don't like the look of these guys," Vernon says, in confidence, outside. They're away from the house, away from the new hires. They're close to Hugh's pool house, but he won't be able to hear them.

"I don't like it either," Stephen says. "I don't like any of this."

"I guess he's just scared, right?" Vernon says. "Scared of this Rollins guy. Of what he might do. He's just covering his ass, right?"

Stephen nods. "I suppose so, but this is an extreme way of going about covering his ass." He looks around at the patrolling men, armed with automatic rifles. "I mean, look at these fucking guys."

"I see them," Vernon says. "Best thing we can do, I reckon,

is if and when the shit starts coming down, we just stay out of the way. Let all these motherfuckers start killing each other while they try to claim the bounty."

Stephen raises an eyebrow. "The bounty?"

"Yeah, didn't you hear? Whichever one of them kills Rollins, they get a bounty. Something like five million bucks – the same amount they put out for the hit on the dark web. If he turns up, I reckon the tribalism's gonna kick in for these guys, each of them desperate to get that cash. They're not a team. Just look at them. They'll turn on each other in a heartbeat."

Stephen hadn't heard. He's beginning to feel less and less like head of security and just another Joe. The bounty sounds like exactly the kind of thing he should've been made aware of. "They look like they'll turn on their *own* crews, let alone each other's," he says. "Jesus Christ, I'm really hoping he doesn't show up, Vern. He does, it's gonna be a bloodbath."

Vernon nods in agreement.

"Keep an eye on things out here," Stephen says. "I've just gotta go into the house, check in on things."

"Sure."

Stephen heads up and inside. He notices how the new recruits side-eye him, like they're trying to work out who he's affiliated with. Their presence makes him feel sicker than he already does.

He finds Cameron and Amy in the living room. There's a guard at the door, and another on each window. Amy is on the sofa, and she looks uncomfortable. She's wearing jeans and a sweatshirt. Her hair is tied back. Stephen doesn't think he's ever seen her dressed so conservatively. He's surprised she's not complaining about the lockdown, wanting to go out to a club or somewhere, to live her life. She looks up as Stephen enters, and she seems almost glad to see him.

Cameron looks back at him. "Stephen," he says. "Help you with something?"

"I'm just...doing rounds. Checking everything over."

"Well, as you can see, everything's looking pretty airtight." Cameron looks pleased with himself. Stephen feels like he's attempting to rub the new recruits in his face.

"Yeah," Stephen says. "Certainly looks that way."

Cameron eyes him up and down. "You aren't going to arm yourself?"

Stephen is armed. He has his Glock. What he doesn't have is an assault rifle. "I'll get on that," he says.

"See that you do," Cameron says, turning away.

Stephen takes that as permission to leave. He takes advantage of it. Outside the living room, he squeezes past a couple of broad Black guys who almost fill the corridor. Stephen heads upstairs. There are more men up here, too. A lot of them stand by the windows, looking out. He sees a skinhead smoking by one of them. Cameron won't like that he's smoking indoors. Stephen doesn't bother to tell him.

There's a palpable air of menace in the house. A tension that grows thicker as Stephen moves through it. All eyes narrow at his passing. He nears the room where Catherine and Kylie are being held. A Latino guy is standing guard. He looks up at Stephen as he nears, regarding him.

Stephen is about to stop, to say he wants to see the prisoners, but he doesn't. He falters for only a moment, and then he keeps going. Finds a bathroom to hide away in. At least here he can be alone. There's no eyes on him.

He sits on the edge of the bathtub and holds his head in his hands. Over and over, he asks himself what he's done. Cameron isn't handling any of this in a way Stephen is comfortable with. He's holding Kylie and Catherine hostage. He's fortified his home with gangbangers, for some reason inexplicably refusing to call the police. In the car, Kylie told

Stephen there was still time for him to do the right thing. Stephen wonders about this. He wonders if it's true. He wonders if he's already doomed the two women. If he were to try and get them back out right now, they wouldn't get very far. There are armed men everywhere, and he doesn't trust any of them.

He splashes cold water into his face, and then he leaves the bathroom. The Latino guy guarding the door watches him again as he gets near, and as he goes by. Stephen imagines them in there. Probably terrified. Kylie, especially, fearing for her life. Not so long ago, she had a gun pointed right at her head.

Stephen feels like a coward. He can't remember a time in his life he ever made a bigger mistake, except perhaps for when he first came to work for Cameron. His stomach sinks. His face burns. He closes his eyes tight as he walks away.

56

I t's getting late. Hugh and Lenny head up to the main house. They haven't been back to it since the altercation with Cameron. Hugh hasn't been wasting the day. He's been making himself friendly with a lot of the new security force. Especially the white ones, with the shaved heads. If Rollins arrives, Hugh wants these guys close to him, keeping him safe. If Cameron tries to pull anything, to give him up or throw him to the wolves, Hugh has consolidated his allies. Hugh has ensured he has backup, and they'll carry through beyond this Rollins problem. Cameron thinks he's going to throw him out? Hugh has other ideas.

Hugh pauses before they go inside. He looks toward the wall enclosing the property. To the closed gate. He looks up at Lenny. "Do you think he'll come tonight?"

Lenny looks out into the darkness. "He didn't come last night," he says. "He might not come tonight. But I think he *will* come eventually. Just biding his time. Trying to make us lax. Make us slip up."

"You think there's a chance he just might not turn up at all?" Hugh knows it's probably just wishful thinking, and the look Lenny gives him tells him as much. "He could just think it's not worth all the hassle, turn around and go home."

"I've seen him up close," Lenny says. "I've seen how he works. I've *felt* it. He's not going to run. And besides that, do you think Cindy would turn and leave?"

"I don't expect her to." Hugh scratches his cheek. "Even if they left, if they run, we'd track them down. It's probably best if they *do* come."

"They will," Lenny says. "And we'll get them."

Hugh nods, then taps Lenny with the back of his hand and heads inside the house. As expected, Cameron isn't happy to see either of them. They find him in the living room, with Amy. Cameron's face sours. "What are you doing here?"

"Just hunkering down for the night," Hugh says. He winks at Amy.

"Don't you fucking look at her," Cameron says, stepping in front of Amy, blocking Hugh's view.

There's a standoff. Hugh notices how the security around the room are watching intently. Half are skinheads, half are Latino.

Cameron speaks first. "It's a big house," he says. "If you're going to stay in it, go find somewhere else to be."

Hugh doesn't leave straight away. He stands his ground, smirking, locking eyes with his brother. "All right," he says, eventually, after the air has become electric with the tension between the two of them. "We'll be in the kitchen."

On their way through the house, they pass Stephen. He doesn't see them, not straight away. He's at the bottom of the stairs, looking up. He's chewing his bottom lip.

"Stephen?" Hugh says.

Stephen gives a start, turns to Hugh and Lenny.

"What are you doing?" Hugh says.

Stephen clears his throat, takes a step back. "Just, uh, just checking things over," he says. "Just looking for weak spots. Anywhere we might be leaving ourselves open."

Hugh isn't sure he believes this. "Okay," he says.

Stephen nods, then turns and hurries away. Hugh looks up at Lenny. Lenny shrugs.

Hugh shakes his head. Whatever Stephen was doing, it doesn't matter. "Let's go get something to drink," he says.

57

Tom and Cindy arrived at the mansion an hour ago. They're still in the car for now. Cindy watches the house through the camera they planted in the tree opposite the gated entrance. She watches the inside of the house, too, through its own security cameras.

"There's not a camera in every room," she says. "It looks like the bedrooms and bathrooms are off limits, apart from that one room where Catherine and Kylie are held."

They know the plan. They've gone over it for the last few hours, until it was ingrained in their minds.

Tom leaves the car. He takes the explosives with him. He goes up to the house. He's dressed all in dark clothes, but he's not ready for the raid yet. He wears an earpiece. Cindy, watching the various feeds through her laptop, keeps him out of view of the security cameras that monitor the immediate outside of the property. Tom follows her directions. Keeps out of their sight. The explosives are C4. Tom plants them against the west wall, spreading them out in four spots, six feet between them. He's planning on going in via the east wall. He returns to the car, again keeping out of view of the cameras, moving when and where Cindy tells him to move.

He doesn't get back in the car. He goes to the rear of it, to the trunk. Where the equipment is stored. He pulls on the body armor, the gas mask. Cindy gets out the car and comes to him. She has the laptop with her. She's wearing a Killing Joke T-shirt, and she keeps running her hands down the front of it, wiping the sweat from her palms. She helps affix the small camera he'll be wearing onto the side of the mask. She checks the feed through her laptop.

"All hooked up," she says. "You ready to go?"

Tom arms himself. He has the M4. His Beretta is on his right thigh, and his KA-BAR is on his left. The smoke grenades are at his right hip. "I'm ready," Tom says.

He goes back up to the house on foot, staying on the road opposite it. No one is patrolling outside the grounds. Everyone is on the other side of the wall. This is a mistake. If they'd been outside, patrolling the parameters, they might have seen Tom planting the bombs. They might have spotted the bombs on the wall. They're not professionals. Cameron and his brother are just a couple of psychopaths who've hired a bunch of gangbangers for security.

Again, Cindy makes sure he moves where the cameras can't see him. She has the detonator for the C4. "You in place?" Cindy says into the earpiece.

Tom doesn't answer straight away. He's in the shadows, beneath the overhanging tree branches. He lowers himself down, bracing himself, preparing to move. The M4 is hanging across his chest. He grabs the smoke grenades, has them ready. "Now," he says.

Cindy hits the detonator. Tom sees the explosion. It's far from him. He can't see the damage it's done. He sees the smoke rising into the night air. His instinct is to run, to get to the wall. But he waits for Cindy to give him the go-ahead.

"Okay," Cindy says. "That's got their attention." He can hear her typing, her fingers moving fast. "They're going to investigate – there's still about a half-dozen of them near where you are. All gangbangers. Be careful. Okay, *aaaaand* – security is down! Go, go, go!"

Tom moves.

"Power is down!" Cindy says.

Tom sees the lights of the house go off, submerging it in darkness. He reaches the wall and throws over three smoke grenades. He starts scaling the wall. He's wearing night vision goggles. When he gets to the top of the wall, he can see the half-dozen men spinning wildly, coughing as they try to see through the smoke. There's one directly below Tom. He drops onto him, crumples him, strikes him in the back of the skull with the stock of the M4 to keep him down.

Tom picks off the furthest gangbanger with a short burst, drops him instantly. He starts moving, running around the outside of the group, sticking close to the wall. They turn on where the gunfire came from, start shooting. They mow down a couple of their own men attempting to shoot up the spot where Tom no longer is. Tom picks off the last of them as he passes.

The gunshots will no doubt bring others running, but all they'll find is the lingering smoke.

Tom reaches the house, gets to a door. There's a skinhead standing guard inside. He fires as he sees Tom's dark figure approaching, not bothering to check whether friend or foe. The glass in the door shatters. Tom goes to the nearest window. He can see the skinhead firing wildly, his face lit up as he shoots. He's roaring. Tom shoots him through the glass. As he goes to the door, the lights come back on.

58

Inside the house, they get the power back on.

Cindy didn't expect it to be down long, but that's fine. All part of the plan. Chaos and confusion. It gave Tom a chance to get inside. Now that they have the power, Cindy can access their security again. She sees Cameron in his living room, surrounded by men. His girlfriend is next to him, clinging to him.

Tom is inside the house. He's in the kitchen. The security are rushing around, trying to find him. Through the camera on Tom's mask, she can see when they do. A gunfight breaks out. At the sound, Cameron and Amy head upstairs with a few more guards.

She spots Hugh and Lenny. They're in a sitting room at the back of the house. It looks like they're arguing. Lenny seems to want to run toward the action. Hugh is preventing him. He grabs him by the arm, jabs a finger into his face. Probably reminds him who he works for, and Hugh wants him to remain by his side. Lenny reluctantly agrees. They head upstairs, too, following after Cameron and Amy.

Cindy checks all the cameras, sees where everyone is and

what they're doing. Catherine and Kylie are still locked away in their room, though they can hear what's going on. Kylie has her ear pressed up to the door. Catherine is at the window, looking out, trying to see what's happening.

"All right, Tom," Cindy says. He's on one knee, taking cover behind the marble island in the center of the kitchen. He looks calm there on the screen, in the eye of the storm. Occasionally he rises, fires back at the men to keep them at bay, then ducks back down and moves, changing position. There's nothing harried about his movements. "The guys who were distracted by the explosion are coming back. They're closing in on your location."

"Got it. Let me know when they're imminent."

"Will do." She sees Tom pull another smoke grenade, and wait. "Almost there now," Cindy says. "Practically on top of you – a dozen paces out."

Tom throws the smoke grenade into the center of the room. He fires over the top of the island at the security in the doorway. They fire back as the others from outside reach the door. They drop some of them. The guards from outside start firing back. They're shooting at each other. Tom throws another smoke grenade into the mix.

"That was the last of them," Tom says of the grenades. He stays low, running around the edge of the kitchen, away from the gunfight. There's another door. He kicks it open. The room beyond – a study – is clear. It's quiet in here. "Targets upstairs?" he says.

"All of them," Cindy says. She checks the cameras. She does a double-take. Something catches her eye. "Oh, shit," she says.

59

S tephen is with Vernon when the battle starts. They're in the security room, watching the monitors. They hear an explosion. The power goes out. They're in darkness. The explosion is followed soon after by the sounds of gunfire.

"Jesus," Vernon says. "It sounds like a war zone out there."

Stephen's mouth is dry. He thinks about Catherine and Kylie, upstairs and alone. Closer, he can hear people crying out.

The power comes back on. Stephen blinks against it. He shakes his head. "Fuck this," he says. "All of our men – none of these questionable new guys – get in touch with them and get them out the back. Get them away from the gunfight. I don't want any of them getting hurt or killed. Tell them to get out and get away from the grounds. Cameron hired these gangbangers to fight his battle, so leave them to it."

"All right," Vernon says, pulling out a personal radio. "What are you going to do?"

Stephen looks to the door, trying to swallow. His throat is too dry. He can hear gunshots and people screaming. Too much gunfire – have the gangbangers turned on each other already in their desperation to claim the bounty? The shooting is close, but not too close. It's not directly outside. If he leaves the room, he doesn't think he'll be in immediate danger. He pulls out his Glock. "I'm going to get Catherine and Kylie," he says.

Vernon looks confused.

"We should never have brought them here," Stephen says. "I made a mistake...I need to make it right."

Vernon doesn't look like he understands, but he doesn't try to stop Stephen. He starts talking into the radio, telling their men to get out. Earlier, Stephen told them to all get on a private channel. He didn't want anything he might have had to relay passing amongst the new recruits, especially if chances were it was going to be *about* the new recruits.

"I'll meet you outside," Stephen says. He goes to the door, his police training coming back to him. He opens it a crack, peers out. The corridor is clear. He slips outside. Vernon follows him out, but then they go in different directions. Stephen goes up the stairs, staying close to the wall and pointing the gun out ahead of him, looking up. All the gunshots are downstairs.

He reaches the landing. There's no one here. It doesn't seem like any security has remained upstairs. All the new guys have gone down, to chase their bounty.

Well, most of them. A Latino guy remains guarding the door where Catherine and Kylie are held, a different man than the one Stephen saw earlier. Stephen swallows with some difficulty, then approaches with authority. "Stand aside," he says. "I need to get the women out of there."

The gangbanger looks him up and down. "Says who?" he says. He's holding an M16. Stephen notices how his finger hovers near the trigger.

"Cameron says so," Stephen says, trying to appear unfazed. "Can't you hear what's going on downstairs?"

"Uh-huh," the gangbanger says. "Mr Brewer told me the only person who takes these women out is *him*."

Stephen opens his mouth to argue, to draw attention to the battle downstairs once again, but he stops. There's no point. This guy isn't going to listen. And it sounds like Cameron may have anticipated Stephen's change of heart. His conflicted conscience. He's probably told the guards to *specifically* not allow him into the room.

Stephen takes a deep breath. "Which gang do you run with?" he says.

The gangbanger looks at him.

"I'm just wondering if, back when I was a cop, I ever locked any of you assholes up."

The gangbanger's eyes flare, and his body starts to move. His shoulders start to twist, but Stephen was prepared for this. He raises the Glock and shoots the gangbanger between the eyes. Blood sprays out the back of his head, splashes against the wall and runs down. The gangbanger hits the ground with a thud, the M16 useless.

Stephen can't think about what he's just done. He moves on from it. Doesn't have time to process what has happened. He tries the handle to the room. It's locked, of course. He looks down at the gangbanger, then searches for a key. He finds it in his pocket. The dead man's eyes are still open, and they look back at Stephen accusatorily. Stephen feels sick. He's tired of feeling this way. Working for Cameron was never supposed to be like this.

As he slides the key into the lock, he hears Cameron's voice behind him. "Oh, Stephen," he says.

Stephen freezes, looks up. Cameron is outside his bedroom. Amy is beside him. She looks confused. Latino gangbangers flank him. He can see Hugh in the background, trying to see over their shoulders, to see what Stephen is doing. Cameron can see what he's done, though, and his new bodyguards can see what he's done to one of their own, and they don't look happy about it. Stephen can't help but feel like he's been lured into a trap.

Or maybe the trap wasn't for him. Maybe it was for Rollins. Whatever, it doesn't matter now. Stephen is the one it's caught.

"I knew you'd disappoint me," Cameron says. "You always do."

Stephen knows what's going to come next. He raises the Glock, but he's not fast enough. The Latino gangbangers are all too eager to waste him for killing one of their own. Their bullets tear through him. They turn him to mush. By the time they're done, there's barely anything left.

60

"Jesus Christ," Cindy says into Tom's ear. "I don't know what was going on, but Cameron's just had one of his own guards killed. Like, they've blasted him into a pulp. Fuck me..." She sounds like she might be sick.

"Keep it together, Cindy," Tom says. He doesn't mean to sound cold, but he needs her to stay calm, in the moment. She can be the difference, for him, between life and death.

"I'm cool, I'm cool," Cindy says, swallowing. "They've taken Catherine and Kylie out of the room and moved them into the master bedroom, with them."

"Where you can't see them." Tom presses his back to the wall, M4 raised, ready to head upstairs.

"Right," Cindy says. "But I *can* see that he's left two men on guard outside the room, and I know that he took a few of them in there with him, and Hugh seemed to take a few of his own, too."

"How many are we talking?" Tom begins his ascent, but he takes his time. One step after another, avoiding making a noise. A Black guy runs into the hallway below. He's carrying a shotgun. He spots Tom on the stairs and raises it. Tom lets loose a burst of fire into his chest, throwing him back into the wall. He waits to hear if anyone else comes, but no one does. He can hear gunfire throughout the rest of the house, but by now the smoke from the grenades would have faded. It's like the guards are fighting among themselves. Gang warfare has broken out on the property.

Cindy waits, watching through the camera on his mask, then says, "Cameron and Amy and three guards with them, then Hugh and Lenny and three guards with them. Plus Catherine and Kylie – that's twelve total."

"It must be a big room."

"Judging by the rest of the house, I'd say so. And don't forget the two guys standing guard outside."

"I haven't forgotten them," Tom says.

Cindy falls silent as he makes his way down the corridor. She's watching. He can hear how she holds her breath. "Hold up," she says suddenly. "Listen, I'm gonna get closer. I'm looking right now and the way is clear. I know which room they're in, and there's a trellis outside the window. I can climb up it. I'm not gonna be able to monitor the rest of the compound, but I *will* be able to tell you exactly where everyone is in that room. But do you hear that? The shootout is dying down. And from what I can see, it looks like they've mostly killed each other off. Give me a couple of minutes, and I'll get eyes on the room."

"Okay," Tom says. He hears her get moving, leaving the car and running.

Tom keeps making his way down the corridor. His footsteps are careful. Measured. Silent. He pauses when he reaches the end. In the corner, opposite him, are two dead bodies. One of them is unrecognizable, lying in a thick puddle of blood. The other is a Latino. Tom keeps his M4 raised, ready. He checks his ammo. Quarter of a magazine remains. He still has his Beretta, and his KA-BAR. "Let me ask you something," Tom says, calling around the corner loud enough for the two guards to hear. He imagines how they stiffen, can almost see how they point their weapons. He's buying Cindy some time to get to the window.

"How much is Cameron Brewer paying you?" he goes on. "How much was he paying your buddies, and the guys you weren't so friendly with? And yet, I'm here. I've got this far. Do you think what he's paying you is worth your life?"

There's a pause, then one of them speaks up. "There's a bounty to the man that drops you," he says.

"You think you can?" Tom says. "There's been a lot of men here tonight. They've all tried, too. You think you're the one?"

There's silence. Hesitation.

"Throw down your guns and I'll let the two of you walk out of here."

Neither of them responds, not right away. Tom gives them time. Lets them think on what he's said.

"How can – how can we trust you?" the same speaker says.

"Because you have to," Tom says. "There's been enough bloodshed here tonight. There doesn't have to be more. Throw your guns where I can see them."

There's another moment of silence. He thinks they're conferring. Then an M4 and an M16 are thrown to the end of the corridor, next to Tom. The two men standing guard come down into view, arms raised. They step tentatively around the corner where Tom is sheltering. Tom points the M4 at the ceiling. If they try anything, he can easily turn it on them, and they know this. They keep their eyes on him as they pass. Tom watches them go. When they reach the stairs, they start running. Tom waits to see if they circle back, if they attempt something. They don't. They're gone.

"All right," Cindy says in his ear, panting. "I'm at the house. I'm climbing up the trellis."

"When you get there," Tom says, staying by the corner, watching the now-unguarded door, "tell me what you see. And be careful, Cindy. Don't let them spot you."

"Got it," Cindy says. "Then what?"

"Then cause a distraction."

61

It's tense inside the bedroom. Hugh stays close to Lenny, and to his skinhead allies. On the opposite side of the room, Cameron is surrounded by his Latino buddies. Amy avoids Hugh's eyes. She stays at Cameron's shoulder, sheltering behind him. Both factions bristle at each other.

In the middle of it all sit Catherine and Kylie. They have their arms around each other.

Hugh attempts to strike up a conversation. "It sounds like it's got quiet out there," he says. "Maybe they got him."

Cameron sneers. "If they got him, then why haven't they dragged his body up here to parade it around?"

"Maybe they've gone looking for Cindy," Hugh says. "If he was here, she was sure to be nearby."

"They're not going to be thinking about Cindy right now," Cameron says. "If they've killed him, they're thinking about the bounty they've just earned."

"Then we need to send them out after Cindy!"

"They haven't brought me Rollins!" Cameron says. "Cindy can wait! Rollins is still out there! Don't you get it, you fucking moron?"

"Fuck you!"

The skinheads with Hugh and Lenny bristle and flex, and the Latinos with Cameron do the same.

Cameron throws up his arms. "Fuck this," he says. "Everyone calm down. He's out there." Cameron runs his hands down his face.

"Why don't you just check the security footage?" Hugh says.

Cameron shoots him a look. "You really are an idiot. Don't you think I'd be doing that already? Don't you think I'd check *exactly* where he is right now, and what's going on out there, if I could? Cindy's blocked me out of my own fucking system."

"How am I supposed to know that?" Hugh says. "How weren't you prepared? Aren't you supposed to be some kind of a tech genius, Cameron? Isn't that what you tell anyone who'll listen?" Hugh smirks. "It's because she's good, isn't she? *Too* good. That's why we chose her in the first place, remember? And now it's come back to bite us all on the ass."

Cameron is about to respond, no doubt to escalate the argument, but Lenny clears his throat. "Everyone needs to calm down," he says. "We should be quiet. We need to listen, and to prepare. We need to take up defensive positions, and we—"

He's interrupted by something smashing through the window behind him. Everyone turns to the sound.

Then there's gunfire, and the door bursts open.

62

The door is locked. Tom points the M4 at the handle and waits for Cindy's signal.

"*Now!*" she says.

She puts a rock through the window. Tom blows out the lock, then kicks the door open. He rolls through and comes up on one knee. Cindy has described the layout of the room to him, has told him where everyone is while the brothers bicker. He brings up the M4, shoulders it, turns to his right and takes out Cameron's Latinos first. They're furthest from the window. The skinheads are closest, and their backs are turned. He fires off short bursts, conserving his ammunition. He doesn't have much left.

The three Latinos go down in a burst of blood. Tom turns to the skinheads. They're spinning from the window at the sound of the gunfire. Tom picks off the first two. The M4 runs out of ammo. Without hesitation, he pulls out the Beretta. The remaining skinhead is pulling up his M16. He's slow, though. Thrown by the deaths of the two to his right. He didn't expect the M4 to run out of ammo. He thought he was eye-to-eye with death. It's taking him a moment to get his reactions back where they need to be.

It takes him too long.

Tom plants three rounds in his chest, dropping him.

Lenny has charged around the outside of the room. He grabs Tom now, lifts him from his feet and slams him against the wall, reaching for his throat. Tom has dropped the Beretta in the impact. He doesn't panic. Doesn't let Lenny get a grip around his throat. He pulls out his KA-BAR and sticks it into the side of Lenny's neck.

Lenny blinks, like he doesn't understand what has just happened. He tries to look down, to where the knife has gone in, but he can't move his head enough. Tom pulls the KA-BAR out. Blood sprays. Lenny tries to keep hold of Tom. His legs buckle under him. He falls to his knees. The knife has hit his carotid. The blood is still spraying. The color has drained from his face. Tom pushes him aside.

Hugh sees what has happened. His eyes are wide. He wasn't expecting Tom to kill Lenny. Hugh spins, reaches for one of the fallen M16s. Before he can pick it up, he realizes Cindy is in front of him. Over him. He looks up slowly. Cindy's jaw is set. She's gritting her teeth. Hugh straightens, holding out his empty hands.

Cindy kicks him, *hard*, between the legs.

Hugh squeals and goes down, clutching himself.

Tom picks up his Beretta. The room has calmed. He looks around, and sees how Cindy was able to get inside. The window is open – despite the broken glass, Kylie and Catherine have slid it fully open.

There's a flurry of movement to Tom's right. Cameron has pushed Amy to the ground. He's trying to escape, bolting for his open bedroom door. Tom blocks his way. Cameron bounces off him. He rolls back, scrabbling toward one of the dead Latinos, reaching for his weapon.

Tom raises his Beretta, but Kylie has charged across the room, tackling Cameron before he can raise the gun. It's between them. They struggle. Tom can't get a clear shot.

"Kylie!" Catherine says.

"Let go of him," Tom says. "Get out of the way."

She ignores them all. Three months of pent-up anger and frustration explode from her as she grabs at his face, claws at his eyes. Cameron tries to fight her off, while trying to swing the rifle around. Kylie grabs it, wrestles him for it. Cameron is stronger. Kylie bites him on the bridge of the nose. Tom sees blood squirt.

They hear gunfire between them. Everyone freezes.

Tom moves toward them, gun raised, stepping carefully. He places a hand on Kylie's shoulder, but she straightens up. She's fine. Tom looks down. Blood is pouring out of Cameron's sternum. The angle of the rifle has fired the bullets upward into his chest cavity. They've killed him instantly.

Amy lowers herself to the ground, holding her head in her hands. Her eyes are wide. Her skin is pale. She's traumatized, in shock. She stares at Cameron's body. Her mouth works like she's about to throw up.

Then she stands. "I feel sick," she says. "Can I go?"

Cindy tilts her head toward the bedroom door, and Amy heads out that way. She's unsteady on her feet. Tom thinks how she looks shell-shocked. When she's gone, Cindy turns to Tom. Tom looks down at Hugh. He's crawling across the ground to Lenny's dead body, where he lies in the pool of his blood. He's whimpering, one hand between his legs from where Cindy kicked him.

Tom speaks to Catherine and Kylie. "We'll find you some car keys and you can split," he says. He motions toward Amy. "You'll have to take her with you. Maybe to a hospital."

Amy tears her eyes away from Cameron. She stares at the

floor. She says something in French, then switches to English. "I feel sick," she says. "I want to go. I need to go."

Tom leans over Hugh, and pulls him up by his hair. "Let's go. You're coming with us."

63

Tom and Cindy have been driving for a while now. Out to the Colorado Desert. They head across it, deep into it. It's still dark.

Catherine and Kylie took one of the cars from Cameron's garage and drove off with the shell-shocked Amy in tow. Tom and Cindy hauled Hugh down to their car. They bound him, and put him in the trunk.

The desert is cool when they finally stop the car and get out of it. They go to the back, to the trunk, but they don't open it immediately. Cindy looks up at Tom. She holds out her hand. "I need your gun."

Tom's been waiting for her to change her mind about this. She hasn't yet. She seems steadfast in her new decision. He looks at her. Doesn't give her the gun, not straight away. "You thought about this?"

"Long and hard," Cindy says, keeping her hand out. "He doesn't deserve justice. This is the only kind of justice I can hope to get for Erica. Prison wouldn't mean anything to him. He doesn't care what he did. It won't gnaw at his conscience, it won't plague him, so what would be the point in locking him up?" She raises her hand.

Tom puts the Beretta into it. Cindy takes a step back. Tom opens the trunk and hauls Hugh out. Hugh is already crying and snivelling. There's snot smeared across his top lip and cheek. Tom drops him onto his knees on the dry, gritty dirt. Hugh raises his bound hands, begging off. He starts to stand, keeping his head lowered.

"Please," he says. He keeps saying it, over and over. "*Please...*"

Cindy doesn't want him standing. She puts a bullet through his right foot.

Hugh goes down screaming, clutching at his leg. He's crying harder. "No," he says, "no, please – please don't kill me..."

Cindy stands over him, squeezing the gun in her hand. "Are you scared, Hugh?"

He doesn't look up. He just nods.

"I want you to be scared," Cindy says. "I want you to be scared, the way Erica would have been scared when you killed her. I want you to beg for your life, the same way she would have." She kicks him, so he has to look at her, but he continues to twist away. He won't meet her eye. He can't.

"How many other women have you killed, Hugh?" she says. "How many other women have you killed the way you killed Erica, you pathetic fucking scumbag?"

Tom stands aside, arms folded. He sees the pain on Cindy's face. Sees how her features twist. Her arm trembles, holding the gun, squeezing it tight.

"Look at me, Hugh," she says. She leans down over him, grabs a handful of his hair, forces him to turn his face to hers. "*Look at me!* I want you to suffer, Hugh. I want you to suffer the same way my sister did, and every other woman you've ever hurt. I want you to suffer, you piece of shit!"

There are tears rolling down Cindy's cheeks. She pushes Hugh away from her and straightens up. She wipes at her eyes.

"If you can't do it—" Tom says, but he doesn't finish.

Cindy doesn't say anything. She doesn't have to. She looks at him. There's a steeliness in her glistening eyes. Her jaw is set. She can do it. She's going to do it. Tom nods, then turns and walks away, leaves her.

He finds a tree and leans against it to wait. He stares off into the night, watches the stars. Soon after, he hears gunshots.

64

Tom buried Hugh's body, then they drove away from the scene. They haven't left the desert yet. They sit together on an outcrop of stones and watch the sun rise. Cindy has her head on Tom's shoulder. He wraps his arm around her.

She sniffs. Tom realizes she's crying still. He doesn't say anything. He rubs her arm and holds her closer.

"When you killed the men that killed Alejandra," she says. She pauses. "When you killed them, did it make you feel any better?"

Tom doesn't answer for a while. He watches the sun. "I..." He takes a deep breath. "No, no, I don't think it did. But not killing them would've made me feel worse. I couldn't leave them alive. They didn't care about what they'd done, either. They'd probably done it before, and they would've done it again, I'm sure. Just like Hugh." He pauses, thinking. "It was necessary. I had to do it. But no, to answer your question, it didn't make me feel any better. But I never expected that it would. I think..." He hesitates, but forces himself to continue. "I think a part of me has been trying to fill that hole ever since I killed them. Before Alejandra died, I thought I knew what I was looking for. I was searching for peace and quiet. For solitude. For...for a *life*. Ever since, I haven't been so sure."

Cindy turns and wraps her arms around him. They sit like this on the rocks for a while, as the day warms up around them.

Eventually, they go to the car and drive back into the city. They call Catherine, and make sure she and Kylie are all right. They are, and they thank Tom and Cindy for their help. Tom asks them where Amy is, and Catherine gives them the name of the hospital.

They go to her room together. Cindy makes sure there is no police presence guarding her. There isn't.

Amy lies on her bed with a drip in her arm. She stares out the window, sedate. Some of her color has returned. She stiffens when Tom and Cindy enter her room. They take a seat by her bed. Cindy speaks. "You saw a lot happen last night," she says. "I want you to understand why."

Cindy tells her the story of her sister. Of what Cameron, Hugh, and Lenny did to her. Amy listens, her eyes never leaving Cindy.

Cindy wraps up. "We didn't plan on killing them. I'm not sure yet if that's what I wanted. But I *do* know that they needed to be punished. When they kidnapped and held Catherine and Kylie captive, we had to make our move."

Amy opens her mouth. She licks her lips and swallows before she speaks. Her voice is a croak. "Why are you telling me this?" she says.

"Because you know who we are," Cindy says. "And you saw us. But we know who you are, Amy. I don't mean that as a threat. I mean, I've read up on you. I've seen you on Cameron's security cameras. I don't believe you're a bad person. I think you got entangled in some things you wanted no part of."

Amy takes a deep breath. "I'm no innocent," she says. "I knew that not everything Cameron was doing was...strictly legal. But I didn't think..." She swallows. "I didn't think he was a *killer*. Recently, he has been so changed. I feel like I have seen a new side to him. A side more like his brother." She bites her lip and stares at the wall.

"We heard on the radio coming here," Cindy says, "the police think it was a gang war. They're not sure how it got into the Hollywood Hills, or how Cameron wound up in the middle of it."

Amy is silent for a while. Finally, she says, "I will not tell them otherwise." She turns back to Cindy. "I am so very sorry for your sister."

Cindy nods. "I hope you feel better soon."

"I feel so tired," Amy says. "I just want to go home."

"Where is home?"

Amy smiles. "Montreal," she says. "I think I am tired of LA. I think I will be tired of it for a long time."

Tom and Cindy leave her to rest. They leave the hospital and return to the car. They have a lot of driving ahead of them. Back to Texas, to take Cindy home. She doesn't plan on staying in her old apartment. She's going to move to a new place. She doesn't feel comfortable staying there, not after it was found and broken into. Despite Hugh and Lenny both being dead now, she doesn't think she'd ever be able to relax in there again.

"What about you?" she says. "Where are you going to go?"

"I don't know yet," Tom says. "But wherever I end up, whenever you get in touch about Malcolm, I'll be available."

Cindy nods. She turns away, curls up and falls asleep. They still have a long way to go.

EPILOGUE

It's a few weeks after Tom leaves Texas that Cindy gets in touch. She's found Malcolm Graves. He's hiding out in a shack in Colorado, out in the middle of nowhere.

It's early evening when Tom reaches the cabin. He leaves his car by the side of the road and continues on foot through trees. He sits at the treeline and watches the cabin until nightfall. Towards evening, he sees Malcolm. He comes outside onto the porch.

Tom watches through binoculars. Malcolm looks dishevelled. He's thinner than he was just a few weeks ago. His hair is unkempt and wild, and his mustache is not as well kept as it was. His stubble is thick, and his cheeks have become bearded. He drinks from a bottle of beer and rubs at the back of his neck. There's a nervous energy about him. Tom can guess why. Cindy found him due to his online activity. He wasn't looking to indulge his sick tastes. Instead, he was trying to find out if his secret had been revealed.

Cindy didn't reveal it. Didn't put out the word of what he is. They didn't want anyone to find him before they did.

Malcolm has probably guessed at the reason his secret

wasn't leaked. He isn't stupid. Either way, he knows what happens for him next. Whether Tom finds him, or the law does, he's a dead man. With the law, he gets another few months of life, but it won't be happy. As soon as they put him into prison, the other inmates will gut him alive.

On one hand, Tom thinks this is what he deserves. Send him to prison and let him live in fear. Have every day filled with dread until the shank finally finds his kidneys.

Tom can't leave it for anyone else, though. Tom was close to him, and he didn't know. They breathed the same air. They were in close proximity to each other. For this, Tom cannot permit him to live. Had he known at the time, he would have killed him through the bars, and damn the consequences.

As it gets dark, Malcolm goes back inside the cabin. Tom doesn't hang around. He crosses the ground and gets close. He looks into a window. The inside of the cabin is all one room – the living room consists of a beat-up old sofa pointing towards a small, boxy television, and there's a cot to one side. The kitchen is just behind the sofa. That's where Malcolm is. He stirs stew in a pot atop the stove. Tom looks around the room. There's a shotgun, but it's next to the sofa. He can't see any other weapons. Malcolm isn't carrying one.

Tom goes to the front of the cabin, up onto the porch. The door is locked. He kicks it open. Malcolm spins around at the stove. He sees Tom. He remembers Tom. He backs up, unblinking, swallowing. His eyes flicker toward the shotgun. It's too far. He'll never make it, though it's the only chance he has. His tongue flickers out over his lips.

Tom has his KA-BAR hidden up his sleeve. He lets it slide down into his hand. Malcolm sees it. Tom advances on him. Malcolm's back hits the wall. His mouth works, he's trying to speak. He can't get any words out. He looks into Tom's face and knows it doesn't make a difference.

"You know why I've come here, don't you?" Tom says.

Malcolm nods, defeated.

Tom nods back. There's nothing else to say. He sticks the knife into Malcolm's gut, then drags the blade up. Malcolm screams, but only briefly. It quickly turns into a choked gurgle. Blood spills from the side of his mouth. His intestines hit the floor.

Tom pulls the knife out and takes a step back. Malcolm falls. He's already dead.

Tom cleans his knife on a nearby dish cloth, then leaves the cabin and walks back to his car. He sits behind the wheel for a while before he starts the engine. He has the window open. It's quiet here. Peaceful. He closes his eyes and breathes deep.

He starts the engine and looks down the length of the quiet road. There's a sign further down, directing to a turn off for New Mexico. Fifty miles.

New Mexico. Tom's home state. It wouldn't take him long to reach his hometown. Tom stares at the sign. He thinks about his hometown. He wonders what it looks like now. Wonders if anyone he knows is still there. It's been half a lifetime since he left. A lot has happened in that time.

Tom deliberates, staring down the road at the sign.

Then he starts driving.

ABOUT THE AUTHOR

Did you enjoy *Hard Target*? Please consider leaving a review on Amazon to help other readers discover the book.

Paul Heatley left school at sixteen, and since then has held a variety of jobs including mechanic, carpet fitter, and book-shop assistant, but his passion has always been for writing. He writes mostly in the genres of crime fiction and thriller, and links to his other titles can be found on his website. He lives in the north east of England.

Want to connect with Paul? Visit him at his website.

www.PaulHeatley.com

ALSO BY PAUL HEATLEY

Blood Line

(A Tom Rollins Thriller Book 1)

Wrong Turn

(A Tom Rollins Thriller Book 2)

Hard to Kill

(A Tom Rollins Thriller Book 3)

Snow Burn

(A Tom Rollins Thriller Book 4)

Road Kill

(A Tom Rollins Thriller Book 5)

No Quarter

(A Tom Rollins Thriller Book 6)

Hard Target

(A Tom Rollins Thriller Book 7)

Last Stand

(A Tom Rollins Thriller Book 8)

Blood Feud

(A Tom Rollins Thriller Book 9)

Made in the USA
Middletown, DE
13 September 2023

38459601R00201